88

88

——

TOM WALLACE

ISBN: 978-1-948374-42-2

Enigma House Press

Goshen, Kentucky 40026

www.enigmahousepress.com

This book is dedicated to Grant Sparks and Jimmie Nell Jenkins, two grand dames and the last survivors of the Bourbon Hill gang. Here's hoping they live forever.

ALSO BY TOM WALLACE

The Jack Dantzler Mystery Series

The Journal (2019)

Heroes For Ghosts (2018)

Murder by Suicide (2017)

The Poker Game (2015)

The Fire of Heaven (2014)

The List (2013)

Gnosis (2011)

The Devil's Racket (2007)

What Matters Blood (2004)

Other Novels

Heirs of Cain (2010)

Divine Rebel (2020)

Sports-Related Books

The University of Kentucky Basketball Encyclopedia

So, You Think You Are a University of Kentucky Basketball Fan

Golden Glory: The History of Central City Basketball

Jeff Sheppard: Heart of a Champion

Embracing the Legend: Jim Harrick Revives the UCLA Mystique (with John McGill)

Inside/Outside: A Behind the Scenes Look at Kentucky Basketball

Travis Ford: Big Blue Dream

ONE

ALTHOUGH HE HAD BEEN ELECTED GOVERNOR OF KENTUCKY in a landslide victory, Mark Baker was a wildly unpopular and polarizing figure. Even among those in his own party—Republican—he was viewed with great skepticism and a wary eye. Among Democrats and Independents he was nothing short of a bully with strong autocratic tendencies. In their eyes, he was Satan in an expensive tailor-made suit.

Baker's personality was inward at best, sullen and angry at worst. He was strictly a my-way-or-the-highway kind of leader. Cross him, challenge him in any way, and you were risking political or business suicide. Landing in his very large doghouse, especially if you happened to be a member of his party could send you into an exile that might never end. Perhaps that's why so few were willing to openly challenge him.

Along with his dark personality there was another reason why he was so disliked and distrusted—he was a carpetbagger from the North. Baker had been born and raised just outside of Boston, where, as a young man in his early twenties he started a small business that quickly grew into a large one. Having made an early fortune allowed him to retire a wealthy man at age fifty, at which time he relocated to Kentucky, where his wife Kathy was from. They had met and married while she was majoring in religious studies at Boston University. She became a teacher, but gave it up when their children—Michael and Kelly—were born.

Now living in his adopted state, Baker sat around doing nothing for five years. He eventually grew bored and decided to make a run for governor, which by any stretch of the imagination had to be seen as a long shot at best. Few had heard of the man, but Baker, using his own money to finance his campaign, put together an outstanding organization that was small, efficient, and in the final analysis, hugely successful.

Baker had been a registered Democrat his entire adult life. However, once he moved to Kentucky and sniffed the political winds he changed his registration to Republican. It was a smart, astute move on his part. With the exception of large, liberal-leaning cities like Louisville, Lexington and Covington, the rest of Kentucky was strongly Republican. And certain areas, particularly in the hills of Eastern Kentucky, could best be described as dead-red. In today's climate, if you had any hope of being elected to a major office in Kentucky, you had better worship the elephant.

Baker had been in office just shy of three years. He had yet to decide on running for a second term but he was leaning in that direction. And despite his unpopularity and the wariness in which he was viewed within his own party he was certain that should he make it official he would be a shoo-in to be re-elected.

In his mind nothing could derail the Mark Baker Express.

That is, until he received the letter.

At that moment everything changed.

Baker had spent the morning and early afternoon hours slogging his way through a series of dreadfully boring meetings. They were precisely the kind of senseless pow-wows high-level office holders had to endure even though every minute doing so was time wasted. Worse for Baker was he did more listening than speaking, which to him meant having to sit quietly while men and women of lesser intelligence droned on about this being a terrific plan, that being a lousy plan. He had to fake being interested in every speaker as if he or she were blessed with insight and wisdom. His biggest challenge during such meetings was managing to remain awake.

The next ninety minutes were spent with lieutenant governor Bradley Cooper, whose primary claim to fame was that he shared the same name with a famous actor. Baker was not close to Cooper, nor did he have much respect for the man. In fact, if he chose to run for a second term, Baker likely would not keep Cooper as his running mate. He did not see Cooper as a particularly bright individual. Also, the two men had virtually nothing in common. Baker only picked Cooper to join him on the ticket because Cooper hailed from Northern Kentucky, an area where his name recognition and his background—he was a three-term state senator—could win votes in what was a section of the commonwealth that might tend toward the liberal Democrat challenger. Cooper's presence on the ticket was a game-changer, picking up enough votes to help earn Baker his victory.

But that was then, this was now. Baker had enough confidence in winning a second term that Cooper had become dispensable. If Baker did decide to jettison Cooper, his new choice for a running mate would likely be Marilyn Lawrence, a Louisville attorney Baker judged to be the polar opposite of Cooper in every way. Baker had privately queried her about possibly being his running mate if he opted to take aim on a second term, and although she was non-committal at the time, he could see in her eyes that she was keenly interested in joining him on the ticket.

After leaving his office in the state capitol, Baker drove to the governor's mansion, showered, changed clothes and downed a small glass of Kentucky bourbon. He and Kathy then drove to

Lexington, picked up her parents and took them downtown to dinner.

Baker always looked forward to spending time with the in-laws, Mary and Ernie Kruger. He particularly enjoyed hanging out with Ernie. The old man was ninety-six but you would never know it by looking at him. He was thin, rigid as a telephone pole, and had a head full of gray hair. It would be easy to mistake him for a man in his seventies. Ernie was originally from Milwaukee and spoke with a heavy German accent, which he came by naturally, his parents having been born in Munich before immigrating to the United States in the early nineteen twenties.

Mary, at eighty-seven, was still in relatively good health but age had begun to wear her down a bit. Her mind remained sharp, but she needed a cane when walking, a requirement that annoyed her to no end. Like her husband, Mary had a strong independent streak, and having the need for assistance while walking was a fact she had yet to come to terms with.

The couple met in what could only be termed a Hollywood-type meeting. Mary was visiting Milwaukee when she had car trouble. The vehicle was towed to the shop where Ernie was a mechanic. Throughout the afternoon, Ernie popped into the waiting area to give Mary an update on how the repairs were going. Each meeting seemed to last longer than the one that preceded it. By the time the car was ready to roll, Ernie felt confident enough to ask Mary if he could take her out to dinner. She agreed. They hit it off well—connected might be the better term—and spent the next two days getting to know each other. When Mary returned home to Lexington, she and Ernie continued to correspond, usually by phone, but sometimes through letters. It wasn't long before they both realized their love for each other. Mary persuaded Ernie to relocate to Lexington, where, with her father's help, he landed a job as a mechanic at the area's largest automobile dealership. They married, and within a few short years

Ernie was the top man in the repair shop. Within a decade, he had saved enough money to open his own place, which he continued to run until he was almost eighty. Mary, meanwhile, spent thirty years working for the local school board. She retired at age sixty-five. Together they often traveled to Boston to visit with Kathy and Mark, and to spend time with the grand kids, Michael and Kelly, both of whom still lived in Boston.

Ernie entertained at dinner, regaling everyone with several of his tall tales. The two women had heard the stories so many times they quickly tuned him out, but Mark was always a captive audience, even though he had also heard the stories on multiple occasions. He didn't care; if he heard them a thousand times that would be just fine with him.

After dinner, Mark told the other three he would head down to the underground parking garage, get the car, and pick them up in front of the building. He did this primarily for Mary, who made the trip without her cane. She would need assistance from Kathy and Ernie to walk the short distance from the restaurant to the street. Mark was only too happy to make it easier for Mary.

When Mark found his car—a Lexus—he immediately noticed a white folder pinned to the front window beneath a wiper blade. He took down the folder, turned it over, and studied both sides. There was no postage and no return address, only his name written with a black Sharpie on the front. He carefully opened the folder and withdrew its contents—a single sheet of white paper with a typed message on it—and read what the few words said.

First, he was confused.

Then he began to tremble.

TWO

Jack Dantzler couldn't recall a time in his life when he was happier or more content than he was these days. His overall health was excellent, and his knees were strong, thus allowing him to continue playing tennis at a high level, which was about as important to him as breathing. He had always had this duel identity—great homicide detective/outstanding tennis player —and now that his days as a cop were in the rear-view mirror, only tennis was left to satisfy his ego. He often wondered what he would be once his days as a tennis player were done. Just another has-been, probably, like a million other guys with nothing left but old trophies, faded glory, and a head filled with ancient memories.

Dantzler was also in good shape money-wise. He had his pension after twenty-seven years as a homicide detective, and he, along with David Bloom and Sean Montgomery, owned the Tennis Center, which continued to turn a nice yearly profit. In addition to that, his first two cases as a private investigator had both ended successfully, and had earned him a healthy paycheck. Thanks to his financial independence he had the luxury to only accept cases that were genuinely challenging. He had no interest in spying on cheating husbands or unhappy wives on the prowl for an outside-of-marriage thrill. Let financially strapped gumshoes take those assignments.

Best of all, though, for the first time in decades he was in a serious relationship. Erin Collins, the assistant district attorney he had met last year while working a case in Cincinnati had been offered—and accepted—a position as the top assistant to Kentucky's attorney general. Although her office was in Frankfort, she purchased a house in Lexington located less than two miles from where Dantzler lived. Not once had the words committed relationship been uttered by either one, nor did they have to be. Their feelings for each other were a given. They did not need to be spoken.

Dantzler had just finished giving tennis lessons to Mayor Elizabeth Anderson's youngest daughter, Heather, a twelve-year-old with dreams of glory that far exceeded her modest talent. She was yet another in a long line of terrific youngsters with marginal ability he had worked with over the years. At best, Heather might someday be a decent player at the high school level. That's about as far as her talent would take her.

It was almost seven and he was less than a mile from his house when his cell phone buzzed. He checked the number . . . it was unfamiliar to him. So was the caller's voice when Dantzler answered. He was both surprised and confused when the man identified himself. Why would this man, of all men on Earth, be calling him? What reason could he possibly have for making contact? Dantzler had rarely been more baffled than he was at this moment.

He had never spoken to Mark Baker, nor had he ever seen the man in person. He had certainly not voted for Baker when he ran for governor. No way was that going to happen. The two men were at opposite ends of the political spectrum. Dantzler was no far-left zealot, but he did tend to be center-left, which was about a million miles from Baker's extreme right-wing agenda.

Baker's views went against virtually everything Dantzler held sacred. Baker was an anti-guy—anti-gun control, anti-science, anti-climate change, anti-union, anti-education, anti-women's rights. In Dantzler's mind, Baker was a Luddite who saw progressives as children of the devil. Didn't the governor understand the root word for progressive was progress, which meant moving forward? And the opposite of progressive was regressive, which translated into moving backward?

To those in Dantzler's camp, Baker was viewed as a Neanderthal hell-bent on taking the commonwealth back to the Stone Age.

And now Mr. Anti-Everything was calling to request an eleven p.m. meeting with Dantzler in the parking lot near the front gate entrance into Kroger Field, home of the University of Kentucky football Wildcats. Dantzler's first inclination, once he got past the shock of hearing from the governor, was to decline the meeting. But for some reason he didn't. Instead, he decided to listen to the governor's pitch.

Baker said the meeting was personal and had nothing to do with his duties as governor. He quickly amended that, saying he wasn't really sure if that was true or not. He told Dantzler about finding a folder on his front windshield, and the single-page note inside the folder. He did not tell Dantzler what the note said, nor did Dantzler inquire about its message. Dantzler would get that information later should he decide to meet with the governor.

Surprisingly, he quickly overcame his skepticism and agreed to the meeting. There was something in the governor's voice—fear, panic, perhaps a combination of the two—that was the deciding factor for Dantzler. He would listen to what the man had to say.

Dantzler got to his house a few minutes later, took a quick shower, dressed in Levis, a T-shirt and sneakers, and then made a call to let Erin know about his plan to meet with the governor. She listened until he was finished, then responded with a single word —"strange." Erin had worked in Frankfort six months, and had met the governor on two occasions, both brief, but she had yet to form much of an opinion on the man. She did know how Dantzler felt about Baker, and even though her political leanings were close to Dantzler's, she was inclined to withhold judgment until she got a clearer impression of the governor.

Dantzler left his house at exactly ten-thirty for the ten-minute drive to Kroger Field. Being early to a meeting was in his DNA, but rarely did he arrive more than a few minutes prior to the start time. But an eleven p.m. meeting in a dark, deserted parking lot wasn't normal, even if he was meeting with the governor. In truth, he couldn't be sure the man who made the call was the governor. Dantzler cursed himself for not asking a question only the governor could have answered. Maybe the call had been made by a man impersonating the governor, perhaps someone Dantzler had arrested and sent to prison years ago. Now the man was seeking revenge. That was a possibility Dantzler couldn't dismiss outright. That's also why he brought his Glock to the meeting. It was never a mistake to be prepared for the worst.

Dantzler parked about one-hundred yards away from where the meeting was to take place. Lights off, he sat in the dark, waiting. At precisely eleven o'clock a black Lexus pulled up near the front entrance and stopped. The driver cut the engine and killed the lights. The Lexus windows were too dark for Dantzler to recognize the driver, or if, indeed, the driver was alone.

Dantzler waited five minutes, then started his car, turned on the headlights, and slowly moved forward, eventually stopping directly behind the Lexus. After cutting the engine and turning off the headlights, he exited his car, walked around to the passenger's side of the Lexus and tapped on the window, which was immediately lowered.

With one hand on his Glock, Dantzler carefully peered into the car and studied the driver's face. It was definitely Governor Mark Baker sitting behind the steering wheel. He motioned for Dantzler to get into the car.

"Turn on the overhead light," Dantzler ordered.

"I would prefer we spoke in darkness," the governor responded.

"I'm not getting in until I'm sure you are alone."

"Who the hell else would be with me?" Baker snapped.

"No light, no conversation."

Baker let out a loud sigh before turning on the overhead light. Dantzler leaned to his left, saw no one hiding in the backseat, holstered his weapon and got into the car.

"I appreciate you meeting me on such short notice and under what can only be termed bizarre circumstances," the governor stated. "I also apologize. Believe me, this is definitely not how I normally do things. Hell, I wouldn't think any sane person would."

"Well, sane or not, here we are," Dantzler replied.

"Yeah, here we are. And to be perfectly honest with you, I'm not sure why."

"It's not by accident, which means you had a reason for the call. Okay, what is that reason?"

"I had dinner last night at Jeff Ruby's new steak place in downtown Lexington. My wife and her parents dined with us. After we ate, I walked down to the parking garage to get the car. My wife and in-laws waited for me to pick them up outside the building. Anyway, when I got to my car, this folder was on the windshield." He removed the folder from the dashboard and handed it to Dantzler. "As you can see, there is no postage and no return address. Inside is a . . . well, you can read it for yourself."

Dantzler opened the folder and removed a single sheet of white paper. Typed on the paper was the following message:

You will pay $5 million dollars: Failure to do so will result in embarrassment for you and your family

Await further instructions

"You're a high-profile politician," Dantzler pointed out. "As such, I'm sure this isn't the first threatening letter you've received. This kind of nonsense goes with the territory, doesn't it?"

"Of course it does. I get letters from crazies on a daily basis. But . . . this one has a different tone to it, a different vibe. I'm not sure I can adequately explain it, but it troubles me."

Dantzler reread the note. "The family reference is what's bothering you, right?"

"Yes. I wouldn't be nearly this concerned if it only threatened me," the governor said. "But including them in the message is worrisome. Any suggestion as to how I should handle this?"

"Don't you have a mechanism in place to deal with threats like this? A security detail, maybe? And what about the Kentucky State Police? Or the FBI? Those folks look into shit like this every day. Why not turn this over to them?"

"It might come to that, but first I would prefer to hire you to look into it. See what you might come up with."

"That's not what I normally do, Governor. I don't think I'm the right person for the job."

"Look, I'm aware of your accomplishments as a homicide detective. And I know about your recent success as a private investigator. Your credentials are impeccable. All I'm asking is that you spend a few days and try to find out who is doing this to me and my family."

"I don't see how I or anyone else can do much until you hear from the note's author again. Unless that happens our hands are tied."

"There has to be something you can do until we get a second message," the governor pleaded.

"The FBI is your best bet."

"Can't do it. Not until I get further instructions."

"And if you do, what then?" asked Dantzler.

"What options would I have?"

"Well, you could simply ignore the message, see it as nothing more than an empty threat. That would be risky, though, should the threat be valid. Or you could pay the five-million. There's an obvious downside if that's the route you choose to take, namely there's a good chance you'll be asked to pay more money in the future. If this person can bleed you for five-million this time, what's to prevent him from thinking he can't do the same at a later date?"

"You paint a very bleak picture, Detective Dantzler," Baker said.

"I'm no longer a detective, remember?"

"Sorry. How should I address you?"

"Jack works for me."

"Okay, Jack, just for the sake of argument, if you do agree to help me, where would you begin?"

"By doing a deep background check on your political enemies. Once that's done, I would zoom in on close friends, co-workers both past and present, and then family members."

"Political enemies, huh? There will be no shortage of names on that list."

Dantzler said, "Can you think of anyone who might have it in for you? Someone with the balls to demand five-million dollars from you?"

"No, I don't know anyone who hates me that much."

"What about something in your past that might prove embarrassing to you or your family? Anything come to mind?"

"I've racked my brain for hours and I can't come up with a thing."

"You ran a successful business in Boston. Did you piss off anyone?"

"Never. I treated everyone fairly and impartially," the governor said.

"What about women? Were you ever unfaithful to your wife?"

"There was an affair with a married lady in the late eighties. But it was very brief, didn't last more than a couple of weeks. We both knew it was wrong, so we mutually agreed to end it. That's the only time I ever strayed."

"Did your wife know about the affair?"

"She did not, thank God."

"Was she ever unfaithful to you?"

The governor shook his head, said, "No way. Kathy is practically a saint."

"Who else knows about this note?"

"Kathy. I showed it to her last night after we got home."

"Not the in-laws?"

"No, I didn't see the need to unnecessarily worry them."

"If I do agree to do this," Dantzler said, "will you make your wife and children available for an interview?"

"That will not be a problem." When Dantzler didn't respond, the governor said, "Does this mean you'll help me?"

Dantzler nodded, said, "Yeah, I'll look into it. But don't expect any miracles."

"What about money," the governor inquired. "How much compensation do you require?"

"We'll work that out later, after we see how much help I can be."

"Anything you want or need, don't hesitate to ask. You will have full access to everyone and everything. You have my word on that."

"Good. I'll phone your wife tomorrow, set a time when I can speak with her. Do your kids live here?"

"No, they are both in Boston."

"I'll need their phone numbers and e-mail addresses." Dantzler paused, then continued, "When I mentioned doing a deep background check, that means I'll be digging into your past and your family's past. If you're keeping any secrets, it would be wise to tell me about them now rather than me finding out later on."

"I'm not hiding anything from you, Jack. I swear."

"Okay, I'll get started on this tomorrow."

"Thanks for agreeing to look into this for me."

"One final thing, Governor. If you do receive a second folder, pick it up using two fingers. When you open it, touch as little of the folder as possible. Also, use the same procedure when removing whatever is inside. If we get lucky, if the person sending it didn't wear gloves, maybe we can lift some prints. That could help us identify the individual who is doing this to you."

"That's a great idea. Yes, I'll be careful when I open it."

Dantzler got out of the governor's car and watched it drive away. As Dantzler got into his own car, one thing the governor said kept running through his head.

"I swear."

Dantzler never trusted anyone who made that statement. It was like the person was trying too hard to convince the listener he was telling the truth. Dantzler always felt telling the truth should be easy.

The truth required no extra push.

THREE

At seven the next morning, Dantzler was sitting with David Bloom and Sean Montgomery in the IHOP on Nicholasville Road. These meetings had become a standard tradition for the trio of long-time friends. Unlike his two compatriots, Dantzler rarely ate a big breakfast, opting instead for a bagel and a glass of orange juice. But for him the food wasn't important. Just hanging out with Bloom, a psychiatrist and Dantzler's old college tennis teammate, and Sean, an ex-homicide cop who was now a successful defense attorney, was the chief reason why he enjoyed being there. Friendship was a more-important sustenance than food.

Erin had been with them until she had to leave for her job in Frankfort. She wasn't a standard fixture at these early morning get-togethers, but when she was it was to the delight of Bloom and Sean, both of whom adored her. The two men were more than pleased to include her in their inner circle. She had quickly become one of the boys.

"You've landed a great lady," Sean noted, moments after Erin departed. "I know this is asking a lot, but try to not muck it up."

Dantzler chuckled, said, "Taking relationship advice from you, Sean, is like listening to a politician's promise—it just doesn't carry much weight. Let's face it . . . you have 'mucked-up' more promising relationships with women than any guy I know."

"Point taken. But like my old man used to tell me, 'Do as I say, not as I do.' That's sage advice, right?"

"Yeah, and it proves once again the old man was far more intelligent than his son."

Bloom said, "Hate to interrupt such a stimulating conversation but I want to hear more about Jack's midnight conference with our esteemed governor. What was your take on the guy, Jack?"

"Worried, definitely scared, unsure what to do next."

"And he has no idea who might've sent the note?"

"Said he didn't."

"You believe him?"

"For the most part, I do. He has no reason to lie."

Sean said, "Guy's got plenty of money. Why not cough up the dough? Put a quick end to it?"

"You know the answer to that, Sean," Bloom said. "If he pays once, he'll likely have to pay again in the future. Maybe multiple times. Blackmailers tend to be rather greedy."

"Know what's interesting?" asked Dantzler. "I got the feeling Baker wasn't nearly as concerned about the money as he was about the fear of being embarrassed."

"If that's true, then Baker is keeping something secret," Sean pointed out. "He has a very big skeleton hiding in his closet. It also means he wasn't being completely truthful."

"Yeah, I came away convinced he was keeping something from me. There was more to his story than he was willing to reveal."

"How do you plan to work the case?" Bloom inquired.

"Start by talking with his family members, then work my way out from there. But what I really need is someone to do computer research. That would help speed things along."

"Has to be someone with access to law enforcement data bases," Sean said, adding, "talk with Eric. He can assign someone from Homicide to work with you. Those folks worship you. Any of them would be more than willing to help out."

Eric Gamble was head of Lexington's Homicide Unit. Dantzler had trained Eric, and was among the strongest voices advocating for him to replace Richard Bird, who had held the position for nearly twenty years.

"Thought about that," Dantzler admitted. "But for now I need to keep a tight circle on this situation. Since this is the governor's problem, I'll ask him to pick someone of his choosing. He shouldn't have an issue with that."

"No disrespect to you, Jack, but the governor is crazy for not turning this matter over to the FBI," Sean noted.

"That's exactly what I told him. He wasted no time shooting down that suggestion. Said he'd rather have me look into it first."

"Insane."

"I don't disagree with you, Sean."

"Good luck with this one, Jack," Bloom said. "Sounds like you're gonna need it."

"Amen to that," replied Dantzler.

DANTZLER LEFT IHOP (after picking up the check), climbed into his car, took out his cell phone and called Kathy Baker. She answered immediately.

"Yes, Mr. Dantzler, Mark told me you would be calling, that you needed to speak with me," she said. "Is that correct?"

"Yes, I do think it's important we talk. When can you be available?"

"What about nine o'clock? Is that too soon?"

"No, it's perfect. Where should we meet?"

"Would it be okay with you if we met outdoors somewhere?" Kathy asked. "It's such a lovely morning. I prefer sunshine to sitting in a room. Is that possible?"

"I rarely say no to sunshine. Where would you like to meet?"

"Do you know where the Vietnam War Memorial is located?"

"Yes, I do. Is that where you want to meet?"

"It's such a lovely place, so yes, if it's okay with you, let's talk there."

"I'll see you at nine." Dantzler paused, then quickly asked, "How will I recognize you?"

"Oh, you won't have to," Kathy stated. "I've seen your picture in the paper enough times to know exactly what you look like. I'll find you."

Dantzler closed his phone, started the motor and began the thirty-minute drive to Frankfort. The Vietnam War Memorial was located on Vernon Cooper Lane, a site he had visited on numerous occasions. He agreed with Kathy Baker—it was a lovely place. The Memorial itself, which honored the more than eleven-hundred Kentucky GIs killed in Vietnam, was laid out like a huge sundial, in which the sundial pointer, or gnomon, touched each fallen soldier's name on the anniversary of his death. It was a neat, respectful tribute to the commonwealth's fallen warriors.

Dantzler arrived at the Memorial nearly ten-minutes prior to the scheduled meeting time with the governor's wife. He was standing in his usual place when he saw a woman walking briskly in his direction. Although he had never laid eyes on the governor's wife, he instantly knew the woman was Kathy Baker. She was dressed casually—white capri pants, blue blouse, flat shoes. Her hair had hints of gray (probably by design, Dantzler concluded), she had on little noticeable makeup, and her eyes were hidden behind sunglasses. Upon reaching Dantzler, she smiled and offered her hand, which he accepted.

"Wish I could say it's a pleasure meeting you, but under the circumstances, Mr. Dantzler, that would be a lie."

"Call me Jack." Dantzler pointed to a name on the Memorial. "He was Mr. Dantzler."

Kathy Baker leaned over, lifted her sunglasses, and read the name Dantzler was pointing at.

John David Dantzler, Sept. 17, 1970

"Your father was killed in Vietnam?" she asked.

"He fought in the Vietnam War, but he actually died in Laos."

"Why would an American soldier be fighting in Laos?"

"Long story."

"I know it's become almost a requirement to say 'thank you for your service' to everyone who has been in the military," she pointed out. "But what can you say for the fallen that even comes close to honoring their sacrifice? What words, what memorials can adequately honor a person's life? Those tributes are nice, but in the end they fail to heal the deep feelings of loss felt by those left behind. How do you handle it, Jack?"

"One day at a time, I suppose. That's really all I can do. All anyone can do. What other choice do we have?"

Kathy reached out and took hold of Dantzler's hand. "I am truly sorry for your loss," she said. "But I'm sure he would be very proud of you. Let me amend that: I'm sure he *is* very proud of you."

"Thank you." Dantzler nodded toward a bench located beneath a tree. "How about we sit over there? Looks like a comfortable spot."

After they were seated, Kathy said, "What do you think of this business concerning my husband? How worried should I be?"

"Honestly, I can't answer that. Not yet, anyway. And I won't be able to until the governor receives another note. Until then, I'm working in the dark."

"So . . . until that happens, there is nothing you can do?"

"I can ask questions, do some digging, but the problem is, I really don't have the resources to do very much. That's why I told your husband his best bet would be to hand this off to the FBI. He wasn't inclined to agree with me."

"Believe me, Jack, I said the same thing. He shut that idea down in a nanosecond."

"Can you think of anyone who could be behind this?"

Kathy shook her head, said, "No, I can't. Mark is the governor, governors make political enemies, they receive hate mail, they garner pages and pages of bad press, and they hear from angry constituents, but . . . that stuff is par for the course. This . . . this is something else entirely. This is beyond hate."

"Not necessarily," Dantzler responded. "It's just as likely this person has no feelings toward your husband at all, that his only goal is the money."

"I wish I could believe that," Kathy said. "But let's face facts. My husband is not a popular governor."

"Take me back to the Boston years. Is there anything in your husband's business past that might come back to haunt him? Can you think of any particular individual who might be seeking revenge?"

"Mark might not be a popular governor, but I can assure you he was an honest businessman. He often went out of his way to help individuals whose businesses were struggling. He made many more friends than enemies. I just don't think our time in Boston has anything to do with this situation."

"I'm inclined to agree," Dantzler admitted.

"Mark is an honest, fair-minded man." Seeing Dantzler smile, she said, "Why the smirk, Jack? Don't you think Mark was being honest with you?"

"Up to a point, yes. But I also had the feeling he was hiding something."

"Did he tell you about his affair?"

"He did," Dantzler answered, trying to hide his surprise. "He also said you didn't know about it."

"Please, I knew about it the day it began and I knew when it ended. My husband isn't quite as clever as he thinks he is. But it was brief, only lasted a couple of weeks, so I chose to let it pass. Had it carried on much longer I would have ended the marriage. If he shared that indiscretion with you, I would have to say he was being totally honest."

"What about the woman? Did you know her?"

"No. And I didn't want to."

"Any chance she could be behind this? Or maybe someone she's familiar with who knew about the affair?"

"My God, that was thirty years ago. If she or anyone else wanted to hit Mark up for money surely they would have done it before now."

"Agreed. Can you think of anything that might prove embarrassing to you, Mark, or any family members? Your kids—what can you tell me about them?"

"They both live in Boston, both are married, and both have two children," Kathy said. "Michael is thirty-one, a Harvard graduate, and a tax attorney. His wife's name is Sheila. They have two sons, Brian and Douglas. Our daughter Kelly is twenty-eight. She graduated from Boston University, and is now a registered nurse. Her husband Paul Snyder is a dentist. They have two girls, Lisa and Stephanie. I dare say you would be hard-pressed to find two more clean-cut, upstanding families anywhere."

"I also informed the governor that I'm going to be doing some serious deep-diving into the past. Is there anything in your background that your husband isn't aware of? Any secrets you are keeping from him?"

"No, most definitely, there are not. I only dated a couple of guys before I met Mark. Once I did all other men fell by the wayside. And in case you are wondering, no, I was never unfaithful to him. Not once was I ever tempted to stray."

"What about Mark's parents? Are they still alive?"

"No, they've been gone for years now. My parents are both alive, though. Dad is ninety-six, but you'd never know it by looking at him. He's a true freak of nature. Mom is eighty-seven, and even though her mind is still sharp as a tack her, body is beginning break down. She requires a cane or a walker to get around."

"Anything in their past that could be troublesome?" Dantzler inquired.

"I don't see how. Dad was a mechanic, Mom worked for the local school board. Neither of those are what can be called glamorous occupations."

Dantzler stood, said, "Like I told you, we're all just whistling in the dark until we receive another demand from whomever is doing this. I can begin doing some preliminary research, but how effective I will be is questionable at this stage."

"Thank you for working with Mark on this dreadful situation." Kathy stood. "I have every confidence you can get to the bottom of this. Don't hesitate to contact me if we need to speak again. I am always available."

Kathy strolled away just as briskly as she had arrived, leaving Dantzler standing alone in the shadows. Watching as she departed, he couldn't help but wonder why she had such confidence in his ability to handle a situation that at this point was a mystery with no possible resolution, successful or otherwise. Her faith in him was, he felt, both misplaced and misguided.

He also couldn't help but wonder if Kathy, like her husband, was hiding something. If so, that didn't lend itself to a successful resolution to this case. What he didn't need was the principals keeping secrets.

Dantzler took out his cell phone called the governor's personal number. Mark Baker answered after three rings.

"Have you set a time to meet with Kathy?" the governor asked.

"Just finished speaking with her. She didn't say much that would be helpful."

"That's not surprising. She has nothing to do with what's happening. This is about me."

"The reason I'm calling is to ask for your help."

"What do you need?"

"Someone who is a whiz at computer research," Dantzler answered quickly. "I have an individual in mind, but since you were adamant about keeping the circle small, I thought you might want to pick someone. Whoever that person is, he or she has to have access to all local, state and federal law enforcement data bases."

"I do know the perfect lady for the job," the governor said. "Her name is Hannah Andrews. She recently left the Department of Criminal Investigations. Hannah would be terrific. And paying her will not be a problem."

"DCI? Those folks work out of the attorney general's office, don't they?"

"Correct."

Shit, that's where Erin works. Hannah Andrews is likely the woman Erin replaced. "If you think she's up to the job, give her a call," Dantzler said. "If she agrees, have her contact me immediately."

"I have to attend a couple of meetings before I'll have time to contact her. But I will the second I'm free. You should hear from Hannah before the end of business today."

"Great. I look forward to it."

Not really, Dantzler thought as he ended the call.

FOUR

BEFORE LEAVING FRANKFORT, DANTZLER GAVE SOME thought to stopping by Erin's office, which wasn't located far from the Memorial, and pay her a surprise visit. However, after thinking about it for several seconds, he quickly nixed the idea. Erin was still relatively new at her job, so his showing up unannounced probably wasn't a wise thing to do. He would have to wait until Erin took her lunch break before he could call and ask his question.

Dantzler decided it was time to get something to eat. He was famished. The bagel and orange juice he had at IHOP were a distant memory. He ran through a host of potential eating places once he got back to Lexington, ticking them off one by one, with none grabbing his attention. Instead, knowing there was plenty of food at his house, he opted to head home and slap together his own lunch. Erin made tuna two days ago, and there was quite a bit remaining. A tuna sandwich, some chips, a sweet pickle and a Pepsi sounded pretty tasty. Plus, it was cheap.

An hour later he was sitting at the kitchen table, his make-shift meal half-finished when his cell phone buzzed. The call was from Erin.

"Hey, are you too busy to talk?" she asked.

"No, I'm sitting at home dining on a tuna sandwich, courtesy of you." Dantzler took a sip of Pepsi, said, "Do you know Hannah Andrews?"

"Of course I do. We were classmates in law school. I now have her old job. You know that. We talked about it prior to me accepting the position."

"Yeah, I remember now. But didn't you tell me she was taking a job with a law firm in St. Louis?"

"That was her original plan, yes. Obviously, she had a change of heart. Hannah is now working for a global private security firm with offices all over the world. She does computer research from her home here in Frankfort. In fact, I saw her two days ago. Why are you asking about Hannah?"

"When I informed the governor that we needed a computer whiz to help with this case he immediately singled out Hannah as the person for the job. He didn't hesitate before tossing out her name."

"Well, he's correct . . . Hannah is a computer whiz. He couldn't have picked a more competent person."

"This means I'll be working with the woman you replaced," Dantzler pointed out. "Is that a problem?"

"Why would that be a problem?"

"I don't know. It just seems strange, is all. What does Hannah look like?"

"She's gorgeous."

"Of course she would be."

"What you're really hinting at is will I be jealous?" Erin asked. "Isn't that what's at the core of your concerns?"

"Well, maybe . . . I suppose so, yes. Will you be jealous?"

"Do you love me, Jack?"

"You know I do."

"Do you trust me?"

"Of course."

"Well, I love you and trust you, so why would you working with Hannah be a problem?"

"You're positive?"

"Jack, if you're in this for the long haul, I'm in it for the long haul," Erin said. "And if we both are, then love and trust are the weapons we'll always have on our side. So . . . you can work with Hannah, or Scarlett Johansson, or Lady Gaga, and I won't give it a second thought. That's because I trust you completely."

"Not sure I'd feel the same way if you were working with George Clooney or Bradley Cooper."

"Trust me, Jack. I have no interest in having a fling with our lieutenant governor. He's definitely not my type."

"He's not the Bradley Cooper I'd be worried about."

"Relax, Jack, and go with the flow. Things are great between us now and they'll be great in the future. Stop worrying, okay?"

"Got it, boss."

"Good. What about meeting later this evening at the Tennis Center?" Erin asked. "Play a couple of sets and then get some supper? Sound like a plan?"

"When can you be there?"

"Sixish. Maybe a little later, depending on how soon certain things get done here."

"I'll see you then."

DANTZLER SPENT the rest of the afternoon at home alternating between listening to music and reading. Under normal circumstances he would have considered such leisure activities as wasting time. He would have felt guilty. But nothing about this was normal. He was locked in a holding pattern that would only end when the next note arrived, if it did. There wasn't much he could do until then.

He left his house at five, drove to the Tennis Center, cut the motor and scanned the parking area, hoping to see if Erin's Audi was there. It wasn't. He was about to the exit his car when his phone rang. The number was not familiar to him but he had a pretty good idea who the caller was—Hannah Andrews.

It was a good guess on his part.

"Thanks for getting in touch with me in such a timely manner, Hannah," Dantzler said. "I'm sure you are very busy, so I appreciate you agreeing to help."

"Aren't you dating Erin Collins?" Hannah asked.

The question caught Dantzler by surprise. "Yes, I am. Why? Is that a problem?"

"Are you aware that our friendship goes back years? And that Erin is now filling my old position?"

"Yes, to both questions. Again, I ask . . . is this going to be a problem between us?"

"Only if you mistreat her in any way. Do that and your punishment will be severe. And I hope you don't think I'm joking. Erin is like a sister to me. I know how strong her feelings are for you. I just don't want to see her get hurt."

"While your concern is touching, it's also misplaced. There is no way I would ever intentionally hurt Erin. My feelings for her are just as strong."

"Terrific. Then let's move forward," Hannah commanded. "Exactly why do you need my help?"

"How much information did Governor Baker share with you when he called?"

"He left a message with your name and number, and insisted I call immediately. That's all he relayed to me. Why? What's going on?"

"What I'm about to share with you needs to be kept in the vault," Dantzler said. "Anything you learn later on comes to me first, and then I'll decide if it should be passed along to Governor Baker. Most . . ."

"If we're working for the governor, why shouldn't he know everything when you and I do?" Hannah interrupted. "What you're suggesting comes across as deceitful."

"I would only keep information from him I judged to be harmful to a member of his family. That's a real possibility in this situation. All I'm saying is it's best that I reserve the right to judge when—or if—Governor Baker sees it. It's for his protection."

"Then you should explain to me what the situation is, because right now I am clueless."

"Do you mind if I ask you a few questions first?"

"No, I don't mind at all. What do you want to know?"

"Initially, Erin told me you were leaving to take a position with a law firm in St. Louis," Dantzler said. "This morning, she informed me you turned down the job, and you are currently working for a worldwide private security firm. Am I correct so far?"

"Yes, you are. I do computer research for International Security, which has its home base in London," Hannah explained. "I work from my home in Frankfort, but I am occasionally required to travel, both here and abroad. My primary task is to gather information on suspected terrorists around the world. We share our findings with governments and with local law enforcement agencies. In case you are wondering why I chose this job over being an attorney, the reason is simple. I am contributing to the safety of millions of people from all corners of the world. That's something no attorney can do."

"How high is your security clearance?"

"There are only one or two levels above mine." Hannah paused, then said, "Now that I have answered your questions, don't you think it's time you fill me in on what's going on, and why I am needed?"

Dantzler said, "Two nights ago, Governor Baker discovered a folder on the windshield of his car. Inside was a single piece of paper with a typed message on it. The message demanded that he pay five-million dollars or embarrassing information about his family would be released, and that he was to wait for further instructions."

"He should have alerted the FBI the second he read the message," Hannah said.

"First words out of my mouth, but he refused. He wants to keep a tight circle until we can come up with some answers."

"You know, some smart people are really dumb."

"I did instruct him how to open a second folder when it comes," Dantzler noted. "If he follows my advice, maybe we'll get lucky and lift a few prints."

"If he'd done that with the first folder, and then called in the FBI, they might have someone in custody by now."

"Too late to play the what-should-have-been-done game."

"So it is. Okay, let's move on."

"Here's what I need from you, Hannah. Do a serious background check on Governor Baker, Kathy Baker, their son Michael Baker, his wife Sheila, daughter Kelly Baker Snyder and her husband Paul Snyder. That last name is spelled S-N-Y-D-E-R. The two kids still live in Boston. I can give you their phone numbers, and e-mail and home addresses, if you need them."

"Not necessary; their names are all I require," Hannah said. "How soon do you need this information?"

"Whenever you can get it to me is fine. I doubt anyone from Boston is behind this, but I need to consider all possibilities before ruling anything out. Once that's done, we can begin to expand our search, which likely means digging into the past of any local individuals who have made threats, verbal or otherwise, against the governor."

"The person behind this will not fall into that group. He won't be a disgruntled citizen."

"Hannah, I think you are exactly right about that. This individual is going to come out of left-field."

"I will get the results of these background checks to you within forty-eight hours, maybe sooner. While you are waiting to hear from the blackmailer, or from me, go ahead and collect the names of the governor's critics who you judge to be worth investigating. In the meantime, you take good care of Erin. She's a diamond."

"You don't have to tell me how lucky I am," Dantzler said, adding, "let me know if you need anything else from me."

"Roger that," Hannah responded before punching off.

DANTZLER WAS on one of the indoor courts exchanging shots with David Bloom when Erin showed up. She watched them for a couple of minutes before heading to the locker room to change into her tennis clothes and to grab her equipment bag. Ten minutes later, ready for battle, she strolled back to the side of the court, went through a few stretching exercises and announced, "Your worst nightmare has arrived."

Dantzler and Bloom laughed out loud, though neither man was overly impressed by her boastful pronouncement. They both knew she was good—she had been an All-America player at Duke University—but she had yet to take a set from either man, although she had come close to beating Bloom on several occasions. She was certain—and so was Bloom—that it was just a matter of time until she raised the flag of victory against him.

A win against Dantzler, however, was a long way down the

road, if it happened at all, which was highly doubtful. His talent level was in a different stratosphere.

"Come on, Bloom, let's do battle," Erin suggested. "That is, unless you are afraid your reign of terror ends tonight."

"Fear is not in my vocabulary, Erin. You should know that by now."

"Then saddle up, cowboy, I'm taking you for a ride."

"I don't see that happening."

An hour later, soundly beaten, Bloom shook Erin's hand at the net, then announced, "That's it for me as a singles player. From now on I play doubles or I'm a spectator."

"Prudent decision, Bloom," Dantzler stated. "We both know you were always better at doubles than you were at singles."

"What about you, Jack?" Erin asked. "Are you up for a set? I'm feeling really confident."

"Where's the honor in defeating a tired opponent?" he replied. "Challenge me when you have fresh legs. Play me now and it will be even less competitive than normal."

"That's what I love about you, Jack. You never take advantage of me."

"And after being sternly lectured to by Hannah Andrews, I wouldn't dare try."

"She has my back, huh?"

"She threatened me with total annihilation if I fail to treat you like a queen."

"You should listen to her. Hannah's tough."

As Erin rose up to give Dantzler a kiss on the cheek, his cell phone interrupted the romance. He looked at the phone but showed no interest in picking it up. A kiss from Erin was far more pleasurable than taking a phone call. Plus, there was no reason to hurry. No need to answer immediately. This call wasn't unexpected. He'd been waiting for it.

And he knew who the caller was, and what the call was about.

FIVE

"I FOLLOWED YOUR INSTRUCTIONS TO THE LETTER," THE governor proudly boasted. "I used two fingers to remove the folder from the windshield, and only used my thumb to open it. I touched nothing inside."

"Excellent," Dantzler said, adding, "What did the note say?"

"That's just it. There was no note, only a cell phone."

"Huh. No Post-it note, no message at all?"

"Nope, nothing but the phone."

"Was the phone still in its original packaging?"

"No, it wasn't," said the governor. "Why? Is that important?"

"Could be?"

"How?"

"It means whoever sent the folder had to touch the phone when removing it from the package," Dantzler pointed out. "It also means there is a very good chance we can lift a fingerprint. That is, unless he wore gloves. We'll get nothing if he did."

"We can only hope for the best," said the governor. "What do you want me to do now?"

"Are you in Frankfort?"

"No, I'm in Lexington, in the parking lot outside of Malone's on Tates Creek Road."

"That's where you found the folder?"

"Yes, I was in the restaurant meeting with some donors. When I came outside, that's when I saw it."

"You aren't far from where I live. Program my address into your GPS and come straight to my house." Dantzler gave him the address. "Did you get it?"

"Yeah."

"It shouldn't take you more than ten or fifteen minutes to get here. Call if you get lost."

"What then?" the governor inquired. "Take the phone to a criminalist to get the prints?"

"No need to do that," replied Dantzler. "I can lift prints, provided there are any."

"I'm on my way."

After ending the call, Dantzler went into the guest bedroom, opened a closet and retrieved his briefcase, the one he used during his final ten years as a homicide detective. In it was everything necessary for the lifting of fingerprints—black powder, a small brush, clear tape, and latex gloves. Lifting fingerprints wasn't a particularly challenging task, but it did require concentration, discipline and extreme attention to detail.

Dantzler carried the materials into the kitchen and placed them in a chair. After clearing the table and wiping it down with a damp rag, he covered the tabletop with a newspaper, plucked a paper plate from the cabinet, placed it on the table, then transferred the materials onto the table.

Everything was in place when Governor Baker arrived eighteen minutes later. Dantzler met him at the door and let him in. The governor entered the house and handed the folder to Dantzler as though its contents were radioactive.

Dantzler took the folder, then led the governor through the

house and into the kitchen. Carefully picking up the folder from the bottom, he turned it upside-down, gave it a gentle shake until the phone slid onto the paper plate. After putting on the latex gloves, he got down to business.

First, he sprinkled some of the black powder onto the side of the phone facing upward. Next, he took the brush and carefully brushed away some of the powder. What remained revealed a clean print. Finally, Dantzler took a piece of clear tape, pressed it onto the surface where the print was visible, and then slowly pulled the tape away.

Studying it, Dantzler said, "This is a near-perfect print. Probably the guy's thumb."

Then he used a spoon to flip the phone over. After going through the same procedure on this side, he commented, "Two more good ones. His forefinger and index finger, most likely."

"Now that we have the prints, where do we take them?" the governor inquired.

"To Hannah. She can run them through her data bases, see if she can get a hit."

The governor looked at his watch, said, "It's almost ten. You aren't taking them to her tonight, are you?"

"I'll give her a call, see if that's possible," Dantzler said. "The sooner she has them, the better."

"Do you also leave the phone with her?"

"No, the phone stays with you in case the guy calls."

"Right. And what if he does? What should I do? Keep him talking so the call can be traced? Isn't that standard procedure?"

"That won't be necessary; he'll use a burner phone. And you can be sure he will destroy it the moment the call ends. If he does call, try to extract as much information as possible. The more he says, the better our chances he'll screw up and reveal something that will help us. Write down everything he says. Remember, no detail is too small or insignificant."

When the governor was gone, Dantzler cleared the kitchen table, again wiping it down with a rag, and then he put the materials back into the briefcase. After returning it to the closet, he went back into the kitchen, opened the refrigerator, grabbed a bottle of Smithwick's, opened it and took a long swig. Then he picked up his phone and punched in Hannah's number.

"Let me take a wild guess," Hannah said. "A call this late can only mean one thing—the governor received a second note. Am I right?"

"Hello, to you, Hannah," Dantzler chided. "And no, you are not right. There was no note. This time the folder contained only a cell phone."

"Darn, a rare miss on my part. How about you give me a Mulligan? You know what that is, don't you?"

"Yeah, but in tennis it's known as a second serve. But sure, go for it."

"You were able to lift a fingerprint?"

"Bingo. And not just one—I managed to get three. All are excellent. When can I get them to you?"

"You have two choices," Hannah said. "You can bring them tonight but I won't be able to do anything with them. A prior commitment will keep me tied up all day tomorrow. Sorry, but it can't be helped. Keep in mind I do have a real job. However, you can bring them tomorrow night, at which time I will be in a position to give them my full attention. Your call."

"What if I bring them tomorrow during the day? That way they'll be there when you do get home. Somewhere inside the house would be best. Is there any way you can leave me a key?"

"Erin has a key to my place. Get it from her. She may not be comfortable giving it to you, so if she does give you a hassle, have her phone me. You can leave the prints anytime tomorrow. I'll be gone all day."

"Just out of curiosity, do you have a key to Erin's place?" Dantzler asked.

"What do you think?"

"Jesus, I had no idea."

"I told you, Jack, she and I are like sisters."

"Yeah, that picture is becoming clearer every day."

"Get those prints to me tomorrow," Hannah said. "I can't promise how long it will take before we get a hit, *if* we get a hit, but I will definitely make searching for them a top priority."

"Oh, we'll get one. A guy who tries to pull off a deal like this is no virgin. He has a past criminal record. You can take that to the bank."

"You're probably right. Get me the prints and we'll find out for sure."

DANTZLER WAS TOO JAZZED to sleep, so he opened a second bottle of Smithwick's, went out to his deck that overlooked the small lake that bumped up against his backyard, sat down and let his thoughts wander. The night was strangely quiet. Absent were the sounds generated by the crickets, frogs and birds who serenaded the evenings on a regular basis. It was a chorus he had come to appreciate.

Being a man of action, a guy hard-wired to always keep moving forward, he found himself frustrated with having to wait before making his next move. Dantzler was pragmatic, if nothing else. He didn't view circumstances through rose-tinted glasses. Whatever it took to bring a bad person to justice was what he did. He didn't believe in grandstanding, hot-dogging or show-boating. Old-fashioned hard work was his ticket to success. Put your nose to the grindstone, keep plugging along, and don't look up until the job was finished. That was his mantra. That was how he had always approached every case. This one was no different.

However, certain cases had sorely tested his resolve. This one had the potential to fall into that category, and lack of forward movement was the reason why. He remained stuck in a holding pattern, totally at the mercy of the governor's blackmailer. There had been two correspondences, yet the only stated demand was to pay five-million dollars. No details, no specific directions. This went against normal. It defied logic. What was the blackmailer waiting for? What was his reason for remaining silent?

Dantzler had to give the guy—and he was sure the blackmailer was male—a certain level of respect. Sending a phone rather than a second note was a smart move. Written or typed messages were more susceptible to being identified by the new breed of modern law enforcement techie geeks than a conversation conducted on a burner phone. Handwriting analysis can provide many clues, as can certain letters typed on an ancient typewriter. Even notes typed on a computer can yield critical clues that might help us identify the note's author.

But this guy, like most criminals Dantzler had confronted over the decades, was far from perfect. Sending the phone was smart, yes, but sending the phone after having opened it, no, that wasn't smart. In fact, it was dumb. And to perform either task without wearing gloves, well, that was not only dumb, it was also a huge mistake. Unless this dude had angel wings his name was bound to be in the system. There was not one chance in a million he didn't have a criminal background. Leaving behind those fingerprints would prove to be his downfall.

That was a major blunder.

But as Dantzler finished his second beer, he was forced to acknowledge that while the blackmailer was no genius, the guy had the makings of a formidable foe.

DANTZLER WAS SITTING on the deck, nodding off when the sound of his phone startled him awake. He initially thought Hannah was getting back to him with fingerprint results. Then he remembered he had not yet given them to her.

He checked to see who was calling this close to midnight, and was surprised to see Erin's name on the caller ID. Immediately, he feared something was wrong and the call was some type of emergency. But he was worried for no reason. Erin was quick to let him know everything was fine.

"No, I just had a sneaking suspicion you wouldn't be in bed," she said. "Looks like I was right. What's keeping you awake? Thinking about the governor's situation?"

"How did you know about that?" Dantzler asked, before answering his own question. "From your pal Hannah Andrews, right?"

"Right. She called to advise me you needed my key to her place. When I asked why, she told me what's going on with the governor, that he's being blackmailed. That's a rather important detail you neglected to share with me, wouldn't you agree?"

"Are you positive I didn't tell you about it? I'm sure I did."

"All you said was the governor needed a computer whiz for a case you were working. You failed to provide full details."

"No, before that. When we were at IHOP with Bloom and Sean. Didn't I mentioned it to you then?"

"You did not."

"An inadvertent oversight on my part," Dantzler said, apologetically. "Trust me, I'm not keeping secrets from you."

"Good to know. Secrets in a relationship are like cancer cells— they rarely lead to a positive outcome." She laughed. "As you can tell, I'm obviously not angry."

"*That's* good to know."

"How soon do you need Hannah's key?"

"When can I get it?"

"Come to my place tomorrow. I'll leave it on the dining rocm table. Keep it as long as necessary. All I ask is I get it back. Deal?"

"Deal."

"Now go to bed. We both need the rest."

"Yes, dear."

"Love you, Jack."

"Back atcha."

SIX

DANTZLER PICKED UP THE KEY FROM ERIN'S HOUSE AT NINE the next morning then drove to Hannah's place in Frankfort and dropped off the fingerprints. He left them on the kitchen table, as Hannah had suggested. On the table was a typed message for him.

"Jack: Background check on the Baker clan was a total bust. I found nothing even remotely close to suspicious or illegal, just three speeding tickets, the most recent being twenty years ago. The Baker family is cleaner than the Brady Bunch. I also checked to see if Mark Baker or his business had been the subject of any lawsuits. The answer is no. Let me know where you want to go from here."

Nothing about Hannah's findings surprised Dantzler, although the fact that Baker's business was free of any litigation did catch his attention. In his experience, virtually every super-successful business person or the business itself was at some point the target of a lawsuit. That neither Baker nor his business had ever been accused or charged with wrongdoing was impressive. Perhaps Kathy Baker wasn't exaggerating when she claimed her husband was an honest, fair-minded man.

Back in Lexington, Dantzler drove to the Tennis Center, parked, and hurried inside. He had business to take care of in his office—checks requiring his signature, along with other forms that needed to be filled out. Once those long-neglected chores were taken care of, he headed to the locker room, changed into his workout clothes, and spent nearly an hour on the treadmill.

Finished, breathing hard, his body coated in sweat, he showered, dressed, and went back upstairs to the lounge area. After grabbing a bottle of water—and paying for it—he sat, took out his cell phone and gave David Bloom a call.

"What's happening, Ace?" Bloom asked

"Are you with a patient?"

"Wouldn't have answered if I were. You know that."

"So, are you free for lunch?"

"Sure. Where did you have in mind?"

"What about the Cheesecake Factory?"

"Sounds like a winner," Bloom said. "I've been craving their potato soup for weeks."

"Great. I'll meet you there in half an hour."

AS DANTZLER WAS LEAVING the Tennis Center, he was ambushed by Randall Dennis, a long-time friend whose only goal in life was to win a single set against Dantzler. This had never happened in the past, nor would it in the future. Some outcomes are firmly fixed by the tennis gods, and nothing or no one can outfox those celestial beings. But none of this mattered to Dennis, a gentle soul who combined boundless optimism with an apparently limitless capacity for disappointment.

"You up for a couple of sets, Jack?" Dennis asked. "I'm feeling lucky this morning. I think my time has come."

"What time would that be?" Dantzler answered.

"Time for me to take a set from you. What else would I be referring to?"

"What have I always told you, Randall? The Messiah will show up long before you ever win a set against me. And I highly doubt he's headed this way anytime soon."

"Yeah, yeah, I know that's your standard line. But who's to say things won't change today?"

"If you want to win a set, here's my advice. Curtis Gibson is downstairs looking for someone to play. Go find him."

"Hell, Jack, he's got to be eighty-five."

"Exactly. You want to enjoy the sweet taste of victory, go beat up on Curtis. I'm confident you can handle him."

"Wouldn't be the same," Dennis proclaimed.

"It's the best you get today, Randall. You're not on my menu. Sorry."

Smiling, Dantzler left the Tennis Center, got in his car, and drove to the Fayette Mall, where the Cheesecake Factory was located. As always, the massive parking area was packed, yet Dantzler immediately spied Bloom standing next to his car. Dantzler pulled parallel to Bloom's Volvo, killed the motor, and got out.

"Sorry for being late," Dantzler said. "I got blindsided by Randall Dennis."

"Let me guess, he wanted to play a set or two against you?"

"Said his time had come, that victory would be his today."

"You have to give the guy credit. He is an eternal optimist."

"He'll need a lot more than optimism if he hopes to beat me." Dantzler pointed toward the Cheesecake Factory entrance. "Come on, let's eat."

Normally at noon it wasn't uncommon to have a wait time before being seated. But that wasn't the case today. Surprisingly, the Cheesecake Factory was light on customers. There were plenty of seats available.

Surveying the dining area, Dantzler noticed a familiar face sitting at a back table. Kathy Baker was seated with a much-older gentleman. She smiled and wave when she saw Dantzler, then motioned for him to join her and the elderly man, who Dantzler assumed was her father.

"Come on, Bloom," Dantzler said, heading in the direction of Kathy's table. "I'll introduce you to the governor's wife."

"How the hell do you know Mark Baker's wife?"

"I'm working a case with him, remember?"

"I know that. I just didn't know you had met Baker's wife."

"Well, now you do."

Kathy extended her hand to Dantzler but didn't rise. "Hello, Jack," she said. "Would you and your friend care to join us? We were about to leave, but since you're here, I would like to ask you a few questions. But first, why not make the introductions?"

"David, this is Kathy Baker," Dantzler said. "Kathy, David Bloom."

As Kathy shook Bloom's hand, Dantzler turned his attention to the old man. "And I'm guessing this gentleman must be your father."

"You are correct, Jack," Kathy said. "This is Ernie Kruger."

"Pleased to meet you, sir," Dantzler said.

Ernie offered his hand to Dantzler but made no attempt to do the same with Bloom.

Kathy cut her eyes toward Bloom, which Dantzler understood as her silent way of asking just how much she could say in front of a stranger

"You can speak freely in front of David," Dantzler said to Kathy. "He is aware of what's going on. As a psychiatrist, he's trained to keep secrets. Plus, he's bound by the time-honored doctor-patient confidentiality agreement. We'll have his license if he breaks his oath."

"Were you able to learn anything from the cell phone sent to my husband?" Kathy asked. "Mark said you found fingerprints. Is that correct?"

"I found three good ones. They have been sent to a lady who will run them through her data bases, see what pops us. If we're lucky, we could have a name by tomorrow morning."

"That sounds very promising, Jack. Once you have a name, what's your next step?"

"Go pay him a visit. Find out if he's the blackmailer, or if he's only working for someone else. Either way, I wouldn't leave until I had some answers."

Kathy looked at Bloom, said, "You're the psychiatrist, so tell me, why does a person engage in such an ugly activity? Is it just for the money?"

"Money is his most-likely motivation," Bloom replied. "But it may be something other than money that drives him. Anger and revenge could also be at the core of what he's doing."

"Anger and revenge . . . for what?"

"You won't know unless he tells you."

"I look forward to that day." Kathy patted her father's arm. "Come on, Dad. We need to get moving."

"Bloom?" the old man said. "That's typically a Jewish name, isn't it? Are you a Jew?"

"Proud to say I am," answered Bloom, startled by the question. "Why? Do you have something against Jews?"

"Not at all. I just don't run into a lot of Jews. Are there many in Lexington?"

"Come to synagogue on the Sabbath. You'll find out for yourself."

Ernie Kruger smiled enigmatically but didn't respond.

"You're accent is German, isn't it?" Bloom inquired. "Where are you originally from, Mr. Kruger?"

"Milwaukee," the old man answered. "But my parents came to

America from Germany. They both lived in Munich. I suppose I inherited my accent from them."

"No more talk, Dad," Kathy said, standing. "We need to get a move on. It was nice running into you, Jack. Let us know if you learn anything from those fingerprints. And it was a pleasure meeting you, Doctor Bloom."

"Likewise," Bloom said.

After Kathy and her father were gone, Dantzler said to Bloom, "I get the distinct impression you didn't much care for Ernie Kruger. Am I reading you wrong?"

"An old German with that accent would make any Jew nervous."

"The guy can't help how he sounds. Come on, let's order."

"I've lost my appetite," Bloom announced.

"Seriously?"

"Yeah. But you go ahead and eat. I'll watch you."

"If you don't eat, I don't eat," Dantzler said. "We might as well take off."

"I don't want to spoil your lunch."

"You aren't. I'll grab something from the machines in the Tennis Center lounge."

"Oh, we both know how nutritious that will be."

"Ah, but it will be tasty and filling." Dantzler stood. "Let's go."

Outside, as they were walking to their cars, Dantzler suddenly stopped, and said, "Casually look around the parking area, Bloom. Tell me if you see anyone watching us or acting suspicious."

Bloom turned his head from side to side as though he was stretching his neck. "No, I don't see anything even slightly off. Why am I doing this?"

Dantzler pointed to his car, where a single piece of paper secured to his windshield by one of the wiper blades was flapping in the breeze. "Looks like our blackmailer has broadened his audience," he said.

"Or maybe Kathy Baker left a note for you," Bloom suggested.

"Do you really believe that?"

"Not for a second. Just being optimistic, like Randall Dennis."

Dantzler removed the folded piece of paper and read the message:

None of this is your concern: Keep your nose out of it

Or else

"A direct threat, Jack," Bloom noted. "Makes it a whole new ballgame, doesn't it?"

"Yeah, now it's become personal."

SEVEN

IF THE BLACKMAILER'S INTENTION WAS TO SCARE DANTZLER then he failed completely. As a homicide detective for nearly three decades, Dantzler had been threatened many times, yet he was never particularly concerned for his own safety. Those threats were typically little more than loud and hollow shrieks from criminals about to be sent away to prison for many years. In essence, they were empty noise.

The blackmailer failed in his primary mission of instilling fear in Dantzler, but the presence of his note made one thing perfectly clear—he had followed Dantzler. How long or how often was unclear at this point. Those questions did trouble Dantzler, and for good reason.

Had he been followed from the very beginning, from his first meeting with Governor Baker in the football stadium parking area? If so, this meant the governor was the blackmailer's original subject of surveillance, and the blackmailer, probably out of curiosity, stopped tailing the governor and shifted his attention to the unknown outsider, who in this case was Dantzler.

If Dantzler's theory was correct, the blackmailer probably

knew where Dantzler lived. Worse still, he had likely followed Dantzler to Frankfort, which meant he knew where Hannah Andrews lived, a fact that did cause concern.

Dantzler tried to tamp down his rising sense of anger—anger was rarely useful when working a case—but he was finding it difficult to do. He was pissed at himself, no question about it. Pissed because he never considered the possibility the governor was being followed. Had he done so, he most certainly would have handled this situation differently, been more cautious, more alert, more vigilant.

Because of this oversight, Hannah's life might be in danger.

That was unacceptable.

THE TWO MEN couldn't have been more different. David Danforth was tall, thin, and elegantly attired in a tailored suit, silk shirt, and expensive shoes. His blondish hair was neatly trimmed, his face clean-shaven, his fingernails perfectly manicured, his blue eyes covered by prescription sunglasses. He had the look of someone who came from money, which he had.

Barry Fleming was short—he might reach five-eight if stretched to the max—with a body that was all muscle. He resembled a tree stump. His outfit consisted of faded Levis, cowboy boots, and a well-worn Lynyrd Skynyrd T-shirt. He had long brown hair, a full beard, and arms covered with tattoos. His eyes were hidden behind off-the-rack sun shades he had probably purchased at Walmart. He looked like a man who had been born many miles from money, which was true.

They were sitting side by side in the bleachers at a vacant youth baseball field. Fleming removed a flask from his hip pocket, opened it, and took a drink. Jack Daniels, his favorite, went down like burning silk. Finished, he thought about offering the flask to his companion, but didn't. He remembered the man didn't drink.

Putting the flask back into his pocket, Fleming asked, "Are you a recovering alcoholic? Is that why you steer clear of booze?"

"Nope, I don't drink for two reasons," Danforth lied. "First, I don't like the smell, so I damn sure wouldn't care for the taste. Second, and more important, I wouldn't like its effect on me. You see, I'm something of a control freak. Pouring that poison into your body makes you drunk. And when you're drunk you aren't in control."

"So, you never drank at all? Not even beer?"

"That's correct. I never drank alcohol, never smoked a cigarette, and never did illegal drugs."

A trio of falsehoods. Danforth had most certainly done them all on many occasions.

"Come on, man, you're telling me you never once smoked a joint?" Fleming said. "That's impossible."

"I feel the same way about pot as I do about booze. It tends to make folks lose control."

Fleming shook his head, said, "You spend a year fighting in Afghanistan, you'll drink booze *and* smoke pot. That much I can promise you."

"What makes you think I wasn't in the war?"

"Guys like you never are."

"Are you implying I'm a coward?"

"No, not at all. But guys with your background rarely join the military. And if the draft was still in play, guys like you would create ways to avoid having to serve. I never served with a single dude who came from money."

"What would you say if I told you I served two tours during the Iraq War?" Danforth said, spitting out another falsehood.

"That you're bullshitting me."

Danforth smiled but said nothing.

"You are bullshitting me, aren't you?" asked Fleming. "You were never in the military. I'd bet my life on it."

Danforth stood, removed his coat, carefully folded it, and laid it on the bleachers. Then he rolled up his right shirt sleeve, revealing a scar two inches below his elbow.

"That's courtesy of shrapnel from an IED," he said, gently rubbing the old wound. "Went straight through. Had it hit bone, the doctors say I probably would have lost the lower half of the arm. Still hurts like a son of a bitch when the weather is rainy and cold."

"Well, I'll be goddamn," Fleming whispered. "I never figured you for a soldier."

Having just told another lie (the scar resulted from crashing through a glass door when he was a kid), Danforth rolled down his sleeve, buttoned it, put his coat back on, sat, and said, "Here's a piece of advice: Never bet your life on anything. You only have to be wrong one time and it's lights out forever."

"Yeah, I hear you."

"Let's talk about more important matters than our military service. How are things going with the guys?"

"Not bad. There have been a few petty squabbles, but nothing serious. Certainly nothing I can't handle."

"Good to hear. That's what you're there for, to keep that bunch in line. If you can't, let me know and I'll find someone who can."

"If the day comes when I can't wrangle that herd I'll gladly step down." Fleming was silent for a moment, then said, "But some of the guys are beginning to wonder what your plan is. They're starting to get a little antsy. I get the feeling they're ready for action."

"Tell them to cool their jets," Danforth said. "The plan is still being finalized. It may be another week, possibly two, before everything is in place. Tell them it's a fluid situation, as if any of those knuckleheads would have a clue what that means."

"Not to sound pushy or anything, but the sooner, the better. Those guys are hungry to unleash terror, to cause damage."

"That day will come. It's just a matter of time. But remind them that being patient, being careful, is more important than being in a hurry. We can't afford to rush things. If we slip up, we all go down. But it will be a glorious day if we succeed."

"I'll drink to that," Fleming said, removing the flask and taking another swig. "To our success."

Danforth said, "Now, what can you tell me about our runaway? Have you or any of the other guys heard from him since he departed?"

"Not that I'm aware of," Fleming answered. "He's a ghost."

"For your information, that ghost is living in an apartment in Lexington. And the word is he has devised a plan he hopes will bring him a small fortune. This is not good news for us. Should he happen to fail in his mission, which will likely be the outcome, and he gets arrested, he'll sell us out to save his ass. We cannot allow that to happen. And if he does succeed, we're screwed."

"How do you know all this? None of us have heard a peep from the guy."

"I know because I have sources you don't have."

"What's his plan?"

"That's irrelevant. What matters is it doesn't happen."

"Why do you think he left us?" Fleming inquired. "He always appeared to be content, happy. He never voiced his dissatisfaction with anything we did, or were planning to do. In fact, he seemed eager to take part in the plan you have in the works, whatever the plan is. Why would he just up and leave? Makes no sense."

"Greed. When we discovered who a certain individual was, that's when he set his plan in motion. He's seeking to take advantage of that knowledge. That can't happen."

"You're right. It can't."

"You do get where I'm going with this, don't you?"

"Are you saying you want me to . . .?"

"That's exactly what I'm saying."

"Jesus."

"Jesus doesn't have anything to do with this," Danforth said. "You do. And it needs to be done quickly."

"Give me his address and I'll take care of it."

Danforth dug into his coat pocket, took out a scrap of paper, and handed it to his companion. "Make it quick, and make it clean," he ordered. "And make damn sure you leave no evidence behind. Wear gloves, use a suppressor, and get out unnoticed. You cannot afford to make a mistake."

"Damn, I never figured on this happening."

"Well, it has. He's a risk that must be eliminated. We can't afford any loose ends." Danforth stood and stared off into the distance. "Get it done. Today."

BORED AT HOME, tired of waiting for a phone call that might not come for days, Dantzler left his house, drove to the Tennis Center, and put himself through another vigorous workout session. After he had finished, he showered, dressed, and went back up to the office he shared with Bloom and Sean.

Sitting behind the big desk he wondered if he had been followed from his house to the Tennis Center, and if so, would he find another note pinned to his windshield when he decided to leave. He doubted the presence of a second note, but when it came to his being followed, he wasn't so sure. He had come to believe he rather than the governor was the blackmailer's primary concern. Surely by now the man had done a background check, and upon learning Dantzler was an ex-homicide detective, that's who he chose to zero in on.

Dantzler wasn't bother by the fact that he was now the center of attention. However, the thought that Hannah Andrews might be in harm's way did trouble him.

Dantzler phoned Sean and asked if he wanted to meet at McCarthy's. Sean, never one to pass on a pint of Guinness, quickly agreed.

"I'm heading out the door at this moment," said Sean, whose office was located two blocks from the pub. "Want me to go ahead and order you a pint?"

"Couldn't hurt," Dantzler replied, his eyes scanning the area as he walked to his car. He saw nothing out of the ordinary, and there was no note on his windshield. He almost wished there had been. That way, he would know the blackmailer was watching him, and that Hannah Andrews was not in imminent danger.

Dantzler entered McCarthy's, stopped and briefly chatted with several of his Irish buddies sitting at the bar before proceeding to the back where Sean was seated.

"You're running behind schedule," Sean noted. "I'm already on my second pint."

"Trust me, I'll catch up."

"What kept you? Run into Randall Dennis again?"

"No. Amy Countzler flagged me down and inquired as to why you continue to take food and drinks from behind the counter without paying for any of it. She thinks you are a worse thief than Willie Sutton."

Amy was the young lady who managed the lounge area at the Tennis Center.

"How old is Amy, anyway? Twenty-two, twenty-three? She doesn't know who Willie Sutton was."

"Maybe not, Sean. But she's all over you."

"I settle up at the end of each month. Amy knows that."

Dantzler chuckled, said, "Apparently, she's not a big fan of your deferred payment plan. She prefers cash at time of purchase."

"God bless that beautiful kid," Sean said. "She's a hard ass, but you gotta love her. Amy could guard the gold in Fort Knox and no one would worry about it being stolen."

Dantzler had just finished his pint of Guinness and was ready to order a second one when his phone dinged. It was a text from Hannah.

"Prints belong to Timothy Ray Nelson, bn. 1989, from Nicholasville, currently lives in Ironwood Apts. on Cambridge Dr., in Lex. No criminal activity, prints came from Army records. Served from 2007-2011, honorable discharge. Hope this helps."

Dantzler responded with a "Thanks" text, then sat back and reflected on what he had just learned. Who was Tim Nelson, and why would he want to blackmail the governor? And the guy had no criminal record? This came as a shock to Dantzler. What would inspire a thirty-one-year-old man with a clean background to suddenly decide to blackmail Mark Baker? What caused him to take such a daring and dangerous leap? It made no sense unless Tim Nelson wasn't working alone. But somehow that didn't ring true for Dantzler. His gut was telling him Tim Nelson was a lone wolf in search of a big payday. He had no accomplice.

Sean said, "Based on that serious look it must have been an important message."

"You up for a ride, Sean?" Dantzler asked.

"Always. Where are we going?" Dantzler handed his phone to Sean, who read Hannah's text message. "Ironwood Apartments on Cambridge Drive? I'm not familiar with the place."

Dantzler laid a twenty-dollar bill on the counter, said, "Do you have your weapon with you?"

"It's in my car," Sean answered.

"Better go get it. There's no telling what evil might be waiting for us."

54

EIGHT

Ironwood Apartments was a three-tier structure with the bottom row of units located below ground level. Dantzler parked in the lot facing the apartment building, then he and Sean exited his car and surveyed the area. This was a part of town neither man was familiar with. On this night, all appeared to be well in the neighborhood. Several residents were milling around, laughing and talking, while music could be heard coming from one of the second-level apartments. All perfectly normal for a warm summer evening.

Tim Nelson lived in the corner unit on the below-ground level. His apartment was the farthest to the right and closest to the stairs leading down to his floor. Dantzler descended the stairs first, followed by Sean. Inside the apartment, the TV, louder than necessary, was playing. It sounded to Dantzler like one of those popular and ubiquitous real-life cop shows was on..

Dantzler knocked and waited for someone to respond. When that didn't happen he knocked again, this time with more force. Again, no response. Dantzler turned the knob, surprised the door was unlocked. He glanced at Sean and nodded. Both men drew their weapons and kept them pointed toward the concrete walkway.

"Tim Nelson, are you home?" Dantzler yelled. "Is anybody here?"

Getting no answer, Dantzler carefully nudged the door with his left hand until it was completely open. Then with his weapon aimed forward he entered the apartment first, with Sean close behind, also with his gun in firing position. All it took was one quick look for both men to realize weapons weren't necessary.

Tim Nelson—at least that's who Dantzler presumed the man to be—was sitting in a chair facing the TV. He was deceased, the victim of a gunshot to the back of his head. Blood dripped down from the wound and onto the floor. The bullet had gone through Tim's head, eventually ending up buried in the opposite wall. His right eye, completely blown out, dangled on his cheek like a marble on a string.

As Dantzler moved closer to the body, he said to Sean, "Check out the rest of the place."

"This is a crime scene, Jack," Sean replied. "We need to wait for the detectives to get here."

"We need to make sure there aren't more dead or wounded in the back. You've done this before, Sean. You know how to preserve a crime scene. Just don't touch anything. And watch where you step."

As Sean made his way to the rear of the apartment, Dantzler began looking around the area where the crime had occurred. The place was, he felt, uncharacteristically neat and clean for a home occupied by a single male. It caused him to wonder if Tim lived with a woman. There were no clothes lying around, no food or dishes in view, the tables, lamps and shelves looked as if they had recently been dusted, and grooves in the worn-out carpet offered signs it had seen a vacuum cleaner within the past few hours.

Dantzler noticed several items he judged to be important to his investigation. Important, yes, but there was no chance he would touch them or move them in any way. Crime scene integrity was always his top priority when he was on the job, and if anyone disturbed that integrity, the person was in deep shit. No way was Dantzler going to break his own rule.

Dantzler was staring down at Tim Nelson's lifeless body when Sean came back into the room. Tim was a decent-looking guy, thin and wiry, with ginger-colored hair and a wispy beard. He wore only a pair of jeans. His entire upper torso, from belt line to his neck, was covered with tattoos, all of which appeared to be professionally done.

Pointing to a prominent tattoo just below Tim's heart, Dantzler said to Sean, "Recognize that, don't you?"

"Yeah, tells us plenty about this poor guy's world view," Sean answered.

"I need to phone Eric, let him know about this. Probably best if we wait outside."

Standing next to his car, Dantzler called Eric, informed him what he and Sean had found, gave the address, and ended the call. He was surprised Eric had not asked for more details.

"Eric said he'll contact Jake and Vee, send them here," Dantzler said to Sean. "He also said he'll have patrol cars here within minutes."

"Don't think it's going to take that long," Sean responded, hearing the sound of sirens in the distance.

"I need to call Governor Baker and fill him in on what we found."

"He should be pleased."

"You'd think so."

Dantzler punched in the governor's number and waited. When Baker answered, Dantzler said, "Governor, I have some good news. The blackmailer's name is Tim Nelson. Hannah got it from prints pulled off the burner phone. I paid him a visit tonight for the purpose of asking him a few questions, but I didn't get the chance—he's dead. Someone shot him in the back of the head. The homicide detectives have been contacted. They are on their way here as we speak."

"That is terrific news," the governor said. "Does this mean the threat is ended?"

"Unless Tim Nelson had an accomplice, which I seriously doubt."

"And you are one-hundred percent positive he's the guy?"

"Yes. There were several items in his apartment that identify him as the suspect. I saw a stack of folders similar to the ones you found on your vehicle, three unopened cell phones like the burner we lifted the prints from, and an ancient Underwood typewriter he used to write the messages he sent to both of us."

"You have no idea how relieved I am to hear this news."

"Listen, Governor, there is another matter I need to discuss with you," Dantzler said. "When the homicide detectives arrive, they are going to ask me why I was first to show up at a murder scene. When they do, I'll have to tell the truth, that I was investigating a blackmail case involving you. I just wanted you to be aware that they will probably have some questions for you. Are you cool with that?"

"Yes, by all means tell them the truth. I have no problem with that. And tell them I will answer any questions they have for me. All they need to do is contact my office."

"I'll pass along the information to them."

"Jack, I can't begin to thank you enough for what you've done," the governor said. "Write up an invoice, put in any amount you deem fair, and send it to me. I will be more than happy to pay it."

"You also need to thank Hannah. Without her efforts we wouldn't have a clue Tim Nelson was the blackmailer. He would be dead, and we might spend years waiting for him to contact us again."

"You're absolutely right. I'll make sure Hannah is fairly compensated for her role in this."

"Gotta go, Governor. Some familiar faces have just arrived."

DANTZLER AND SEAN stepped away from the car and greeted Jake Thomas and Vee Jefferson, both of whom had been specifically handpicked by Dantzler to join the Homicide Unit. Jake was a war hero with a slew of medals to prove it, while Vee, a tall, elegant black woman—and Eric's cousin—had already proved herself to be a huge plus for the department.

Moments earlier, two patrol cars had showed up, lights flashing, tires screeching, coming to a stop in front of the apartment complex. The two officers bolted from their respective vehicles and quickly made their way to Dantzler, who recognized both men but didn't really know either one. He informed them Eric Gamble had been alerted to the situation, then led them to Tim Nelson's apartment, where he waited at the door while they took a look inside. After a brief stay in the apartment one of the officers went back to his vehicle, grabbed a roll of yellow crime scene tape, and with the help of his fellow officer began securing the scene. They had just finished when Jake and Vee showed up.

"Vee, you're running with a shady character," Dantzler said, giving Vee a gentle hug.

"Same goes for you, Jack," Vee replied, nodding at Sean.

"What are we looking at inside the apartment?" Jake asked Dantzler.

"Deceased male, name is Tim Nelson, age thirty-one, single gunshot to the back of his head."

"Sounds quick and efficient."

"You'd be right."

"How do you think it went down?" Vee inquired.

"Best guess, the shooter was known to Tim, Tim was watching TV, hears a knock on the door, recognizes the guy, probably a friend, so he has no qualms about letting him in. They sit and talk for a while, all buddy-buddy, then at some point the visitor excuses himself to go to the bathroom, or maybe he goes into the kitchen for a drink of water, takes out his weapon, comes up behind Tim, puts the gun a few inches from the back of Tim's head, and squeezes the trigger. Tim never knew what happened."

Jake looked at Vee, said, "What the hell are we here for, Vee? Seems Jack has it all figured out. Now, if he would only tell us who the shooter was, we could wrap up the case and put a ribbon on it. Can you do that for us, Jack?"

"Nah, you guys have to do the heavy lifting," Dantzler said. "I'm no longer in your line of work."

Vee said, "Hard for me to believe no one heard the shot. In a place like this I would think that's next to impossible."

"Shooter used a suppressor. Plus, the TV volume was high. When you canvass the place, I'll bet no one admits to hearing anything resembling a gunshot."

"Would you guys mind sticking around until Vee and I take a look inside?" Jake asked.

"We live to serve, my liege," Dantzler said.

As the two detectives ducked under the crime scene tape and entered Tim Nelson's apartment, Dantzler and Sean waited next to Jake's vehicle. With all the recent commotion, a growing crowd, drawn by the patrol cars' flashing lights and the arrival of an ambulance, had gathered at the scene. Some were standing in the lawn, while others were peering down from their second- and third-floor railings. Few things draw a big crowd faster than the buzz of police activity.

"Jack, you did this for a million years, so far be it from me to doubt anything you say," Jake said, as he and Vee approached, each one removing their latex gloves. "But I do have a question for you, and I have a hunch you know what it is."

"How is it we're the first ones at the crime scene, right?"

"Bingo. A dude gets murdered, and you and Sean, two ex-homicide detectives, discover the body. I find that very interesting. Explain how this came to be."

"Tim was blackmailing Governor Baker. I was asked to investigate, and in the process of that investigation, Tim's name came to my attention. I learned his identity about thirty minutes before Sean and I got here. When we arrived, I knocked on the door a couple of times, got no response, so I tried the door handle. It was unlocked. We went inside and found Tim's body."

"How long were you in the apartment?"

"Maybe five minutes. Does that sound about right, Sean?"

"No more than five minutes," Sean answered.

Jake said, "How long has this blackmail scheme been going on? And how much did Tim get from the governor?"

"Not long, and he got nothing," Dantzler replied.

"Dude gets murdered for nothing tags him as a two-time loser in my book," Vee commented. "He should've chosen a different avenue for his criminal pursuit."

"Do you suspect Tim's death is somehow connected to his blackmail plan?" Jake asked.

"Probably, but I wouldn't swear to it," Dantzler replied.

"How did Governor Baker find out he was the target for blackmail?"

"Last weekend, after dining in downtown Lexington, he found a folder pinned to his windshield. Inside the folder was a note demanding the governor pay five-million dollars or else he and his family would be greatly embarrassed. No date, time, or location was included in the message, only to await further instructions. He found a second folder two days ago, this one containing only a cell phone. I was able to lift fingerprints from the phone. That's how I got Tim's name."

"What do you know about Tim?" Vee asked.

"Not much. He's originally from Nicholasville, had no criminal record, served four years in the Army, and received an honorable discharge. The prints came from his military records. That's the extent of what I know about the guy."

"Has Governor Baker been made aware of what happened here?" asked Jake.

"Yes, he has. I phoned him a few minutes before you guys showed up. Naturally, he was relieved."

"Are you positive Tim was working alone?" Vee said. "Maybe a disgruntled partner is good for this murder."

Dantzler nodded, said, "Sure, that's a possibility, but I don't see it. Tim was looking for a quick payoff, what he figured would be an easy five-million bucks. But he didn't plan things out. Had he been more astute, he would've used an accomplice, someone with a bigger brain and a smarter plan. No, the way I see it, this has all the earmarks of a one-man operation."

"Well, you and Sean are free to take off," Jake said. "Vee and I will handle things from here. If we come up with anything, or if we need further help from you guys, we'll be in touch. And if you come across any evidence helpful to our investigation, please make sure we get it."

"It's your headache now, Jake. My work is done." Dantzler shook Jake's hand and gave Vee another hug. "Good luck, guys."

When he and Sean were back in Dantzler's car, Sean said, "There is no way you're done with this, Jack? I know you better than that."

"Not by a long shot. Not after seeing that tattoo on Tim's chest."

NINE

Beginning at nine the next morning, Dantzler and Sean spent two hours at Police Headquarters giving a full statement concerning the previous night's events. Along with giving their account for the official record, they both answered additional questions posed by Jake and Vee, none of which added further details to what they had already written down. The process was tedious, took longer than necessary, but essential to the investigation into the murder of Tim Nelson.

After their civic duty was finished, Dantzler, Sean, and Eric Gamble went for an early lunch at Cheddar's. Most of the conversation was between Dantzler and Eric, and it primarily concerned Vee and how she was handling her job as a homicide detective. According to Eric, Vee had exceeded his expectations, a fact that didn't surprise Dantzler. But it did please him to learn his judgment had been vindicated. He had gone out on a limb when he chose her to join the homicide squad, a move he knew was bound to be met with skepticism by many of those on the force who had more experience and more time on the job than Vee. Plucking Vee, a young, black female from relative obscurity meant risking an uprising among veteran officers, black, white, and Hispanic, who felt resentment toward Dantzler for the choice he made. Were Vee to fall short, or worse, fail at the job, it would have left a dark stain on Dantzler's legacy. Hearing she passed the test with flying colors was music to his ears.

Dantzler left Cheddar's, drove to the Tennis Center and went directly to his office. He didn't have time for small talk, or to be invited to play tennis. He was in no mood for any of that. Once inside the office, he closed the door, something he only did when he, Sean, and Bloom had important Tennis Center matters to discuss.

David Bloom showed up fifteen minutes later looking gloomier than normal. He plopped down on the couch, glanced at Dantzler, but remained uncharacteristically silent.

"What's that old joke about a horse entering a bar and the bartender asks, 'Why the long face?'" Dantzler said. "Okay, Bloom, why the long face?"

"Are you inferring that I look like a horse?" Bloom asked.

"Well—if the bridle fits . . ."

"You're a funny guy, Jack, a real comedian. The truth is I'm bummed because I can't shake that brief exchange I had with the governor's father-in-law. It sticks with me like a terrible odor that won't go away."

"Come on, Bloom, the old fart can't help how he sounds. His parents came from Germany, so it's only natural that he has a German accent. How is that any different from your situation? You've lived in Lexington since your college days, yet you haven't lost your accent. You still sound exactly like a Brooklyn cabbie in one of those old forties' movies. Give the guy a break."

"It's not his accent that troubles me; it's what he said. '*Bloom? That's typically a Jewish name, isn't it? Are you a Jew?*' Why would he even bring that up? Answer that for me. If my last name was Garcia, would he have said, 'Garcia? That's typically a

Spanish name, isn't it? Are you Spanish?' I seriously doubt he would have made a big deal of it. What's that word you cops use —*hinky*? I'm telling you there is something hinky about that old man."

"Here's what I think, Bloom. You are making a mountain of manure out of a single turd. And for your edification, hinky is used more by cops in movies and on TV than in the real world."

"Want to know about the real world, Jack?" Bloom said, standing. "I have a two o'clock patient, a sixteen-year-old female who has twice tried to commit suicide, once by cutting her wrists, and once by overdosing on sleeping pills. How sad is that? And how sad is it that teenage suicide has become so common in this country?"

"Good luck with that one, Bloom. At least she's got the right person trying to help her."

"Only time will tell how 'right' I am," Bloom said as he left the office.

When Bloom was gone, Dantzler put in a call to Hannah Andrews and left a message on her answering machine, asking her to dig deeper into Timothy Ray Nelson's background. Dantzler was aware that Jake and Vee were doing their own routine background check, and he could get the information from them if he wanted to. But he didn't want them feeling like he was hovering over their investigation. No, any information he got would come from Hannah and not the homicide detectives.

What Dantzler didn't know at the time was that virtually all the information he sought would soon arrive at his office.

AT FOUR, just as Dantzler was preparing to leave—he had a dinner date with Erin scheduled for six—a man appeared at his office door. Dantzler recognized the man, but couldn't recall his name, or if they had ever been introduced. But Dantzler was certain he had seen the man in the Tennis Center at some point in the past.

"What can I do for you?" Dantzler inquired, still trying to put a name to the man's face.

"If you can spare a few minutes, I would like to speak with you," the man said. "However, if you aren't free, it can wait. We can meet at your convenience."

"No, come on in," Dantzler said. He motioned to the chair across from his desk. "I know you from somewhere, but I don't think we've been officially introduced. You've played tennis here before, haven't you?"

"Yes, on several occasions, usually as a doubles partner with Chris Blake," the man answered. "My name is Robert Nelson."

"What can I do for you, Robert?"

"A police detective, Jake Thomas, informed me you were the person who found my son's body last night. I would like to ask you a few questions, if you don't mind."

Stunned by the news, Dantzler said, "Tim Nelson was your son? I had no idea. I'm very sorry for your loss. I can't begin to imagine how painful this is for you."

"It's beyond painful, if you want the truth. I'm in total shock, and my wife is absolutely shattered. Tim was our only child, and he was especially close to his mother. I'm not sure she will ever recover from this."

"How can I help?"

"Detective Thomas indicated Tim was involved in a scheme to blackmail Governor Baker, and you were the investigator looking into the case. What can you tell me about that?"

If any other individual had made that request Dantzler would have shut down the conversation. But how could he say no to the victim's father? He couldn't. Robert Nelson had a right to know all the details.

"A little more than a week ago, the governor found a note demanding that he pay five-million dollars," Dantzler said, adding, "and if the payment wasn't made, the governor and his family would be terribly embarrassed. The note ended by telling the governor to await further instructions."

"And were those instructions delivered?"

"No. A couple of days later, the governor found a second folder, one that contained only a cell phone. Your son made a mistake by not wearing gloves when he handled the phone. We were able to lift your son's fingerprints from the phone. That's how we identified him."

"But Tim had no criminal past that I'm aware of. So, how did you get his prints?"

"From his military record."

"Oh, yeah, right, I forgot about that. And you are positive those prints are Tim's? No chance you could be wrong?"

"Fingerprints don't lie, Mr. Nelson. Sorry."

"Please, can the formality. Call me Robert."

"Tell me about your son, Robert."

Robert Nelson drew a deep breath before answering. "Tim was a terrific kid growing up, never got into trouble, never did anything to challenge, harm, or embarrass either my wife or me," he said. "He was an honor student all through school, and an excellent athlete, particularly when it came to football. Tim was a wide receiver, good enough to earn scholarship offers from a half-dozen mid-major colleges. We really thought he would accept one of those offers and continue as a football player, but Tim, like many young men at the time, was drawn to the military. He wanted to go fight the bad guys, to kill the enemy, to be a patriot. So, he turned down the chance to play football and became a soldier instead. Diane—that's my wife's name—and I weren't pleased that he was so hell-bent on going to war, but we never expressed our concerns. We supported his decision."

Dantzler said, "It's my understanding that Tim did serve overseas. Is that correct?"

"Yes, it is. Tim was in the Army for four years, spent eighteen months in the Middle East. He was in the infantry, saw plenty of action, but rarely spoke about what he witnessed or what he did. Naturally, as his parents, Diane and I were desperate to know the details. You know, experts often say it is better to talk about certain potentially life-altering moments than to keep them locked up inside. But we didn't press him on it. We felt it had to be his decision whether or not to talk about his combat experience."

"Would you care for something to drink?" Dantzler asked. "I can call down to the lounge, have a bottle of water or a soft drink sent up. Care for anything?"

"No thanks, I'm good."

"Combat can have a dramatic impact on an individual's life. Did the war change Tim?"

"Oh God, did it ever. Before he deployed overseas, Tim was a talker, a real chatterbox. When he came home, he was silent, almost to the point of being sullen. His energy level dropped, he had no ambition, and, well, he just wasn't the same kid anymore. We urged him to enroll in college but he declined. And then there were the tattoos, which I loathe. He had one on each arm when he came home. Although I disapproved, I didn't make a big deal of it. He was a soldier, and I am well aware many of those guys get a tattoo. I chalked it up to that. Then we didn't see Tim for several months. When he finally showed up at home, he was literally covered with those damn atrocities. I asked him why he had done it, but all he did was shrug and walk away."

"Did you happen to see the tattoo next to his heart?"

"If I did I didn't pay any attention to it. Why? Does it have a special meaning?"

"Yeah, it does."

"I'm aware of your reputation as a homicide detective, Jack, and that causes me to wonder why you mentioned a specific tattoo," Robert said. "Are you saying the meaning of that tattoo might tell us why Tim was killed?"

"Impossible to say," Dantzler replied, ready to change the subject. "Let's go back a second. You said Tim was gone for several months. Any idea where he was during that time?"

"He never said, but if I had to make a guess I'd say he was spending time with a group of young men he had begun to hang around with. God only knows what nonsense they were up to."

"Did you ever meet any of those guys?"

"Two or three, very briefly, and I can tell you I didn't much care for what I saw. Shaved heads, tattoos everywhere, beefed up like they were on steroids, nothing but foul language . . . not at all like the friends Tim ran around with when he was younger."

"Did you happen to catch any of their names?"

"No, I didn't. But I might be able to get them for you."

"That would be a plus," Dantzler noted. "Did Tim ever talk politics with you or your wife? Ever express any particular ideology?"

"No, never. I couldn't tell you if he was a Democrat, Republican, or Independent." Robert's eyes filled with tears. "The sad truth is I didn't really know my son anymore. He had become a stranger to us. And now I'll never have the chance to bridge the gap."

"Like I said, Robert, I'm truly sorry."

"You know what really puzzles me, Jack? The five-million dollars. That makes no sense at all. If Tim needed money all he had to do was come to me. I'm not a wealthy man, and no, I couldn't fork over five-million bucks, but I'm not a pauper either. I've done okay in life. I would have helped him out. He had to know that. So why turn to blackmail for the money?"

"We may never know the answer to that question."

"Do you think the money played a role in his death? Maybe he had an accomplice, and things went sour between them? Maybe the guy got greedy, wanted all the money for himself? Is that plausible?"

"There is no evidence pointing in that direction. I'm one-hundred percent certain Tim acted alone. And no, I don't think money played any part in his death. He was killed for other reasons."

"Any idea what those reasons might be?"

"No, I don't."

Robert looked at his watch, said, "Oh my, I have taken up far too much of your time, Jack. I had no idea we've been talking this long. I need to get out of your hair and let you get on your way. I apologize for overstaying my welcome."

"No need to apologize," Dantzler said. "Actually, you've done me a huge favor by sharing your thoughts about Tim. I was planning on doing some research into his background and now I won't have to. You've told me more about your son than I could ever hope to find in my research."

Robert stood and extended his hand to Dantzler. "If you were planning to do more research, does that mean you are still investigating the case?" he asked.

"Not in any official capacity, but yes, there are questions I need to find answers for. I'm not sure how successful I'll be, but if I do learn anything new, you will be the first one to know. That's a promise."

"Thank you, Jack. And God speed."

Dantzler felt great empathy for Robert Nelson. The man had suffered a wound to the depths of his soul, a wound that can never be healed. His only child was gone, killed in a brutal manner, leaving behind only grief and a hundred questions that will likely never be answered. A violent homicide had once again shattered a decent, close-knit family. Dantzler had seen it happen too many times in the past, too many murders, each one a singular event that left a permanent mark on his own soul.

Would human beings never learn?

However, empathy for Robert Nelson hadn't prevented Dantzler from keeping some information close to the vest. He hadn't gone into detail about the meaning of the tattoo next to Tim's heart. Robert didn't need to know what it stood for. It would only further his anguish if he did know. Nor did Dantzler mention a woman's name he found on an envelope in Tim's apartment. Becky Prescott. Maybe Tim had a lady friend who could shed some light on why he changed so drastically after returning from overseas. Or perhaps Becky Prescott fit into Tim's life in other ways. That was an avenue Dantzler would follow.

But that journey would have to wait. He had but one goal at the moment, to make his way to the restaurant before Erin decided she had been stood up. This would not be a good thing. Keenly aware the clock was ticking, he left his office, hurried out of the Tennis Center, and jumped into his car, a single thought running through his head.

Being late was not an option.

TEN

Dantzler had just showered and dressed when he heard a car pull into his driveway. Barefoot, he made his way to the living room, pulled back the curtains, and looked to see who his guest was. He was surprised to see Governor Mark Baker heading for the front door. Little early for a visit, Dantzler thought, especially one from the commonwealth's highest elected official. Dantzler opened the door before the governor had time to knock.

"You're maybe the last person in Kentucky I expected to see this early in the morning," Dantzler said. "I'm hoping you didn't bring another blackmail note with you."

"No, happy to report I'm not bearing more bad news," Baker replied. "Hope I'm not putting you out with my unannounced arrival. I'm early for a big shindig at Heritage Hall, felt the need to escape Frankfort, so I decided to come by and settle up with you."

"Please, come in, and no, you aren't putting me out." Dantzler motioned for Baker to enter. "What are we settling?"

The governor reached into his coat pocket, took out an envelope, and handed it to Dantzler. "You haven't sent me an invoice for your services," he said, "and I have a hunch you never intended to do so. Therefore, I felt the need to take matters into my own hands. There is a check in the envelope. If you deem the amount to be insufficient, just say so and I will write one you feel is more appropriate."

Dantzler laid the envelope on an end table without opening it. "I'm sure it's more than fair."

"You are a rare specimen, Jack, a genuinely honest man. I can see why you were such a great representative of law enforcement."

"Would you care for something to drink, Governor? I'm not a coffee guy, but I do have orange juice. Or water, if you prefer."

"I'm good, thanks. Unfortunately, I am a coffee drinker, and I've had about a gallon of the stuff this morning."

"Unless you are in a hurry, have a seat, stick around for a while." After the governor sat on the sofa, Dantzler said, "What's going on at Heritage Hall?"

"A luncheon honoring Mayor Elizabeth Anderson for her work with Special Olympics," the governor replied. "It's a good cause, one I fully support, but the only reason I'm attending is because the optics would look shitty if I didn't show up. It would just provide more ammunition for the press—and my many critics —to savage me in the newspapers, on TV, and on social media. I don't need that. So, I'll make an appearance, even though the mayor and I are not friendly. We disagree on virtually every issue. Do you know her?"

Dantzler nodded, said, "I've given tennis lessons to both of her daughters."

"Sorry if I offended you, Jack. That wasn't my intention. I've learned over the years that in certain instances silence is a better policy than honesty. I tend to spout my views when I would be better served by keeping my trap shut. The truth is I should be more like my father-in-law. That man never reveals anything important to strangers."

"I met him at the Cheesecake Factory a few days ago. He was there with your wife. He didn't say much while I was there."

"You were a stranger, so no, he wouldn't. He'd view you with a wary eye." The governor smiled and shook his head. "But once he gets to know you, to trust you, he becomes a different man, a truly interesting and engaging man. And he is easily the best storyteller I've ever been around. He has hundreds of great tales he'll tell. I've heard them all at least a dozen times, yet I crack up with every telling. Ernie's an amazing guy."

"Came from Milwaukee, right?" Dantzler inquired.

"Yes, he was the only son of immigrants from Germany who came to our country with nothing but the clothes on their backs and a single suitcase. Like most immigrants, they couldn't speak a word of English. But they had that steely determination to make a go of it. They dug in, connected with other German families that had arrived earlier, and persevered. By the time Ernie was born they were doing all right."

"Sounds like the classic success story."

"Yeah, it was. And the timing was right, too. They got out of Germany after the first war ended, before Hitler took over and practically destroyed his country. Ernie was born in nineteen twenty-five. He was an only child."

"How did Ernie make a living as an adult?" Dantzler asked.

"He was a mechanic," Baker noted. "There is no piece of machinery Ernie can't fix. He's kind of a savant when it comes to working on automobiles. That's how he met Mary. She was visiting Milwaukee and her car broke down. The vehicle was towed to the shop where Ernie was a mechanic. He repaired the car then asked Mary out for dinner. She agreed. They eventually got married and he relocated to Lexington, where, with her father's help, he took a job as a mechanic in an automobile dealership. Wasn't long before he was practically running the repair shop. Over the years he saved enough money to open his own place, which he continued to run until he was almost eighty. Like I said, Ernie is an amazing man."

"Is Ernie a religious man?"

"Wow, that's an out-of-the-blue question. Why does that matter to you?"

"Just curious."

"I would say religion is a mixed bag in our family. Kathy, Mary, and our two kids are Baptists. I was raised Catholic, but I'm not a very good one. I only attend Mass on special occasions. As for Ernie, to be perfectly honest with you, I can't recall him ever setting foot inside a church. Funny, how I never thought about that until now. In answer to your question, I don't really know anything about his religious background. That's never once come up in any of our conversations. Why? Are you a religious man, Jack?"

"I'm more of a believer than I am religious, if that makes any sense. For me, organized religion tends to get in the way."

"You need to talk to Ernie about that stuff. Hell, I'd be curious to know his thoughts on the subject."

"But that won't happen, will it? I'm a stranger, remember?"

"We need to rectify that," Baker noted. "I'll have you over for supper one night, and I'll make sure Mary and Ernie are also there. Once he gets to know you, becomes more comfortable around you, he'll open the door and let you in. Can't promise it will happen, but we won't know until we give it a try."

"I'm all in," Dantzler said. "You name the time and date, I'll be there. I never pass on an opportunity to listen to a great storyteller. I would love listening to Ernie's tales."

"I'll get with Kathy and set it up." Baker stood, straightened his coat, then looked into a mirror and adjusted his tie. "I had better make a beeline to Heritage Hall. It would be poor form to arrive late. The press would surely accuse me of grandstanding, of attempting to draw attention away from Mayor Anderson and to myself. That would, of course, be nonsense. There is no way I have to make an effort to upstage the mayor. Hell, my presence alone does that."

Governor Baker opened the front door, turned, and patted Dantzler on the shoulder. "I will contact you with information about dinner," he said, pointing at the envelope Dantzler had placed on the table. "And don't hesitate to let me know if you disagree with the amount I paid for your services. I'll be more than happy to up the ante."

After the governor drove away Dantzler picked up the envelope and opened it. The check was for fifty-thousand dollars, an amount that stirred feelings of guilt. But they only lasted for a split second. The way he looked at it, the money was for future services as well as past services. There was no chance he would walk away from this case.

He had too many questions that needed to be answered.

DAVID DANFORTH, tall and elegantly attired as always (even when slumming, he was dapper looking), had to make a serious effort to keep his road rage in check. He was on a winding, two lane country road, his BMW convertible hugging the back bumper of a nice-looking late-model Ford Focus being driven by an elderly lady who looked like she might have been in kindergarten with Moses. Unable to pass on the surprisingly busy road, Danforth made good use of his horn, which only seemed to encourage the old biddy to drive even more slowly.

"Goddammit, woman, either shit or get off the pot," Danforth screamed, again pounding on his horn. "How did you even get a driver's license? Give a blow job to the cop who administered the test?"

Danforth knew she couldn't hear him but that didn't matter. He just had to vent his frustration.

He was on his way to meet Barry Fleming, his second in command, on a large piece of property owned for generations by the Danforth family that had been handed down to David. The place, once the site of a successful tobacco and hemp farm, was now little more than a ghost of the past. Everything had been torn down—the main house, a smaller house, garage, storage shed, barn, an old outdoor privy. All traces attesting to the fact that two generations of Danforth's once lived there in regal splendor had vanished. The only remaining reminder of the past was a large pond located two-hundred yards from where the main house once stood.

There was one structure on the property, a recently constructed Quonset hut paid for by Danforth. The hut served as a meeting place for a small group of men, none of whom had ever laid eyes on him. To them, he was little more than a phantom, a myth, which was exactly how David wanted it. Barry Fleming was the only one who knew Danforth's identity, or that he owned the Quonset hut.

Danforth had more money than he could ever hope to spend, and he'd come by it the best of all possible ways—he inherited it. He had the good fortune to be the great-, great-, great- grandson of an old codger who discovered gold in California, and then, as if God hadn't already touched him with one blessing, the guy was lucky enough to strike oil in Texas. In less than two years, Luther Danforth became one of this country's wealthiest men. With all that inherited money, David Danforth, Luther's lucky descendant, often joked that his blood was green, not red.

Befitting his wealth, Danforth attended the best prep school, then an Ivy League college, earning a degree in Anthropology, an area of study he conceded would provide little in the way of job opportunities. But he pursued the subject simply because he found it interesting. Anyway, did it matter what he studied? He never intended to work for a living, and, indeed, he had succeeded in that endeavor.

And contrary to the tall tale he told his pal Barry Fleming, he had certainly never served in the military, or fought in Afghanistan. Put his life on the line for . . . who? Our government? There was not one chance in a million he would ever be stupid enough to go that route. Hell, if he had fought in the war he might've actually been hit by a burning piece of shrapnel. Then his scar would be legitimate. But it wasn't, and telling Barry he had been wounded in war was just another lie, like the one about never drinking alcohol or doing drugs. In truth, he'd been imbibing in booze since before he was a teenager, and he'd snorted enough coke to fill a large bathtub.

Danforth's singular goal in life was to enjoy it. And he most certainly had, living in a multi-million-dollar house in Lexington, dining in the best restaurants, taking regular trips abroad, spending time with beautiful, glamorous, sexy women, all of whom he regarded as short-term business transactions. Nothing permanent, nothing serious . . . just bang them, pay them, and send them on their way.

However, in recent weeks and months, having fun had become boring and unfulfilling. Danforth recognized the reasons why his feelings and thoughts had altered. Times had changed in the past two decades or so, and those changes had not gone unnoticed by him. America, the country he grew up in, was rapidly becoming a place he no longer knew or appreciated. It was as if a great monument had suddenly been defamed, or the Earth had shifted beneath his feet. His equilibrium had become unstable.

It was a situation that had to be addressed.

This was the reason for his meeting with Barry Fleming.

At a crossroad several miles from Danforth's destination the old lady in the Focus made a left turn, thus clearing the way for him to crush the accelerator. Barring no future highway snails he should be at the Quonset hut in ten minutes.

BARRY FLEMING'S red F-150 truck was the lone vehicle parked outside the Quonset hut when Danforth arrived. He parked, quickly got out of the Beemer, and went inside. Fleming was shooting pool on a Brunswick table, one of the many luxuries Danforth had purchased to keep the group occupied when they were present.

"You winning?" Danforth asked, as he came inside.

"As Fast Eddie said to Minnesota Fats in *The Hustler*, 'How can I lose'?"

"You would lose if you played me."

"You sure about that?"

"Oh, yeah."

"Okay, I'll take your word for it."

"Smart guy." Danforth sat on a stool at the small bar he had installed to the delight of the men. It was easily their favorite of all the luxuries. "Sit, we need to chat."

"Want a beer? I'll grab you one. Oh, I forgot, you don't drink."

"That's correct."

Fleming sat on the stool next to Danforth. "What's so important that you'd drive all the way out here to discuss?" he asked.

"We'll get to that in a minute," Danforth answered. "But first let's talk about other matters. I read in today's Lexington newspaper that a certain Tim Nelson met with a grisly demise. Know anything about that?"

Fleming smiled, said, "Not a thing."

"Am I correct in assuming everything went as planned? That there were no problems?"

"Nah, the poor shmuck never saw it coming."

"And you left nothing behind? Nothing that could incriminate you?"

"No, it's all good."

"And the weapon you used?"

"At the bottom of the pond out back."

"Excellent." Danforth cracked his knuckles, said, "Now, for the real reason why I made the trip out here. Within the next week we are going to have a visitor. You won't like him, and that's all right, because, frankly, I don't much care for him either. But he is a valuable piece of the puzzle I'm putting together, so you will treat him with respect, however distasteful that might be. And when I say you, I mean only you. While he is here—and it will only be during the daylight hours—no one else is permitted to be on-site. Under no circumstances will the men be allowed to see him, or to know he is here. I'm aware this isn't going to be easy, but you have to make sure he is not seen by any of the guys. Can you do that?"

"Damn, David, you're asking a lot," Fleming replied, shaking his head. "Guys are in and out of here all during the day."

"That cannot happen. Not for the time he is here. I'll make sure he's gone each day by four thirty. The guys can come any time after five-thirty."

"If that's what you want I'll make it happen. But . . . why won't I like the guy? Why don't you like him?"

"His name is Muhammed."

"A brown skin from the Middle East?"

Danforth nodded.

"Why the fuck would you bring a damn towelhead to this place?" asked Fleming. "What's he gonna do for us?"

"He possesses certain skills regarding very large firecrackers," Danforth said.

"And how many firecrackers are we talking about?"

"Not sure at this point. Maybe one, maybe three."

"And you won't tell me more than that, will you?"

"Not at the present time." Danforth paused. Then: "Who do you regard as the most intelligent man in the group?"

"That would be a toss-up between Luke Rogers—he's better known as Roadkill—and a relatively new dude named Mickey Wilson. It's a close call, one I'm not sure I can make. Can't you use both of them?"

"Could, sure, but I choose not to. Let me put it to you another way . . . which one do you trust the most?"

"Well, Roadkill is fairly intelligent, but I wouldn't trust him to bring back correct change for a quarter. He'd short you by a nickel or a dime. If trust is what you're looking for, I'd have to go with Mickey."

"Good. The next time you and I meet, which should be within three days, he needs to join us."

"That won't be a problem."

Danforth stood and stretched. "It's all coming together, Barry," he said, making his way toward the front door. "Just hang tight and wait to hear from me. And in the meantime, begin letting the guys know this place will be off-limits during the day, beginning tomorrow. Remember, whatever you do, don't breathe a word about our brown-skin guest. That would not go over well."

"Sure you aren't interested in a game of pool before you leave?" Fleming asked, picking up a cue stick. "Nine-ball, ten bucks?"

"Playing you would be like robbing a blind hooker. Keep your money, Barry. You never know when you might need it."

ELEVEN

BECKY PRESCOTT WORKED FOR A VETERINARIAN LOCATED ON Wellington Way. Dantzler had gathered this information from Becky's Facebook profile, along with further details relating to the vet clinic's phone number and its hours of operation. He phoned to make sure Becky was at work; she was. Then he asked when she normally took her lunch break. Between noon and one, he was told, although that was subject to change, depending on whether or not there was an emergency situation requiring all hands on deck.

Dantzler arrived ten minutes before noon, parked, went inside, asked the receptionist to let Becky know he was there, and he would like to speak with her. The receptionist, her name was Norma, managed a polite smile, but Dantzler could tell she wasn't pleased with his request. She told Dantzler to have a seat in the waiting area. At five minutes past twelve, Becky Prescott emerged from a door marked Clinic Personnel Only, saw Dantzler sitting in the back, and began walking toward him.

Becky Prescott was small—no taller than five-two—slim, with blonde hair and a light complexion that was virtually indistinguishable from her white lab coat. She wore Levis, sneakers, and a dark blue cotton shirt under her coat. But it was her eyes that caught Dantzler's attention. They were perhaps the saddest eyes he had ever seen on another human being. Two clear blue pools of pain. Becky was, Dantzler concluded, a deeply depressed young lady.

Dantzler stood, introduced himself, and waited until she sat before returning to his seat. Although smoking in public places in Lexington was strictly forbidden, Becky reached into the pocket of her lab coat, extracted a single cigarette, and put it in her mouth.

"Don't worry," she said, after removing the cigarette from her mouth and looking at it with longing and desire, "I won't light it. I quit smoking cold turkey five years ago. Much as I hate to admit it, I crave the damn things like crazy. Every second of the day I want one."

"Never smoked a cigarette in my life," Dantzler said.

"Smart man. Once they get their hooks in you it's all over." Becky cast those sad eyes on Dantzler. "Are you another cop here to talk about Tim? I've already spoken with Detectives Thomas and Jefferson. Did they send you?"

"Once upon a time, I was a homicide detective but not anymore. Now I'm a private investigator. But yes, I do want to ask you about Tim Nelson, beginning with what was your relationship with him?"

"If you were a cop, surely you must know the detectives I spoke with. Why not get the information from them?"

"Because I would be getting their version of your story. I prefer hearing it directly from you. That way it's unfiltered."

Becky absent-mindedly began turning the cigarette over and over in her hand. Finally, she said, "If you aren't a cop, why are you interested in Tim?"

"I'm the one who found Tim's body," Dantzler replied. "He was involved in something I was looking into at the time. I went to his apartment to ask him a few questions. But . . . he was deceased when I got there."

"Was the 'something' illegal?"

"I'm afraid it was."

"Why am I not surprised?" Becky put the cigarette back in her coat pocket. "So . . . how did you get my name?"

"Same way the detectives did—from an envelope in Tim's apartment. Your name was on the return address."

"I can't believe he kept that letter. I sent it almost a year ago."

"Tell me about Tim," Dantzler prodded. "About your relationship with him."

Becky let out a long sigh, then said, "We started going steady during our junior year in high school. We were deeply in love. I mean, totally into each other. Our relationship continued right up until he came back from overseas, from the war. We had planned on getting married after he left the military. It was to be a big church wedding. But . . . best laid plans, right?"

"Why not? What changed?"

"Tim changed. When he returned home, he became more and more distant, from me, from his family, from his friends. His entire attitude was different. He was reserved, had this faraway look in his eyes, never laughed or joked like he did in the old days. I can't explain it. It was like an alien had taken control of Tim's mind and body."

"Sounds like he was suffering from PTSD."

"That's what I initially thought, but I don't believe it was PTSD. I think it was something else entirely, something much deeper and more personal."

"Like what?"

"I'm no shrink, so I'd only be speculating."

"That's okay, Becky. You probably knew him better than anyone. I'd like to hear your thoughts on what happened to Tim."

"His attitude toward people changed," Becky said. "You know, toward foreigners, people of color, immigrants. Tim never felt that way before going off to fight in that damn war. He always got along with everybody."

"Did he express racist views to you?"

"You haven't been listening—Tim *never* expressed anything to me after he returned from overseas. That's when he broke off our relationship. But he didn't have to talk . . . those tattoos said it all. I still can't believe he put that vile shit on his body. And then there were those men he began to associate with. There was nothing good about that bunch."

"Did you happen to catch any of their names?" Dantzler asked.

"There was one guy they called Roadkill. He was a big guy with a shaved head and a full beard. And another one, his name was . . . wait, give me a second, it'll come to me. Yeah, it was Barry. Those were the only two I ever met. They were at Tim's apartment the last time I saw him."

"Any idea what those men were up to?"

"No, I don't. Sorry. Really, all I can tell you is I'm positive they didn't belong to a church group."

Becky glanced up at the clock on the wall inside the receptionist's office. "I really need to get back to work," she said, standing. "I only have a few minutes to eat lunch, so is it okay if we cut this short?"

"Sure. And I didn't intend to keep you this long." Dantzler stood, took out a business card, and handed it to Becky. "Call me if you happen to think of anything that might be important. And thank you for speaking with me. You've been very helpful."

"And you won't tell me what illegal activity Tim was involved in?"

"Better not, Becky. That's something you don't need to know. Anyway, it's old news now. It would be best if you forget I brought it up."

IN THEIR QUEST for answers relating to Tim Nelson's murder, Detectives Thomas and Jefferson had questioned Becky Prescott two days before Dantzler met with her. During the interrogation, which took place in Becky's condo, they had been professional and courteous, just the way Dantzler had trained them. Their conversation with Becky had elicited facts similar to the ones Dantzler had gathered.

Save for a single important piece of information:

Jake and Vee neglected to ask Becky about the names of the men Tim Nelson had begun to hang out with.

Because of that oversight, Jake and Vee did not know about Roadkill or Barry.

This was information Dantzler learned only seconds before Becky disappeared into the inner sanctum of the veterinary clinic. He asked her specifically if she had given those two names to Jake and Vee, and she told him she had not, that they hadn't inquired about Tim's new friends. Dantzler had no choice but to share this information with Jake and Vee. Keeping them in the dark could hinder their search for Tim's murderer.

Dantzler's gut was telling him Roadkill and Barry were somehow linked to Tim's death, which, by extension, meant they were likely involved in the blackmail scheme, or at the very least, they were aware of it. If this was true, Dantzler had been wrong to assume Tim was working a one-man operation. Either way, they were probably connected to the murder, and this was information Dantzler could not withhold from Jake and Vee. After all, his main concern was the blackmail scheme, whereas their primary task was Tim's murder. Therefore, he was obligated to give them those names.

MUHAMMED SENT a text to David Danforth informing him his ETA in Lexington would be delayed three days, meaning he would be in town by the middle of next week rather than late Sunday evening as planned. This news did not sit well with Danforth. It messed with his schedule, made the situation more difficult. There was a tribe of crazy bastards hanging out at the Quonset hut who were bound to have questions. They'd be hungry for an explanation as to why they weren't being permitted entry into a place they had come to regard as their personal sanctuary.

And God only knows how they might react upon learning they were barred from the place because a Muslim was present. That would most assuredly lead to a full-scale riot, which could prove disastrous.

But Danforth had no control over Muhammed's travel plans. The man would arrive when he arrived and Danforth had no choice but to live with that fact. He just had to make double sure Barry Fleming understood how important it was to keep a potential explosion from occurring.

An event that seismic would ruin everything.

DANTZLER WAS NOT by nature a paranoid man. Having dealt with hundreds of criminals over the years, he was naturally wary, cautious, and always alert. Those traits went with the territory. But he had never been a guy who constantly looked over his shoulder, fearful bad news was trailing close behind.

Not until today, anyway.

Leaving the veterinary clinic, he had the feeling he was being seen by watchful eyes. He saw nothing suspicious as he looked around the parking area, but the feeling lingered even after he got into his car and began driving back to the Tennis Center. He now suspected he was being followed. Checking his rear-view mirror and his side mirrors he again saw nothing out of the ordinary. Traffic was light, so he reasoned if he were being followed, the suspected vehicle ought to be easy to spot. But it wasn't. He concluded there was nothing to be alarmed about. No one was tailing him. Shaking his head, he chalked it up as a moment of temporary insanity and nothing more.

He shouldn't have, because he was being followed.

TWELVE

Dantzler spent an hour at the Tennis Center, left around seven forty-five, stopped by a liquor store, purchased a bottle of The Famous Grouse scotch, and then headed for home. It was almost eight-thirty when arrived at his house.

Having shaken the feeling he was being followed, he pulled into the driveway not expecting anyone else to show up. He was wrong. A few seconds after he cut the engine and climbed out of his vehicle a black Lexus slowly pulled up behind his car.

Dantzler turned to see a man emerge from the Lexus. He was of medium height, had brown hair and a neatly trimmed beard with specks of gray in it. He wore a blue suit, white shirt (no tie), and black loafers. A smile crossed his face as he started walking toward Dantzler.

The man held up both hands in an I-surrender pose, and said, "I come in peace."

"You've been spying on me for the past couple of hours, haven't you?" Dantzler asked.

"Spying sounds so nefarious, so unsavory, so covert. I would feel much better if we could agree I was keeping an eye on you. Sounds less suspicious, wouldn't you agree?"

"What reason would you have to watch me under any circumstances?"

The man pointed at the sack Dantzler was carrying. "What's in your poke?" he asked.

"A bottle of scotch."

"Splendid choice . . . I truly enjoy scotch. What do you say we go inside and continue our conversation there? I'm a creature of comfort, and standing outside in the on-coming darkness and the warm weather is not my idea of comfort."

"I'm not in the habit of inviting complete strangers into my house, much less having a drink with them," Dantzler pointed out. "Telling me your name will greatly increase your chances of getting the comfort you so desperately seek. In other words, no name, no drink."

"Samuel Rosen. And you need not identify yourself. I know who you are—Jack Dantzler. I'm also well aware of your reputation as a homicide detective, and that you recently retired." Rosen reached back inside his car and took out a leather briefcase. "Now that we're old pals, can we move inside?"

"What do you want to talk about?"

"Inside, I'll tell you everything. And trust me, we'll definitely need the scotch. What I have to say could take a while."

Saying nothing, Dantzler turned, unlocked the front door, and went inside. Rosen followed seconds later. Dantzler led his visitor through the living room and into the kitchen. He set the sack containing the scotch on the table, looked at Rosen, and shrugged his shoulders.

"Is this comfortable enough for you?" Dantzler inquired.

"Perfect," Rosen replied. He opened the sack, removed the bottle of scotch and read the label. "The Famous Grouse? Never heard of it. Any good?"

"I wouldn't be drinking it if it weren't." Dantzler grabbed a glass from the cabinet. "Straight, or with soda?"

"Straight, no ice."

Dantzler poured scotch into the glass and handed it to Rosen. Then he took a second glass, filled it with ice, poured the scotch, added some soda, and stirred. "Back to my previous question—why do you want to talk to me?"

"Well, for starters, how about the death of Tim Nelson?" Rosen said. "What can you tell me about that?"

"Tim is dead and I haven't a clue who killed him. But I'm no longer a homicide detective, which means I'm not involved with that case."

"His murder, yes, I'm aware you aren't involved. However, you are investigating, ah, shall we say, certain tangential aspects of the case."

"Enough of this bullshit," Dantzler said, after taking a sip of scotch. "What are you, a cop, PI, FBI . . . what? Who do you work for?"

Rosen took a long drink, then said, "For the past eight years, I've been with the Southern Poverty Law Center in Montgomery, Alabama. Prior to that, I spent a dozen years at the Simon Wiesenthal Center in Los Angeles. Going back even farther in my past, I was a young attorney in L.A."

"Southern Poverty Law Center? That's Morris Dees, right?"

"Yes, that's correct."

"I heard him speak in Atlanta a few years ago. A very impressive man. And Simon Wiesenthal was famous for tracking down ex-Nazi war criminals, wasn't he?"

"Correct on both counts." Rosen took another drink. "Based on what I just revealed and the men I work for then and now, are you beginning to get a feel for where I'm heading with this?"

"You're telling me Tim Nelson was a neo-Nazi, just like all

those new friends he had begun to spend time with. Am I getting warmer?"

"You're as good a detective as advertised. Yes, you are not only warm, you are scalding hot."

"And next you're going to tell me Tim was killed by someone in that group, aren't you?"

"That's precisely what I'm going to tell you."

"Then you have no choice but to share this information with the local homicide investigators," Dantzler said. "You can't keep them in the dark. They should know this."

"What good would that do?" Rosen asked. "I have no hard evidence, only a hunch. But it's a strong hunch."

"On what basis do you connect the group to Tim Nelson's murder?"

"That brings us full circle, back to the reason why you were investigating Tim Nelson." Rosen emptied his glass with a final swallow, picked up the bottle, and poured the scotch. "The men in that group discovered the identity of someone they could worship and idolize. But they also knew to keep this discovery secret. His name could not be revealed under any circumstances. Leaking what they had learned would lead to a terrible outcome, so they were all sworn to silence. Tim Nelson had other ideas. Being the greedy type, he wanted to use that information to make money. So . . . he split from the group and became a free-lancer by black-mailing the governor. That's how you got involved. That's also what got him killed."

"How do you know all this?"

"We have our ways." Rosen took another drink. "But am I wrong so far?"

"Tim's note threatened to embarrass Governor Baker's family if five-million dollars weren't paid. Okay, let's say I agree Tim was a neo-Nazi. But I'm still unclear how any of this ties into the governor."

"Why are you so sure Tim was a neo-Nazi?" Rosen asked. "Don't forget, he left the group. Maybe he disagreed with their beliefs."

"No, he was a neo-Nazi. I know because of his tattoos. Tim was only wearing a pair of jeans when I discovered his body. I saw most of his ink."

"Including the one close to his heart?"

"The number eighty-eight? Yeah, I saw it."

"Do you know what it means?"

"H is the eighth letter in the alphabet," Dantzler noted. "Many neo-Nazis and skinheads tattoo the number eighty-eight, which stands for HH, on their bodies. In their twisted world, the double H translates to Heil Hitler."

"Very good, Jack. Yes, that's exactly what it stands for."

"Okay, Tim Nelson and his friends worship at the altar of Adolph Hitler. But once again I have to ask . . . how does any of this tie into Governor Baker? Or why the group wanted Tim Nelson dead? Those are big holes you need to fill."

Rosen lifted his briefcase off the chair next to his, opened it, and took out a Manilla folder. Inside the folder were a dozen or so photos, all 8x10's, all black and white, all showing various German soldiers in uniform, some laughing and joking, others with a stern, hateful, arrogant look on their faces.

Rosen thumbed through the photos until he found the one he was looking for. He removed it, placed it on the table, and turned it around so Dantzler could view it. He put the other photos back into the folder, then placed the folder inside the briefcase, and closed it.

The photo, obviously taken in the evening, showed four German soldiers dressed in heavy winter overcoats standing around shooting the breeze like soldiers from every nation have done for centuries. Judging by the smug look on their faces they had not a single care in the world.

"Recognize anyone in that picture?" Rosen inquired.

Dantzler studied the faces. "This guy, second from the left, that looks like Josef Mengele. The first guy in line is Hermann Goering, right?"

Rosen nodded.

"The fourth man, I recognize his face but I can't recall his name. Help me out."

"Albert Speer," Rosen said. "What about the third man in line, the one standing between Mengele and Speer? Recognize him?"

Dantzler studied the man's face for almost a minute then finally shook his head. "Obviously, he's much younger than the other three," he said, "but no, I don't know him."

"You not only know the man, you've spoken to him. His name is Franz Kindler. You know him as Ernie Kruger."

"That can't be right," Dantzler protested, again studying the photo. He flipped it over. Auschwitz 1944 was stenciled on the back. "This picture was taken seventy-seven years ago. There is no way any of these men are still alive."

"Three of the four are dead," Rosen conceded, after taking a drink. "All except Franz Kindler . . . Ernie Kruger. He was nineteen when that picture was taken. That makes him . . ."

"Ninety-six. That's exactly how old Mark Baker said his father-in-law is."

"What else did the governor tell you?"

"Ernie was from Milwaukee, his parents came from Munich, and he had never visited Germany. He was a mechanic, he met Mary in Milwaukee when she had car trouble, they began dating, they eventually got married and relocated to Lexington, where he ran a successful auto repair shop until he retired."

"All good liars and con men include just enough truth in their story to mask the lies." Rosen finished his drink, thought about a refill, but decided he'd had enough for now. "Did you happen to run a background check on Ernie Kruger?"

"Gave it some thought, but canned the idea when Tim Nelson was murdered," Dantzler said. "Didn't see the need at that point."

"Then let me give you the real truth about the man. Franz Kindler was born and raised in Munich. From youth, he seemed to have a special knack for working with machinery, particularly automobiles. His family was poor, and that played a big role in his joining the Nazi party. As we know, the Versailles Treaty was not kind to Germany. Kindler very quickly became a zealot, blaming much of Germany's financial and cultural woes on the Jews. At some point, and we aren't sure when, he met Mengele and became his protégé. He was with Mengele, who was known as the Angel of Death, when Jewish prisoners were unloaded from the rail cars at Auschwitz. Mengele would direct each prisoner to move left or right, either to become a working slave, or to be led into the gas chamber. Kindler also assisted Mengele, a physician, with his horrific experiments on prisoners, especially with twins. We also have records verifying Kindler shot at least seven Jewish prisoners in cold blood. In short, he's a bad man."

"But a hero to the group Tim Nelson belonged to, right?"

"An actual Nazi butcher living just a few miles away? You bet he's their hero."

"Was Ernie aware they discovered his identity?"

"No, and we have no idea how they found out."

Dantzler said, "He has to be one of the last surviving Nazis. Are you planning to arrest him anytime soon?"

"We're in no hurry to do that," Rosen commented. "He's not going anywhere. And should he die before we do take him into custody, then we'll release the information about the atrocities he committed. His name and reputation will be ruined forever."

"How did you learn his true identity?"

"About forty years ago, a lady living in Los Angeles, a Holocaust survivor, attended the Kentucky Derby. Walking around Churchill Downs, she saw a familiar face, the man she recognized as Franz Kindler. She had a camera, and she snapped a pretty decent picture of Kindler. After returning to L.A., she wrote in her diary that she had seen Kindler. Unfortunately, she was killed in an automobile accident before she could get the photo to Simon Wiesenthal. Five years ago, her granddaughter, whom I knew, was clearing out some boxes that had been stored away. When she ran across the photo and her grandmother's notation in the diary, and knowing I had once worked at the Wiesenthal Center, she sent the information to me. My initial thought was the same as yours— Kindler was surely dead. But I was intrigued enough to begin a serious investigation. My search took me to Germany to Argentina to Milwaukee, and then here, to Lexington. Last December, I followed the governor and his family into a restaurant, where I was able to collect a glass with Kindler's fingerprints on it. They were a perfect match to the ones in his Nazi file. What was for the most part an exhausting journey ended up being exhilarating."

"Do you suspect Kindler's wife and daughter are aware of his past?"

"Oh no, they don't have a clue. There is no way he would share that with them."

"This will devastate his wife and daughter."

"Here's another piece of Kindler's past that will shatter his wife, his daughter, and the governor—Mary was his second wife. His first wife, her name was Lisa, whom he married in nineteen fifty-four, died in nineteen fifty-nine from a fall down the stairs in their house. Her death was ruled accidental, although local detectives had their doubts."

"You mentioned Argentina. Is that where Kindler lived immediately after the war?"

"Yes, along with Mengele and dozens of other Nazi war criminals. He lived there for approximately seven years." Rosen, deciding it was time for more scotch, refilled his glass. "Here's what you would have learned had you run a background check on

Ernie Kruger. No records of him living in this country existed prior to nineteen fifty-three. That was the year he got a driver's license, a job, paid taxes, and had a physical address. It was also the year he became a citizen. You might say it was the year he was born."

"You are sharing all this information with me about a Nazi war criminal, yet you aren't prepared to take him into custody," Dantzler stated. "That begs the question—why *are* you telling me all this?"

"Because I'm going to ask a huge favor from you, which I'll get to in a minute," Rosen answered. "But first, I need to tell you what brought me here in the first place."

"I had a sneaking suspicion there was more to your story. What is it?"

"We've heard whispers this group Tim Nelson belonged to is planning some type of event. We don't know what the event is, or when it is scheduled to take place. Now, maybe it's a group picnic. Maybe it's a church outing and nothing more. Or maybe it will be an attack meant to take lives. We just don't know for sure. Obviously, we will alert local law enforcement if we do learn an attack is inevitable."

"How do you know this?"

"We've been able to glean the information from overheard scraps of conversations."

"You keep saying 'we.' Who are you referring to?"

"I have a man planted inside the group," Rosen said. "His real name is Mike Watkins, but within the group he is known as Mickey Wilson. He's been in for almost nine months."

"Getting accepted into a group like that couldn't have been easy. What did he have to do to prove himself?"

"We created a background that made him look like a superstar Nazi disciple. We even forged a prison record for him. Then we went to Hollywood and had an artist give him a bunch of phony tattoos. Mike moved down here when that was taken care of. Didn't take long before the word got out about him, about how he was the real deal. Not long after that he was invited to meet with the group's leader. They chatted and Mike was accepted into the group. Now he's considered one of the top guys."

"Is this a large group we're talking about?"

Rosen shook his head, said, "It's a very small group, no more than twenty-five or thirty members."

"Who's the leader?"

"That's a very interesting question, Jack. The truth is we don't know."

"How is that possible? Didn't you just tell me your undercover guy met with him and was accepted into the group? How is that possible without meeting the leader?"

"Mike met with Barry Fleming," Rosen said. "But he's only second in command. Fleming is ninety-percent muscle and ten-percent brains. He lacks the intelligence to mastermind a big plan of any type. What we need is the name of the individual who is ninety-percent brains and ten-percent muscle. The actual leader."

"And how do you plan to learn this man's identity?"

"We have now arrived at that moment when I ask you for a favor." Rosen pointed at the bottle of scotch resting on the table. "Make yourself another drink, Jack. You'll probably need the alcohol when you hear what I'm going to say."

Dantzler touched the bottle, nudged it away, and said, "I don't need another drink. Just tell me what you have to say."

"Our immediate goal is to identify the man running the group. The brains behind whatever it is they have planned. Mike can't do that—asking too many questions would make them suspicious. That's a risk we can't afford to take. So . . . we need to go at it from another angle. We need someone else to make contact. We were hoping that someone would be you."

"No more alcohol for you. That's the most insane idea I've

ever heard. Look, I don't know Barry Fleming, and I doubt I know any of the men in that group. But I can promise you at least one of those guys knows who I am. Probably more than one. There is no way they'd allow an ex-cop to join the group."

"That's where you're wrong, Jack. Think about it—you have the perfect story to tell, one sure to interest them. And you know what I'm talking about."

Dantzler nodded, said, "How do you plan to get a message to them?"

"Mike will set up a meeting with Barry Fleming. You and Mike will have worked out a back story—how you met, became friends, spent time together, that sort of thing. Before the meeting, Mike will sell your story to Fleming, really push you as a man who could be a big plus for the group. I have no doubt he'll be interested."

"Where does this group meet?" Dantzler asked. "Where is the actual headquarters located?"

"In a Quonset hut on a piece of property in Jessamine County."

"If I agree to do this I'll have to play it the way I see it."

"Wouldn't expect anything else," Rosen said.

"It would be a mistake to come across as too anxious to join. Even a man with only ten-percent brains would be suspicious."

"You're on-board, then?"

"It's an insane idea, but yeah, I'm in. How soon can I meet with Mike?"

"You mean Mickey. You might as well start referring to him by his group name. That's how you need to know him. Are you available tomorrow?"

"Yes."

"Then let's meet here at noon. Will that work for you?"

"Noon is perfect."

"We'll be here." Rosen stood and began walking toward the

front door. "And thanks for volunteering to help. We have to find out about their plan, whatever it is. Having you on our side is sure to be beneficial."

"I'm not as confident as you are."

At the front door, Rosen turned, extended his hand to Dantzler, and said, "See you tomorrow, Jack. And thanks for the scotch. It was damn good."

Dantzler watched Rosen drive away, turned, went back inside, closed the door, and locked it. He turned off the living room lights, and then headed back to the kitchen, a lone thought running through his head:

What have I gotten myself into?

BARRY FLEMING'S cell phone buzzed seconds after he had just finished having sex with a woman he met earlier at the Malabu Pub. He lit a cigarette before answering. The caller was David Danforth.

"Did I catch you at a bad time, Barry?" Danforth asked.

"Actually, you caught me at the perfect time. A minute earlier would have been a bad time."

"Have you spoken with Roadkill and the new guy . . . what's his name?"

"Mickey Wilson."

"Did you talk to them about meeting with me?"

"No, not yet."

"Don't. There has been a change of plans. Seems our brown skin visitor's arrival in Lexington has been pushed back until the middle of next week. I don't see the need to meet until the day before he gets here. That is, if I still deem a meeting necessary. Either way, don't say anything about it until you hear from me."

"Got it." Fleming brushed ashes into an empty coffee cup.

"What about the other thing? The guys not being allowed in the Quonset hut? Is that still good?"

"Tell them they can be there after five-thirty. But no sooner than that."

"Got it," Fleming repeated, seconds before Danforth ended the call.

THIRTEEN

"I KNEW THERE WAS SOMETHING OFF ABOUT THAT OLD MAN," David Bloom stated. "His hatred for Jews was blatantly obvious. I could see it in his eyes, hear it in his voice. And it's a hatred that goes far deeper than typical cookie-cutter anti-Semitism. It's in his DNA."

It was nine on a Saturday morning and Bloom, Dantzler, Erin, and Sean were sitting in a booth at IHOP, having just finished eating breakfast. Now three of the four were drinking coffee—Dantzler was working on a second glass of orange juice—their minds reeling from what they had just been told.

Sharing the information hadn't come easy for Dantzler—he'd done so knowing it probably violated his own personal book of rules. It was never wise to relay details to those who had no legitimate reason to be in the loop. But these were the three people he trusted most, so he told them about Ernie Kruger, and about his conversation with Sam Rosen.

"Damn, a real-life Nazi evildoer living right here in our backyard," Sean said. "I would've bet a small fortune all those sick bastards had died off by now."

"Most of them have, Sean," Dantzler acknowledged. "And the world's a better place without them. So far, though, the Grim Reaper has spared Ernie Kruger."

"I hope they take him into custody before he checks out," Bloom said. "If he dies before that happens, he will be spared the indignity of having been revealed as the monster he is. Indignity is a small price to pay for what he did, but if worse comes to worse, it's better than nothing."

Erin said, "Did you have relatives who died in the Holocaust, David?"

"My mother's grandparents and two of my uncles died in Dachau."

"You know what I thought about when Rosen told me who Ernie Kruger was and what he had done?" Dantzler asked. "Hannah Arendt's phrase 'the banality of evil', which she introduced at Eichmann's trial in Israel after he displayed no guilt for his actions, and for how he claimed to have simply been following orders and just doing his job. She said he was an average person whose his actions were ordinary. He did not resemble the monster everyone expected him to be."

"There's nothing ordinary about what Eichmann, Kruger, and their fellow thugs did," Bloom argued. "If there is any room left in Gehenna, I pray there's a spot reserved for Ernie Kruger."

Sean said to Dantzler, "What do you know about Sam Rosen?"

"He likes scotch."

"You think he's legit?"

"I did some research after he left last night," Dantzler replied, "and yeah, he checked out as the real thing. He currently works for the Southern Poverty Law Center. Before that, he worked at the Simon Wiesenthal Center in Los Angeles. Everything he said was easily corroborated."

"Here's the problem I have with the plan you two cooked up."

Erin said. "If Sam Rosen has even the slightest inkling an attack is possible he needs to give that information to the local authorities. Frankly, Jack, I'm surprised you didn't make that argument."

"I agree with you, Erin," Dantzler said. "But I want to get a better handle on the situation. After meeting with Mike Watkins, and later with Barry Fleming, if that does happen, and I'm not one-hundred percent comfortable with the way things are playing out, I will talk to Eric Gamble. Then he can put local law enforcement on alert. I'm not going to let something bad happen if I could have prevented it."

"Mike Watkins has no shortage of courage if he's willing to live in a lions' den with a group of neo-Nazis," Sean said. "It's not an undercover job I'd have any interest in accepting."

"You don't anticipate having to go undercover with that bunch, do you, Jack?" Erin asked. "If I have any say-so on the matter, you won't."

"A lot of pieces would have to fall into place before that happens," Dantzler replied. "And if the plan I've come up with works, I doubt I'll be going anywhere."

"Make it work," Erin ordered. "I don't want anything bad happening to you."

"Better heed her advice, Jack," Sean said, standing and picking up the check. "Just like it came down from God in heaven."

SAM ROSEN AND MIKE WATKINS, aka Mickey Wilson, showed up at Dantzler's house precisely at the designated time. Rosen brought a bottle of The Famous Grouse, telling Dantzler that, "After the damage I did last night, I felt the need to replenish your stock." Dantzler didn't disagree.

Inside the house, Dantzler got his first real look at Mike Watkins. He was indeed an impressive-looking man, and he definitely fit the mold of the standard-issue neo-Nazi/skinhead type. Watkins was about six-one, had the full unkempt beard, a completely shaved head, and a muscled body covered with ink. Dantzler quickly decided those tattoos were indistinguishable from the real thing; the Hollywood individual who did the work was a true artist. Watkins had blue eyes, a quick smile, and a soft voice. Dantzler liked the man immediately. He also knew there was nothing soft about Watkins other than his voice. He'd be the first man you would pick if you were heading into a rumble.

Dantzler and Watkins settled in on the deck, then spent the next hour developing a realistic back story they could use if the meeting with Barry Fleming materialized. Except for two occasions in which he offered suggestions, Rosen remained silent, content to let Dantzler and Watkins create a comfortable and shared history.

Dantzler's cell phone rang seconds after he and Watkins finalized fabricating their fictional past. He answered, and was surprised to hear Kathy Baker's voice.

"I hope I'm not catching you at a bad time, Jack," Kathy said. "But I was wondering if you would care to join Mark and me for dinner this evening. Mark indicated you expressed an interest in hearing my father's tall tales. You'll have your chance tonight. Unfortunately, it won't be in the Governor's Mansion. Instead, for convenience sake we'll be eating at my parents' house on Raintree Road. I'll text the address. Are you available, and are you interested?"

Dantzler smiled at Rosen and Watkins, then said, "Yes, I would be honored to have supper with you guys. And, of course, to meet your dad."

"Excellent. Will six-thirty work for you?"

"I will be there."

"Oh, I almost forgot," Kathy practically screamed. "Mark informed me you have a lady friend. He also told me her name, but darn it, I've completely forgotten what he told me. I'm telling you my brain has turned to mush."

"Erin Collins."

"Yes, of course. How could it have slipped my mind? Anyway, please feel free to bring her with you tonight. She will be more than welcome."

"I'm sure Erin will be eager to join us."

"We'll be expecting both of you at six-thirty. Have a great day, Jack."

When the call ended, Dantzler looked at Rosen and Watkins, and said, "Looks like I'll be dining with an actual Nazi tonight."

"You have my sympathy," Rosen said.

———

THE OLD MAN'S EYES, unblinking and colder than a reptile's, never wavered, staying locked on Dantzler the entire three hours he and Erin spent with the Mark Baker clan. Nothing else seemed to interest the old man other than Dantzler. It was unnerving, as though Ernie was aware his true identity had been compromised.

Or, as Dantzler silently acknowledged, maybe he was projecting. Maybe the old man suspected nothing.

But one fact became clear very early on: Despite constant pleading by Mark, Ernie was in no mood to tell his stories on this night. Each time the governor suggested a story, Ernie's reply was either, "Nobody wants to hear that damn story again," or "I've told that damn story so many times I'm sick of it."

And, of course, with each reply his eyes were staring directly at Dantzler.

The evening's conversation was basically one-sided. Although Kathy and her mother offered a few comments, Mark did most of the talking. Primarily, he was interested in gathering information about Tim Nelson's murder. Were the cops any closer to finding his killer? Do the cops think Tim might have had an accomplice? Have they figured out what Tim meant when he threatened to embarrass the governor and his family?

Dantzler's answered each question with a shrug of his shoulders, or "I'm not familiar with what the detectives know, or where the investigation currently stands."

An hour after they had eaten dinner and had moved into the living room, Erin abruptly shifted the conversation to World War II by asking Mark if his father had served in that conflict. Dantzler cringed when he heard the question, fearing Erin had ventured into dangerous territory.

"Yes, as a matter of fact, he did," the governor said. "He served from forty-two until he was wounded in the Battle of the Bulge in early forty-five. A lot of men were killed in that battle. He was lucky to survive."

"Both of my grandfathers were in the war," Erin said. "Both were in the infantry. Wendell fought in the Pacific, Richard fought in Europe. Richard was with the 45th Infantry Division that liberated Dachau. He always said that was the worst and the best day of his life."

As Erin spoke, Ernie kept his eyes locked onto Dantzler. Rather than avoid eye contact, Dantzler opted to stare back at the old man. If this had been a pissing contest it would have been declared a tie.

"I can understand that sentiment," Mark commented. "Those camps were horrific, arguably the low point in human history."

Dantzler stood, said, "We need to get going, Erin. It's getting late, and we don't want to overstay our welcome." Then to Kathy: "It has been enjoyable, Kathy. Thanks for having us. And it was a pleasure meeting you, Mary."

"You are welcome back anytime," Mary said. "You make a lovely couple. I'm sure things will go well for the two of you in the future."

"I'll walk you to the door," Mark stated.

When he, Erin, and Dantzler were outside, the governor said, "I apologize for Ernie's behavior tonight. He just wasn't his usual self. Normally, you can't shut him up, especially when he starts telling his stories. Tonight . . . I don't know. He seemed out of sorts. Maybe next time he'll be in a better frame of mind."

"Not a problem, Governor," Dantzler said, shaking Baker's hand. "A man who has lived ninety-six years has earned the right to behave anyway he wishes."

In the car, Dantzler said to Erin, "Why the journey into World War II history? That seemed a little risky to me."

"I wanted to see his reaction."

"And?"

"There was none. His eyes never left you."

"Yeah, all night."

"He knows that *you* know."

Dantzler didn't respond. He suspected Erin was right.

AFTER RETURNING HOME and Erin had gone to bed, Dantzler opened a bottle of Smithwick's, went out to his deck, his thoughts still on Ernie Kruger's bizarre behavior earlier in the evening. Dantzler wondered why the old man acted the way he did. Was it because he genuinely suspected his identity had been uncovered? That was the most-likely reason, Dantzler concluded. But was that an accurate assessment on Dantzler's part? It was just as likely that Ernie suspected nothing. After all, how could he know?

But if that were the case, why was the old man's attention focused solely on Dantzler?

Maybe Ernie Kruger, after a lifetime of constantly looking over his shoulder, had developed a sixth sense, an internal warning system alerting him to possible danger. Maybe he was uncomfortable being in the presence of a former law enforcement official. That might explain his edginess. Maybe he didn't know for certain, yet he was searching for clues in Dantzler's eyes.

Maybe . . .

Dantzler's thoughts were interrupted when his cell phone went off. The call was from Mike Watkins.

"Hope I didn't wake you," Watkins said. "I realize it's late. Sorry if I got you out of bed."

"No, you didn't," Dantzler said. "What's up?"

"Our meeting with Barry Fleming is on. Tomorrow, ten p.m., Shamrock Bar in Patchen Village. Are you familiar with the place?"

"Yeah."

"Good. Should we revisit any part of our story before the meeting?"

"No, I'm locked in."

"Okay, Jack, see you tomorrow night," Watkins said before ending the call.

"Who was that?" Erin asked. She was standing in the doorway wearing only one of Dantzler's T-shirts. Dantzler was positive he had never seen a sexier or more-beautiful woman in his life, or that such a creature even existed. At that moment he had his doubts.

"Mike Watkins. He and I are meeting with Barry Fleming tomorrow night. Sorry if the phone woke you up."

"It didn't. I needed a drink of water.

"Need anything else?"

"I could be persuaded."

FOURTEEN

BARRY FLEMING LEANED OVER, SIZED UP HIS SHOT, EIGHT-ball in the corner pocket, a simple shot straight in, took in a deep breath, slowly exhaled, and drew his cue stick back. If he made the shot, which he had full confidence he would, he'd win five dollars off Shane Crosby, aka Sarge, given his name after he had reached that rank in the Army before getting kicked out and handed a dishonorable discharge.

But Barry never got to take the shot.

"Why the fuck wasn't I allowed in the Quonset hut until after five-thirty?" Skunk asked. "Why the fuck weren't any of us allowed in before five-thirty? Answer that for me, Barry. I really want to know. Hell, we all want to know."

Skunk, real name Dwayne Fedderson, had gotten his nick-name because of his breath, which was so bad it could knock over a bull elephant. No one wanted to be within five feet of the man, and when they were they did their best to face away from him. His preferred method of attacking his halitosis was to constantly have a breath mint in his mouth. Unfortunately for him, not a single person felt the mints were working.

"I don't know, Skunk," Barry replied, turning his face away from Skunk. "The order came from high up. I'm just doing what I was told to do."

"Whoever gave that order cost me money, time, and gas," Skunk argued. "I always get here at four or four-thirty. You know that. Today, I show up and see that damn *No Admittance Until 5:30. No Exceptions* sign on the door, I have to get back in my truck, drive all the way back to town, and hang out with my crazy uncle. That sucks."

"This situation is only going to last for a few days, maybe a week," Barry pointed out. "Things will go back to normal after that. Now . . . will you please shut up and let me take this shot? I could use the five bucks."

"A week? Are you shittin' me?" Skunk moaned as he walked away.

After Barry made his shot and had been paid the five dollars, Sarge asked, "Who did give you that order, Barry?"

Barry shrugged, said, "You'll find out when he wants you to know."

"The goddamn prick needs to take down his sign," Skunk said, having returned after getting a bottle of beer. "Why'd he put the damn thing up in the first place?"

Barry, clearly exasperated, said, "I don't know, Skunk. I'm not in charge. I just follow orders."

Sarge put his cue stick in the rack on the wall, turned back to Barry, and said, "What can you tell us about this plan that's in the works?"

"At this point, nothing," Barry answered.

"Not even a hint?"

"When I know, you guys will know."

"But we'll all be involved, right?"

"Far as I know, yes."

This wasn't exactly a lie, but Barry was far from certain it was the truth. Fact is he didn't know the answer to Sarge's question. Initially he had concluded—or had been led to believe—that whatever the plan was it would be big, complicated, and deadly. But now he wasn't so sure, not after his latest conversation with David Danforth, who stated this guy Muhammed might only be building a single bomb. This caused Barry to re-evaluate his earlier belief. How many men were required to transport and plant one bomb? Certainly not twenty-five, the number of men currently in the group. What . . . maybe two men? Three, tops? If so, this meant far more than half the group would be sitting on the sidelines. And that would make for a lot of angry, pissed-off dudes.

Barry knew he would have trouble trying to keep those men in line if it did turn out that way. He doubted he could do it by himself. This was an issue he needed to bring up to Danforth. Not that Danforth would care. Barry had a strong suspicion Danforth really didn't give a shit about the group. He was only using it for his own purposes, whatever they may be.

Barry knew plenty of men in similar groups across the country, and compared to those groups this one didn't amount to much. In Barry's view it ranked as little more than an outlaw biker gang. He genuinely liked a couple of the guys, and barely tolerated the rest, most of whom were born losers guided by some phony neo-Nazi ideology they knew absolutely nothing about. Primarily, their only goal was to guzzle free beer and spout tough-guy lingo.

As Barry's grandfather often said, "There is no vaccine that will cure stupid."

Anyway, Barry thought, what kind of a legitimate group would allow a guy like Skunk to be a member? None, that's how many.

Barry checked his watch—it was eight-twenty. Still plenty of time before his ten o'clock meeting with Mickey Wilson and the man Mickey thought might fit into the group. Well, Mickey, the bar for admittance isn't set too high. Not if Dwayne Fedderson, aka Skunk, could slip under it. No, if your guy has any intelligence at all he's a shoo-in for acceptance.

———————

WAITING DID NOT TOP the list of things David Danforth cared to do. Being wealthy, he was accustomed to getting things done with the snap of his fingers. Or by flashing a big wad of cash. Certainly not by waiting.

Now, through no fault of his own (nothing was ever his fault), he was sitting on his ass, waiting, at the mercy of others.

This was not a feeling that brought him great joy.

But at the moment waiting was all he could do.

First, there was the Muhammed issue. That goddamn towel head was supposed to be in town tomorrow—Sunday—but now he wouldn't arrive until Wednesday. Despite being slightly peeved by the inconvenience, Danforth was inwardly pleased by this change of plans. Muhammed couldn't have known it, but his delayed arrival worked to Danforth's advantage. The additional time was favorable to his plan. A three-day delay changed everything. There was no time for Muhammed to build three bombs; that idiotic plan was now dead. No matter. Danforth never intended to have three bombs built. Instead, he would direct Muhammed to build a single bomb, which is what Danforth had in mind from the beginning. His reason for lying was to better entice Muhammed to accept the job. More bombs, more money. That had been his sales pitch to Muhammed.

Of course, Danforth had yet to settle on a suitable location for placement of the bomb. Unlike the insane original plan, which called for bombing a synagogue, a Christian church, a mosque, or a predominately black church, he was still working his way through a list of possible sites. But more important to him than location was the bomb must cause massive damage.

The original plan calling for three bombs had been the idea of the man Danforth was now waiting to hear from. It was nine-twenty; the man was supposed to have called by nine. How much longer should he have to wait? Danforth wondered.

Waiting was bad enough; waiting for a man Danforth had little use for was especially infuriating. It was almost demeaning to someone with Danforth's arrogance. He wouldn't have been pleased waiting for a call from Jennifer Lopez, much less this silly bastard, a man he judged to be weak and unimpressive.

But the man did have serious clout and prestige, so . . . why not play along with him?

Danforth's phone sounded. "Bout time," he said, barely able to hide his scorn. "I was beginning to think you'd forgotten me."

"Never. How are things progressing?"

"Not very well, thanks to that damn camel jockey you're sending us. We are running behind schedule."

"He will be in town tomorrow. What's the problem?"

"Obviously, you aren't up to date on his change of plans. He won't be arriving until sometime on Wednesday."

"My, my . . . that does alter the circumstances."

Danforth said, "Beginning with, he'll only have time for one firecracker. He needs to build it, and get it done in a hurry."

"In spite of my disappointment I must concur," the man said. "Our next issue, then, is to decide on an appropriate location."

Danforth smiled, said, "That's your call to make."

"Let me think about it for a day or two. When I decide I'll get back to you and we can begin devising a plan."

Take all the time you want, fool, because what you decide doesn't matter. "Don't take too long coming up with your plan," Danforth said. "The men are getting restless. Make them wait too long and they might riot."

"Those men are your concern, not mine."

"Just keep in mind I'll require payment before anything happens. That was our deal, remember?"

"You'll get the money," the man said. "Just sit tight and wait to hear from me."

When the call ended, Danforth flipped his phone onto the sofa, anger rising in his blood like bile in his throat. He wasn't used to being preached to by anyone; having to listen to a weak, ineffectual weasel made him nauseous. With more money than he could ever hope to spend he had to ask himself why he was doing it in the first place. His answer was simple: he loved the challenge, the excitement.

And as he saw it, where was the crime in playing God? What was wrong with that?

After all, wouldn't the world be a better place without certain individuals?

Goddamn right, it would.

FIFTEEN

At ten p.m., the Shamrock Bar & Grille was surprisingly busy. The majority of patrons sat at the bar, drinking, talking, or watching TV. Two couples were playing darts, and several others were sitting at tables in the dining area. It had been years since Dantzler had been there, but the place had changed little during that time. It still seemed to be a decent place to eat, drink, and have a good time.

Dantzler and Mickey Wilson entered then waited a minute or so to let their eyes adjust to the darkness. After a while, Wilson pointed to a lone male sitting in a back booth against the far wall.

"That's Barry," Wilson said to Dantzler. "You ready for this?"

"As I'll ever be," Dantzler replied.

They wound their way through a maze of tables until they arrived at Barry Fleming's booth. Wilson slid in next to Fleming, Dantzler sat across from the two men. Wilson made the introductions. Neither Dantzler nor Fleming made an effort to shake hands.

Dantzler was wearing worn-out Levis, a long-sleeve denim shirt, and a pair of engineer boots he borrowed from Sean. Dark stubble attested to the fact he had not shaved for three days. His appearance was meant to make an impression on Fleming, to come across as resembling a potential group member, although Dantzler had no clue what the standard-issue neo-Nazi look consisted of these days.

The waitress came to take their orders. Dantzler and Wilson each ordered a Diet Pepsi, Fleming a second beer.

"How long have you guys been friends?" Fleming asked, after the waitress had gone.

"Longtime, Barry," Wilson responded. "But we aren't here to chat about our friendship. So let's put the conversation on speed dial."

"Fine by me," Fleming said, turning his attention to Dantzler. "I heard about your situation. It's . . ."

"I have a lot of situations," Dantzler said as their drinks arrived. "Which one are you referring to?"

"The one where you spent all those years as a successful cop only to be passed over for the top job when it became available, a job you had earned and had every right to have, a job that was ultimately given to a young spade instead. That's not fair, not the way it should have gone down. By all rights that job should have been yours."

"Nobody ever said life is fair, Barry. Anyway, there was nothing I could do. Way of the world these days."

"Ain't that the damn truth? Sad, if you want my opinion. I'm tellin' you, this country is being invaded by people who ain't like the three of us, you know, white. Whites built this country. Anybody with a smidgen of smarts will agree with that. What do we have now? A damn rainbow of invaders, black, brown, yellow, who are taking over our way of life. Stealin' our country right out from under our nose. Do you realize that in the next twenty or thirty years whites will be in the minority? When that happens, guys like us will be royally fucked."

After taking a sip of beer, Fleming continued his tirade. "Think about it—Muslims want to kill us, gooks and chinks all think they are more intelligent than we are, and the blacks, well, all they do is lounge around and live off welfare rather than get an actual job. And Catholics? The only thing they are good for is preying on young boys. Women? Their goal is to cut off our balls and turn us into subservient, neutered weaklings. Then we come to the Jews; they are the worst of all. They control the money and run most big businesses while looking down their crooked noses at us. What did any of those types contribute to the greatness of this nation? The United States would be nothing if it weren't for white people. And now our country is crumbling under the weight of too many foreigners. Yeah, I know the liberals' argument that all of us who aren't Native Americans came from somewhere else. Hell, I'd bet most Native Americans came from Mexico or Alaska. But I don't give a shit about any of that, 'cause it don't matter. The people who made this country great were white Protestants. You agree, Dantzler?"

"Like I told you earlier, it's the way of the world," Dantzler repeated. "I don't concern myself with things I can't control."

"Well, there's your first mistake," Fleming said.

"Barry, I agreed to this meeting because Mickey said we might find some common ground on certain issues. But I didn't come here to listen to you whine and moan like a little bitch. I . . . ."

"Hey, you can't talk to me like that," Fleming protested. Then to Wilson: "Mick, if your friend is trying to impress me, he ain't doing . . ."

"I'm not here to impress you or anyone else," Dantzler interrupted. "And I have no interest in talking about the past, or how you think this country is heading downhill. Instead, what I would rather do is to hear what plan you have—if you have one—that will change things in this country more to our liking. Ways to make the United States great again."

"So . . . you do agree that our country is in bad trouble?"

"Do you have a plan, Barry? Simple question. Or are you strictly a talker?"

Fleming looked at Wilson, said, "What did you tell Dantzler, Mickey?"

"Only that the two of you might have overlapping interests," Wilson said. "That maybe you guys could work together."

"I don't know, Mickey. He seems to know a lot more than he should. Plus, he comes across as a hardass."

"But a hardass with intelligence, which is what the group needs. We can do better than all those morons we currently have."

"Come on, Mickey. We have some smart guys in the group. You know that."

"Barry, I can count the number of smart guys in the group on maybe three fingers. And that's being generous."

Dantzler said, "Let me make this perfectly clear, Barry. If you don't want me, no problem, we shake hands and part company as friends. Sometimes things just don't work out, two people don't click. Happens all the time. However, if you are interested, if you see a way we can work together, then I'm willing to follow where the road takes us."

"Let me think about it," Fleming stated. "I'll have to talk to someone first. Then I'll get back with you."

"Mick, I was under the impression Barry made the call," Dantzler pointed out. "Now I find out he's not the guy? What's the deal here?"

Wilson shrugged. "I thought Barry could make the decision. Obviously, I was wrong."

Dantzler stood, said, "You do whatever it is you need to do, Barry. When that *someone* makes a decision, tell Mick. He knows how to get in touch with me."

As Dantzler headed for the door, Fleming turned to Wilson,

and said, "I don't know about him, Mickey. He doesn't strike me as our kind of guy."

"He's exactly our kind of guy, Barry," Wilson said, standing. "You'd be nuts to turn him down. He's an ex-cop. Think of the tactical and strategic expertise he brings to the table. That kind of knowledge is priceless."

"He's not an easy dude to like."

"You don't have to like him, Barry. You only have to use him."

"Okay, Mickey, I'll make the case for him. But the final decision isn't mine to make. The outcome is not in my hands."

"Do your best, Barry," Wilson said. "We can use Dantzler. Make your guy understand that."

OUTSIDE IN THE CAR, Mike Watkins chuckled, and said, "He's right, Jack. You did come across as a real hardass. I'm surprised he didn't tell you to fuck off."

"I wanted to play hard to get," Dantzler said. "He didn't need to think I was begging to join the group."

"I'm pretty sure you're reticence came across loud and clear."

"Think there's any chance Barry knows what reticence means?"

"Not a chance in hell." Watkins started the car and pulled away from the curb. "Did anything he said stand out for you? Catch your attention?"

"The mention of a plan sure struck a nerve with him. His reaction left no doubt something is in the works."

"I'll keep my ears close to the ground, see if I can get lucky and learn what they have in mind. But I'll have to be careful. Asking too many questions will risk drawing unwanted attention."

"Don't take any unnecessary chances, Mike." Dantzler was

quiet for a few seconds, then said, "When can you and I meet with Sam again?"

"What about tomorrow?"

"Sounds good. Give me a call, let me know the time. We can meet at my place, if that's agreeable."

"That should work. I'll contact Sam and set it up."

They drove in silence during the remainder of the trip back to the Tennis Center, where Dantzler left his vehicle. Dantzler had no idea what Mike Watkins was thinking, but for Dantzler it was less about what he was thinking and more about what he was feeling.

A rising sense of urgency.

SIXTEEN

Erin Collins's eyes snapped open. Rolling over, she looked at the clock next to the bed. Three o'clock. Rolling back over, eyes wide, she stared up at the ceiling, trying to recall what it was that brought her from deep sleep to fully awake in a matter of seconds. The answer came quickly—a name she had come across at work.

Timothy Nelson.

Being a stickler for detail, and as the new kid on the job not wanting to be blindsided or caught lacking pertinent information, Erin had spent many extra hours in her office studying hundreds of files, active and inactive, in an effort to have a better understanding of what her office had been involved in during the past several years. The older files were read mostly for her own enlightenment, knowing it was highly unlikely any of them would be of future use. The current or active files were most important to her.

But this turned out to be a wrong assumption on her part. It was in one of the inactive files that she came across Timothy Nelson's name. She read the file several weeks before Nelson was murdered and his name meant nothing to her. Even after Nelson's death she failed to make the connection.

Until tonight . . .

Then, like a siren had gone off in her head Tim Nelson's name shattered her sleep.

But what was in the file that was so important? she silently asked herself. Why did his name suddenly spring to the forefront of her consciousness? What was it that now had her searching through the fog of memory trying to find the answer? In an effort to recall anything specific—date, subject of the file, other names— she let her thoughts drift back, hoping to solve what had now become a perplexing mystery.

Frustrated, her thoughts did nothing but bring up more questions.

The first thing she realized was Dantzler had to be told. But after rolling that notion around in her head for a few seconds, she decided to hold off telling him until she went back to her office, located the file, and gave it a more thorough reading. Perhaps a detailed study would indicate her concerns were unwarranted, and Tim Nelson was only a periphery figure in a meaningless investigation.

However, Erin didn't think that was the case. There had to be an important reason why his name was mentioned. If it wasn't important, why did it claim a place in her memory bank? Why was it at the forefront of her thoughts? Why had it caused her to suddenly wake up?

Those were questions she had to answer.

DANTZLER WAS SITTING ALONE at a table in the Tennis Center lounge reading Time magazine when his cell phone rang. It was a few minutes past noon. He was fairly certain the call was from Mike Watkins, who had promised to get back in touch once he heard from Barry Fleming. But the call wasn't from Watkins. It was from Erin.

"Hey, this is quite unexpected," Dantzler said. "And a pleasant surprise. To what do I owe this honor?"

"I need to run something past you," Erin stated. "Are you busy?"

"No, not at all. You sound serious, Erin. What's up?"

"Last night, I woke up with a name rattling around in my head. It was a name I ran across while reading a file a few days after I started the job. At the time, his name meant absolutely nothing to me. Now, though, after recent events the name takes on an entirely different meaning."

"Whose name are you talking about?"

"Tim Nelson."

"Why would his name be in one of your files?" Dantzler asked.

"Because he was working for the FBI," Erin replied. "And unless I'm badly mistaken, he was a confidential informant."

"Tim Nelson . . . a CI? That makes no sense. Almost all those guys have a criminal record, which is why they become CIs in the first place. They're seeking a better deal, a lower sentence, maybe even to avoid jail time. But that doesn't fit with what we learned about Tim. We ran his background, spoke to his parents, and he came up squeaky clean. Not even a parking ticket."

"Did you ever consider his record might be a little too clean?"

"What does his file say?"

"Not much, because about eighty-percent has been redacted. I would also bet the redactions came after his death."

Dantzler said, "Confidential informants have a handler. Does the file say who was handling Tim?"

"Glenn Rigby."

"I know Glenn. Been a long time, but we worked together on a couple of cases. He's a good guy, a real pro. He is also considered one of the FBI's top profilers." Dantzler was silent for several seconds, then said, "And there is nothing in the file detailing what Tim's crime was?"

"If it's in the file it has been redacted," Erin responded.

"Whatever it was would almost certainly have been after he was discharged from the Army. After he returned from Afghanistan. That's when everyone says he changed. Maybe that change had less to do with the war and more to do with his being nabbed for committing a crime."

"Think maybe he was planted in the group to spy on their activities? Maybe they found out and that's why he was murdered. No one likes a snitch."

"That's a possibility, Erin, but I'm skeptical of that theory. He was definitely killed by someone in the group, I'll give you that. But not because they found out he was a CI. Don't forget, he was no longer in the group at the time of his death. His blackmail scam against the governor and his family posed a threat to expose a name the group leaders didn't want revealed. That's what got Tim killed."

"Well, I can't take the file out of my office, so if you want to go through it, you'll have to come here," Erin said. "I'm not sure it would be worth your time, given so much is redacted."

"No, I'll contact Glenn, talk to him. He'll fill me in on the details."

"Gotta run, Jack. My stomach is rising up in anger and I only have a few minutes to eat lunch. I'll see you when I get home."

"Love you."

"Love you back."

DANTZLER HAD NOT LAID eyes on Glenn Rigby in more than a decade so he was shocked to see the man who walked into Wendy's. The man was virtually unrecognizable. Dantzler did a double-take before realizing the man was indeed Glenn. The change in his appearance was startling. Glenn's hair had turned snow white, he was painfully thin, there were dark circles under his eyes, and his skin, a terrible looking yellowish color, hung more loosely than old wallpaper slowly peeling away.

Dantzler quickly concluded Glenn was not a healthy man.

"Damn, Glenn, what's going on with you?" Dantzler asked, as Rigby pulled back a chair and sat. "You don't look for shit. Everything okay?"

"Getting stronger every day, Jack," Rigby replied, settling in. "Think I look bad now? You should have seen me a month ago, hell, two weeks ago. Compared to what I looked like then, I'm Charles Atlas these days."

"Cancer?"

"Yep, the Big C. Colon. Went through surgery, chemo, radiation . . . the whole package. Had to crap in a bag for three weeks. Then they went in, reattached all the pipes back to the way they were supposed to be. Now I can once again crap like a normal person. You have no idea how thrilled I was to sit on a commode. It was heavenly. Anyway, I look like a bag of bones, but I'm cancer free."

"Good for you, Glenn."

"Just lucky, I guess. Who knows? That nasty shit could come back anytime."

"You want a Coke, Glenn? Something to eat?"

"Nah, I'm good." Rigby leaned back and looked out the window as the rain began to fall. "What was it you wanted to ask me about, Jack? And didn't I hear you retired and became a private investigator?"

"You heard right. But this isn't a police issue. It's personal."

"Okay."

"What I need from you, Glenn, is information about Tim Nelson."

"Ah, Tim Nelson. I understand you found his body."

"That's correct, I did. But what I want to know is was he working as a confidential informant for you?"

Rigby shook his head and again looked out the window. "Damn, Jack, how did you find out about that?"

"So . . . you just answered my question. He was working for you."

"Yeah, for about fifteen months."

"I checked his record, talked to his parents. The man came across as a saint. Obviously, that wasn't true, was it? His crime has been erased from his file."

"That was part of the deal," Rigby stated. "In return for helping us he not only avoided prison time, he got a clean slate. That's standard operating procedure in those types of situations. You know what's weird, Jack? The damn kid *was* practically a saint until a short time before he was discharged from the Army. At that point, for stupid reasons he took a wrong turn."

"What did you nail him for?" Dantzler inquired.

"Nelson had taken Social Security cards from seven soldiers killed in action, brought the cards back to the states, and attempted to either open checking accounts or apply for credit cards. A dumb plan, I grant you, but nobody ever said criminals are intelligent. We had him in custody a week after he put his plan into action."

"Then you turned him?"

"That was an easy call, really. I felt right away Tim wasn't a bad kid, he simply made a stupid mistake. I decided if he would help, if he wanted a pathway to greener pastures, I would give him the opportunity to make it happen. He jumped all over it."

"Did you plant him in the group?"

"We did, yes."

"Why?"

"How much do you know about this group, Jack?"

"Not much. Why don't you fill me in?"

"As far as these types of groups go—neo-Nazis, skinheads, white supremacists—it's a pretty sorry outfit. It's small, peopled by wannabe tough guys who are probably better suited for the Hell's Angels or the Outlaws, not that either of those biker gangs would ever accept these clowns. But you get the picture. Mainly, the group consists of loud, vulgar, hard-drinking idiots."

"There's more to it than that, Glenn, or you wouldn't have placed someone inside. Come on, man, give."

"We suspect, and it's only a suspicion at this point, the group is purchasing guns—pistols, long rifles, automatic weapons—and selling them to far-right leaders in foreign countries, which is helping fuel the extremists ideologies popping up around the globe. It's almost impossible to have a successful uprising without serious firepower. We suspect the group of supplying that firepower."

"How are they able to purchase weapons without being flagged by the Feds? I'd bet most of those guys have a criminal record. They shouldn't be allowed to buy guns."

"Come on, Jack, you know better than that. In this country, about the only requirement for purchasing a weapon is to be breathing. Anyway, here's how we think it works. Each group member goes to different venues in different cities, different states, where guns are sold—stores, gun shows, street dealers—and they buy one gun at, say, three or four different places. Never more than one, which might raise those red flags you mentioned. Do the math, Jack. If twenty-five guys each buy three weapons, you now have seventy-five. We also suspect friends and family members are also involved, although they probably don't have a clue where those guns are headed. The group gets a hundred-plus weapons each month, jacks up the price, and sells them at a nice profit."

Rigby took a deep breath, sat back, and said, "Mind if I get a drink? I'm parched."

"No, what do you want?" Dantzler asked. "I'll get it."

"Coke."

Dantzler left, then came back a few minutes later carrying two Cokes. He handed one to Rigby and returned to his seat.

Rigby sipped, said, "Here's the problem we run into . . . there is not a single person in that group with enough intelligence to conceive of and pull off a plan that intricate. Which means someone else is running the show. That's the guy we want."

"And Tim was tasked to do that?"

"Yes. But he failed to get a name for us.'

"What did you think when he left the group?"

"I didn't know about it until he was murdered," Rigby said. "I'm assuming the man we are after found out Tim working for us, and that's what got him killed."

"You'd be wrong, Glenn," Dantzler pointed out. "Tim was attempting to blackmail Governor Baker for five-million dollars. That's why he was killed. not because he was working undercover for the FBI."

"What reason would Tim Nelson have to blackmail anyone, much less the governor of Kentucky? That's insane."

"Members of the group identified an individual whose name had to be kept secret. Tim felt otherwise. He wanted to use that knowledge to make a fortune. Obviously, that couldn't be allowed to happen . . . so they silenced him forever. That's why he was killed."

"So, Tim's greed led to his death?"

Dantzler said, "Are you aware someone is already planted within the group?"

"No, I'm not. Who?"

"Someone from the Southern Poverty Law Center."

"That makes sense. Knowing what they do, who they go after, that gives me some idea what you've been hinting at."

"I'm not clear on all the details, Glenn, but I can promise you if I do gather more information, I'll share it with you. Trust me that may be sooner rather than later."

"You think they have something in the works?"

"Can't say for sure, but yeah, that's what I've been hearing."

"You'll have to let me know when you find out for certain. We can't hide on the sidelines with our thumbs up our ass while bad shit is happening. You'll also need to tell the local cops as well."

"If I know, you'll know, Glenn. That's a promise."

Rigby slid his chair back, stood, and stretched. "I can count on you, Jack. I know that," he said. "Same goes for me. If you require the Bureau's help, I'll bring all the resources you'll need."

"You got it, Glenn," Dantzler said. "And keep kicking cancer's ass. Guys like you need to stick around a while."

SEVENTEEN

"Jack *fuckin'* Dantzler? A celebrated ex-cop? That's who you want to bring into the group? What's wrong with you, Barry? Have you completely lost all your marbles?"

David Danforth and Barry Fleming were the only ones in the Quonset hut. It was four in the afternoon and the rain was coming down in sheets, pounding on the roof like a mad carpenter hammering nails. Danforth shoved his chair back, stood, went behind the bar, and grabbed a plastic cup off the counter. After filling the cup full of Diet Sprite, he returned to his seat and took a drink.

"You didn't answer my question, Barry," Danforth said. "Have you lost all your marbles? I'm waiting."

"No, I have not," Fleming answered. "I'm being perfectly serious. We should let Dantzler join."

"Why? What possible reason would Jack Dantzler have for wanting to be part of our group? Wait. I'll answer that one for you, Barry . . . no reason at all."

"You're wrong, David. He has a perfectly legitimate reason for wanting to join. And even though he didn't come right out and say it, I could see in his eyes he's interested."

"Oh, so now you're an eye-reader," Danforth said. "That certainly makes me feel a lot better."

"Make fun all you want, David, but I know I'm right."

"Clue me in, then, if you don't mind. What's this legitimate reason you're referring to?"

"He was passed over for the position as head of the Homicide Unit, a job he wanted and deserved to have. After almost thirty years on the police force, after all he had accomplished, Dantzler gets screwed over by the very people who should have made him the top dog. But they didn't. Instead, they royally fucked him over. And who gets the job? A young coon with less than half the experience Dantzler had. Dantzler loses out to reverse racism, political correctness, and affirmative action . . . all the bullshit ideas that are turning whites into second-class citizens in the country we built. Dantzler feels betrayed. That's why he's interested."

"Barry, do you ever watch the news on TV? Ever read the newspaper? Ever pay attention to what's happening around you?"

"Only if it has to do with sports. Why do you ask?"

"Because, Barry, if you were the least bit informed, you would know Dantzler didn't leave the force because he was pissed off or felt betrayed. He retired. They had a big ceremony, pinned medals on him like ornaments on a Christmas tree. And furthermore, if you kept up with the news you would also know Dantzler brought Eric Gamble, the black dude, into the Homicide Unit, trained him, and then pushed hard for Gamble to get the top spot. So . . . I think your eye-reading skills need some work, don't you? Bottom line, Barry—you got played."

"Damn."

"This guy who brokered the meeting, the new guy . . . what's his name?"

"Mickey Wilson."

"How long has he been in the group?" Danforth asked.

"Nine or ten months," Fleming replied. "Close to a year now. Not long enough to be involved in our gun business."

"What do you know about him? Did you thoroughly dig into his background?"

"Of course I did, David. And everything about him came up clean. I even spoke to a guy who spent time in prison with Mickey. He said Mickey was the kind of man we could use."

"Did you talk to this man face to face or over the phone?"

"Phone."

"So, in truth, you don't have any idea who was on the other end of that call, do you, Barry? For all you know, you might have been speaking with the director of the FBI. Or maybe it was Dantzler. Did you ever consider that possibility?"

"It wasn't Dantzler. The voices were different."

"Oh, so you're a voice-reader, as well? Good to know." Danforth laughed but it came out hollow. "You need to keep a close eye on Wilson, Barry. If he's not on the up and up, we'll have to get rid of him. Just make sure you don't reveal any important information until we find out for sure where his loyalties lie."

"How do you plan to do that?" Fleming inquired.

"By feeding him some misinformation, see what he does with it. His response will tell us all we need to know."

"Okay, that sounds solid. As for the other thing, I'll tell Mickey to inform Dantzler he doesn't get in."

"No, don't do that. Give Dantzler the green light," Danforth ordered. "Better to keep him close. That way, we can monitor his behavior, see if he's really in or if he's a plant."

"And what if he is a plant? What then?"

"Simple . . . he and Wilson disappear." Danforth finished his drink, crushed the cup, and tossed it into a garbage can. "On to other matters. How many guns have we collected this month?"

"Hundred and ten."

"Break it down for me."

"Thirty-one handguns, twenty-eight long rifles, nine hunting rifles, thirty-one AR15s, and eleven M16s."

"Great. But let's cut back next month. Make it between fifty and sixty."

"Where is this shipment headed?" Fleming wanted to know.

"Palestine. Hamas needs them in their war against those Zionist Jews," Danforth said.

"What they could really use are RPGs."

"They're not easy to come by, but I'm working on it."

"What about that other thing? You know, the situation involving our brown-skin visitor? When is he supposed to show up?"

"In two days." Danforth stood. "Get back in touch with Wilson and tell him Dantzler is approved for membership. But share nothing important with either man. We clear?"

"We're clear."

"Take it easy, Barry," Danforth said, heading for the front entrance. "Just remember it only takes one slip of the tongue for everything we've built to come crashing down. And what I have planned is far too important to fail. We cannot let that happen."

Fleming silently nodded, still unsure what Danforth's big plan entailed.

MIKE WATKINS PHONED LATE the previous night to let Dantzler know he had been accepted into the group. Hearing the news, Dantzler suggested he, Watkins, and Rosen get together as soon as possible to discuss working on their next move. Now, after meeting for breakfast at Denny's, and then making the trek back to Dantzler's house, they were sitting on the deck as the rising sun burned away the early morning fog. Watkins and Rosen each had a bottle of water, Dantzler a Diet Pepsi.

"What's the next step?" Rosen asked.

Watkins said, "I'll take Jack to the Quonset hut later this evening. He can personally thank Barry Fleming for getting him accepted into the group. Then I'll introduce Jack to the guys."

"Why wait until this evening, Mike?" Rosen said. "If time is a factor, why not take him in this afternoon?"

After taking a drink of water, Watkins said, "For some unknown reason there is a sign on the Quonset hut door saying no one is allowed inside until after five-thirty. Been that way for about a week, and I have no idea why. But I would love to know what's going on inside the hut during daylight hours."

"Same here, Mike," Rosen agreed. "Finding the answer has to be a top priority." Then to Dantzler: "You up for going in tonight?"

"I think it would be a mistake on our part," Dantzler answered. "Here's why I say that. If I show up just hours after being accepted, it might cause Barry to wonder why I went from indifference to suddenly being anxious to get into the group. It might cause him to suspect I'm still a cop, and I'm going in undercover. However, if I say I'm not interested, well, I'll be more believable in his eyes. And it will also serve a double purpose for us. First, it will tell us if they truly want me in, and second, if I'm reluctant, that should reduce any concerns Barry might have about my motive for joining. It will give him confidence in me and it should bolster my credibility with him."

Rosen looked at Watkins, shrugged, said, "Makes sense to me. What about you, Mike? What are your thoughts?"

"It's a smart play but a risky one," Watkins pointed out. "What if Barry says, 'Okay, he doesn't want in. Fuck him.' Then our plan would be DOA."

"If that's his reaction, you'll continue to lobby on my behalf,' countered Dantzler. "And if he doesn't come around within a few days, I'll reach out to him and say I've changed my mind."

"Can't hurt to give it try," Watkins conceded.

Dantzler said, "Okay, now I have some information to pass along to you guys. But before I do, let me ask you a question: Are either of you aware the FBI had someone inside the group?"

"No," Rosen said. "Who?"

"Tim Nelson. He was a confidential informant."

"That kid was a CI for the Feds?" Watkins said, clearly stunned by the news. "That's pretty damn hard for me to believe. Who told you that?"

"Glenn Rigby. He's a veteran FBI agent. Glenn was Tim's handler."

"A confidential informant had to have committed a crime," Rosen said. "What was Tim Nelson charged with?"

"Identity theft, among other things," Dantzler replied. "He stole Social Security cards from seven deceased soldiers, came home with them, and tried to open checking accounts or secure credit cards. The Feds pinched him almost immediately. Then they cut a deal with him. No jail if he went undercover for them."

"Damn, robbing soldiers killed in action is a sleazy thing to do," Rosen said, disgust registering in his voice. "I'm not sure I could make a deal with a dirt bag like that. Not sure I'd want to."

Watkins said, "Obviously, I'm surprised to learn he was a CI, but I do remember Tim being a little different than most of the guys in the group. He was quiet, stayed to himself, and just came across as more intelligent than most of the other guys. Do you think Barry Fleming found out Tim was a snitch, and that's why he was killed?"

"Apparently Sam hasn't passed along this little nugget to you, Mike. No, Tim was killed because of a blackmail scheme he was working."

"Nelson was blackmailing Governor Mark Baker," Rosen said to Watkins. "Sorry for not telling you sooner."

"You're kidding," Watkins said. "And I thought he was intelligent. I'd better walk back that assessment."

"Something else Rigby told me," Dantzler said. "The group members are purchasing guns and selling them to radical far-right extremist factions in countries all around the globe."

"Not *all* group members are buying guns," Watkins challenged, "because I haven't been. Hell, this is the first I've heard about it."

"You haven't been in the group long enough to have earned their complete trust," Rosen pointed out. "Until they are fully convinced you're for real, they'll always keep you on the outside."

"The gun issue is important but it's secondary to uncovering whatever plan they have in the works," Dantzler said. "That has to be our primary area of focus. We can't lose sight of that."

"Then let's get on with it," Rosen stated. "Mike, make the call to Barry Fleming and tell him Jack is not interested in becoming a member of the group. We'll go from there, depending on his response."

"I'll phone Barry within the hour," Watkins said. "Then I'll call you, Jack, and let you know what he said."

"I'll be here," Dantzler said.

EIGHTEEN

DAVID DANFORTH WAS ANGRY WHEN HE SHOULD HAVE BEEN pleased.

Muhammed finally arrived in Lexington at four-thirty Tuesday afternoon. This was what pleased Danforth. Muhammed was two days late, but his tardiness was now forgiven. He was here; now he could get to work.

Muhammed phoned to let Danforth know he was in the McDonald's parking lot on Nicholasville Road. Danforth was on Tates Creek Road heading toward town when he took the call.

"It's good you are finally here," Danforth said, adding, "I have you registered at the Hyatt downtown."

"That is not where I will be staying," Muhammed stated.

"Why not? It's a very nice hotel."

"I prefer to stay in a place of my own choosing at a location you don't need to know about."

"Well, I do need to know, Muhammed. I have to know where to pick you up in the morning and where to drop you off at night."

"I have a better plan. We can meet here every morning. You may not approve, but this is how I want it to be."

"You're a cautious man," Danforth said, clearly frustrated by Muhammed's intransigence. "If that's what you prefer, so be it. For now, though, stay where you are. I'll be there in twenty minutes. I have a few questions that need to be cleared up. What are you driving?"

"White Honda Accord."

Danforth pulled into the McDonald's lot eighteen minutes later. He immediately spied the Honda. He saw something else as well—Muhammed was not alone. That's when his anger kicked in.

A petite woman sat in the passenger's seat, a grim look on her very attractive face. She appeared to be nervous and unsettled. Danforth discerned from her brown skin and the hijab covering her head that she was also Muslim. Perhaps she was Muhammed's wife or girlfriend, Danforth concluded.

"Thought you would be alone," Danforth said, after pulling next to the Honda and lowering his window. "I didn't count on you having company."

"As you can see, I'm not alone," Muhammed stated, sounding somewhat testy. "Is this a problem?"

"No, not at all."

It just means I now have two people to make disappear rather than one. "Will we need to purchase any materials before you get started?" asked Danforth.

"No, everything I need is in the trunk," Muhammed answered. "Much more than enough for the three objects you requested."

"There has been a slight change of plans concerning the number of objects needed. Now, I'm only going to require one . . . a very powerful one."

"I will expect the same amount of money for one that I was promised for three."

You'll be dead, motherfucker. You won't see a penny. "Your payment is not an issue." Danforth said. "You'll get what you deserve. That's a promise."

"Half tomorrow morning, the remainder after the job is completed. This was our arrangement."

"That remains unchanged. Regarding tomorrow, it's a twenty-to thirty-minute drive to the location where you'll be working," Danforth said. "Can you be ready by eight in the morning?"

"Eight o'clock is fine," Muhammed replied.

"Sure you won't tell me where you are staying?"

"Where I stay is not important to you." Muhammed paused, then said, "One more thing. When I do finish working on the object, one piece of the puzzle will be missing before it can be fully armed. Only I will know what that piece is. I will be long gone at the time, which means if you want the object to do its damage, you'll have to make a call to me for the necessary information. The reason I take this precaution is simple: To make sure that once I am no longer needed I don't become dispensable."

"Why would you even think that, Muhammed? What reason would I have to harm you? Hell, I might require your expertise again in the future."

"Civilians who hire me to build a WMD are typically not good or trustworthy individuals," Muhammed flatly stated. "And like you said, I am a cautious man."

With that, Muhammed put the window up and drove away.

Being cautious will not keep you alive, you fuckin' camel jockey, Danforth whispered under his breath.

———

DANFORTH GAVE some thought to following Muhammed but opted not to. He figured Muhammed, being a suspicious man, would drive around long enough to make sure he wasn't being tailed. Anyway, the reality was, Danforth didn't really give a damn where the bastard was staying. Muhammed was in town (finally), ready to begin work, and that's what mattered.

Instead, Danforth took out his cell phone and punched in Barry Fleming's number.

"Been wondering when I would hear from you," Fleming said.

"Just wanted to let you know our brown-skin visitor hit town a few minutes ago and is ready to begin work. I'll have him at the hut by nine tomorrow morning, maybe a little earlier," Danforth said. "Make absolutely sure no one else is on the premises, or attempts to enter. Keep the damn doors locked tight. You get him anything he wants or needs. I understand this is a distasteful assignment for you, but it has to be done. Since he's only making a single firecracker, he shouldn't be around very long."

"What's he like?'

"Arrogant, smug, cautious . . . and not alone. There was a Muslim chick in the car with him."

"Will her presence impact our plan later on down the road?"

"No, it won't. It just means we eliminate two, not one."

"Right."

"See you tomorrow morning, Barry."

"SO DANTZLER DECLINED to join our merry gang?" Danforth said. He was sitting in the entertainment room watching a late-night rerun of *NCIS*. Switching the phone to his left-hand, he used his free hand to pick up his glass and take a sip of the Macallan 25 he had heard somewhere that James Bond preferred. "That tells us all we need to know, Barry."

"Not sure I'm catching your drift," Fleming responded. "Clear me up on what it tells us."

"That Dantzler intends to spy on us. He's working undercover for someone."

"Who?"

"Don't know. It could be the local cops, the FBI, ATF, Homeland Security. But you can be sure it's one of those outfits."

"But he declined our offer, David. What reason would he have to be working undercover if he doesn't even want to be in the group? That makes no sense."

"Trust me, Barry. He wants in."

"Then why did he decline the offer?" asked Fleming.

"The answer to that question is obvious," Danforth noted. "He doesn't want to come across as being too eager to join."

"Man, I'm not following this at all."

"Think about it for a second, Barry. Dantzler knows if he comes across as being too eager to get in we'll be suspicious of his motives, his real purpose for being in the group, which is to spy on us. He'll figure we suspect he's still involved with law enforcement, which would put him at risk should we find out. He knows that. So, what's his best plan for downplaying our concerns about him? By declining our offer and playing hard to get. It's what I would do if I were in his shoes."

"Okay, but he's out. We have no reason to worry about him, do we?"

Danforth took another sip of Macallan, said, "He's betting you will get back in touch and plead for him to join."

"And what if I don't? He's screwed, right?"

"No, Dantzler will simply wait two or three days and if you haven't contacted him, either he or Mickey Wilson—and I'm betting on Wilson—will contact you and say that Dantzler, after giving it more thought, has had a change of heart and now would like to accept your offer."

"You really think Dantzler is that intelligent?"

"No, Barry, I think you're that dumb."

"That's a cruel thing to say, David," complained Fleming.

"But truthful, Barry. Only a dumb man would fail to see through that scheme. It's as obvious as the nose on your face."

"Okay, I didn't see it. I'm dumb, stupid, whatever. Now what do you want me to do?"

"Sit tight and wait for Dantzler or Wilson to get in touch with you. When that happens, tell them Dantzler is still welcomed to join. Let them think they're winning."

"If you say so."

"Until then, make sure Muhammed has everything he needs," Danforth ordered. "The sooner he completes his task, the sooner he and his lady friend can be eliminated."

A thought came to Danforth seconds after ending the call—Muhammed's safety net. Muhammed had mentioned a final piece of the puzzle only he would know about before the bomb could be fully armed, and he'd be a safe distance away before revealing the key piece of information. That was his plan for staying alive in the event Danforth considered taking him out.

Thinking about it now, Danforth didn't see this as much of a problem. In fact, he saw it as no problem at all. Extreme torture has a way of inducing even the toughest guys to talk.

And Danforth doubted Muhammed was all that tough.

NINETEEN

DANTZLER READ THE BRIEF NOTE FOR THE THIRD TIME:

**Resign within 30 days.
If you don't, your family will face extreme
embarrassment.**

"LOOKS like you were wrong about Tim Nelson," Mark Baker commented. "Seems he did have an accomplice after all."

Dantzler and David Bloom had just finished easily taking two sets of doubles against Randall Dennis and Grady Franklin when Dantzler's cell phone buzzed. The call was from Baker. According to the governor, he and Kathy, upon exiting a Lexington movie theater, discovered the note pinned to their windshield just like the previous one had been. Dantzler suggested they meet at his house.

Dantzler glanced at the note again, pondered what the governor said, then answered, "You're correct, Governor. I was wrong. Dead men don't leave blackmail notes. But if Tim wasn't working alone, the question becomes who was his accomplice? Who was the source of his information? Based on this second note, the individual who left it is a much better writer than Tim was."

"But this note is exactly like the first one, isn't it?" Kathy asked.

"No, they aren't exactly alike," Dantzler pointed out. "In fact, there is a huge difference between them."

"Well, they sure look the same to me," countered Kathy.

Dantzler handed the note to Kathy. "Look at the note closely, and then compare it to the first one. Tim demanded money. He wanted cash, a big score. That was his motivation. Whoever sent this note has no interest in money. He's thinking long-term. He wants the governor gone."

As Bloom took the note from Kathy and studied it, Dantzler continued, "And there are other differences as well. This one has a comma, and there's a period at the end of each statement. The first note had no punctuation at all. Also, the first note was written on a typewriter, this one on a computer."

"What the hell does that tell us?" Baker asked.

"The person who sent this note is better educated than Tim Nelson," answered Dantzler.

"Earlier, you mentioned that Tim got information from someone," Kathy said. "Information about what, specifically? And in what way would that information cause great embarrassment to our family?"

Dantzler realized his slip of the tongue placed him in a precarious situation. He had to make clear this latest note did come from someone associated with Tim, while at the same time keeping Kathy in the dark about her father. He was in no position to reveal the truth about Ernie Kruger to the Bakers. It wasn't his place to do so. No, when that time came, it would be Sam Rosen who claimed the honor.

Bloom, realizing Dantzler was in a bind, came to the rescue.

"Blackmailers almost always exaggerate their threat by giving the appearance of having more knowledge than they actually have," he said. "It's a classic scare tactic. In this case, the blackmailer knows Mark is an independently wealthy man. Therefore, my guess is, he is hinting that Mark didn't earn his money in a completely honest way. He's throwing darts at an invisible target hoping one of them will be a bulls-eye. He is betting Mark has skeletons hiding somewhere in his closet."

"But like Jack said, the author of this note doesn't ask for money," Baker pointed out.

"No, you're correct," Bloom responded. "But if you don't resign, this individual just might conjure up a phony event in your past business dealings and spread false rumors about what went down during that transaction. Even if it's a lie it would cause you and your family great embarrassment."

Dantzler eyed Bloom, impressed by how he had come to the rescue, and by the line of serious BS he was laying on the Bakers. He knew Bloom wouldn't let him forget about this saving intervention for weeks. Dantzler would be on the financial hook for untold pints of Guinness at McCarthy's. That was fine; Bloom deserved it for his quick-thinking diversionary tactics.

"The big question, Governor, is who benefits the most if you were to resign?" Dantzler asked, taking over from Bloom.

"That's a tough one to answer," Baker said. "Well, on second thought, it really isn't all that difficult. About half the politicians in Frankfort have an eye on replacing me. But I don't see any of those yokels going down this path. They'd rather use the ballot box to unseat me."

"What about the lieutenant governor? Wouldn't he benefit the most—and the fastest—should you leave office?"

"Bradley is lazy, lacking ambition. He's not motivated enough or greedy enough to pull off a scheme like this. I don't see him as a viable suspect."

Dantzler said, "It's got to be somebody. Can you think of anyone who hates you enough to try and blackmail you into vacating your office before your term is up?"

"You're damn right I can," Baker snapped, turning to his wife. "And you know who I'm talking about, don't you, Kathy?"

"Preston Combs," Kathy quickly answered.

"Preston Combs?" Dantzler echoed, looking at Bloom. "David and I know him, Governor. He's a long-time member of the Tennis Center."

"Yeah, well, that bastard has enough money to buy your Tennis Center twenty times over. And if he did buy it, he would still have more money than God. He's worth far more than I'll ever be, that's for sure."

"Why does Preston hate you?" inquired Bloom.

"Politics, why else? He and I differ on virtually every issue, big or small. Let me fill you in on just how badly he wants me gone. He backed my opponent in the Republican primary, spent a small fortune trying to help the guy get the nomination. And when that didn't work, when I kicked their ass, what did Preston do? He spent another fortune backing my Democrat opponent. Switched sides like a true traitor. Didn't work out too well for him, did it? I'm the one sitting in the big chair."

Dantzler looked at his watch, then said to Bloom, "It's only nine-thirty. Preston tends to play later in the evening. There's a good chance he might still be there. Why don't you give Amy a call, find out for sure?"

Amy Countzler was the young woman who managed the Tennis Center lounge.

Taking out his cell phone, Bloom punched in Amy's number, and waited. After a few seconds, he said, "Hey, Amy, it's David Bloom. Quick question: Does Preston Combs happen to be on-site? He's in the lounge now? Do me a favor. Ask him to stick around for a while. Jack needs to speak with him. Thanks, Amy. You're the best."

"You're going to talk to Preston tonight?" Kathy asked.

"Why not?" Dantzler replied. "Come on, Bloom, we need to hurry. He won't stick around all night."

"Don't let that Benedict Arnold con his way out of this," the governor barked. "If he's responsible, I want him prosecuted to the fullest extent of the law."

"*If* he's guilty," Dantzler commented, leading the quartet out the front door.

"IT'S AFTER TEN, Jack. Little late for a chat, isn't it?" Preston Combs asked.

Combs, a beefy man with white hair and prominent jowls, settled into a chair in Dantzler's office. Dantzler sat behind the small desk. The two men were alone, Bloom having opted to sit this one out.

"I appreciate you staying around, Preston," Dantzler said. "It is late, so I'll get straight to the point."

"I'm not remiss in paying my membership dues, am I? I pay those at the beginning of the year. Well, my secretary does. Did she forget to pay?"

"No, this isn't about your dues. This is about something else."

"Okay, what's on your mind, Jack?"

Dantzler paused, aware he had to be careful with his next few words. Preston was known for being an ill-tempered man, and it didn't take much to set him off. The wrong choice of words could ignite the fuse.

"You're not a big fan of Governor Baker, are you, Preston?" Dantzler finally asked.

"That's putting it mildly," Preston answered. "No, fact is, I detest the man and everything he stands for. He's a cancer on the soul of Kentucky, and a phony Republican to boot. Why are you asking me about him? I'm on record as being vehemently opposed to the man. That's not big news."

If an explosion were to occur, Dantzler knew, it would come with his next statement.

"Someone is blackmailing the governor, threatening to expose him and his family to great embarrassment if he doesn't resign within thirty days. I'm certainly not accusing you of . . ."

"The hell you aren't or we wouldn't be having this conversation," Preston said, forcefully.

"You're dead wrong, Preston," Dantzler responded, hoping to calm a potential storm. "I am not accusing you of anything. I don't think for a second you would do anything like that. But you do have plenty of important contacts, folks who follow your lead. Can you think of anyone with enough hatred—and the balls—to blackmail the governor?"

"No one I know is stupid enough to take part in a criminal act that might land him in prison. My friends—followers, as you call them—are much smarter than that." Preston stood and leaned forward. "Are we done with this interrogation, Jack?"

"It wasn't an interrogation, Preston. And I'm sorry if you saw it that way. But yeah, we're done. Again, thanks for sticking around and meeting with me."

Preston started for the door, stopped, and turned back to face Dantzler. "You make it clear to the governor that if I do attack him he'll see me coming," Preston warned. "I won't take the coward's way and send a damn blackmail note. That's not my style. No, I'll look him squarely in the eyes, man to man."

Preston took a step toward Dantzler. "I'll let you in on a little secret, Jack. If I wanted to bring down the governor, I could do it with the snap of my fingers. A simple phone call to the newspaper would do the trick. And should I ever choose to do that, his family would know what genuine embarrassment really feels like."

Dantzler listened but didn't respond. He could sense Preston wasn't finished with his rant.

"Mark Baker is the biggest hypocrite to ever sit in the governor's chair," Preston continued. "All his pro-life talk, how the unborn must be protected, how life is God's most-precious gift to us. That's pure hypocritical bullshit coming from his lips. His pro-life stance was built on sand once his nuts got caught in the crosshairs. Then he sure changed his tune."

"What are you saying, Preston? That Mark Baker got a woman pregnant?"

"And paid for her to have an abortion. You think cages wouldn't be rattled if that information ever got out to the public? Not to mention the humiliation and sense of betrayal it would bring to the governor's family. But out of respect for the woman, I haven't told anyone other than you."

"How sure are you about this, Preston," Dantzler asked, sounding skeptical.

"If you doubt me, Jack, just mention this woman's name to the governor and watch what his response is."

"What name?"

"Hannah Andrews."

TWENTY

Shit! Hannah Andrews? Erin's BFF? Why couldn't it have been anyone other than her? Talk about a sick joke.

Dantzler sat in his office, alone now that Preston had departed in an angry huff. But he hadn't left before having passed along his shocking—and unwanted—bit of news. It was news that caused Dantzler to cringe upon hearing it.

Dantzler's shock was accompanied by a series of questions, none of which were easily answered. Does Erin know about this? Would she be surprised to learn her best friend had hidden a pregnancy—and abortion—from her? Would a best friend keep such a secret to herself? Would she completely shut out her best friend? Keep her totally out of the loop? None of this seemed plausible, Dantzler decided.

Deeper questions lingered: Should he bring it up to Erin? Would it be wrong to keep it from her? How would Erin react if she found out Dantzler had kept her in the dark? No doubt, she'd be pissed.

What about Hannah? Should he discuss it with her, find out for sure if it's true, or simply a malicious rumor? And if it is true, how deep should he probe into her relationship with the governor? But would bringing it up with either woman really matter in terms of the investigation? Would it be beneficial? He couldn't see any obvious way that it would.

His conclusion was to not say anything to Erin or Hannah for the time being. He simply couldn't persuade himself that to do so was in anyone's best interest. At least for now. That decision was subject to change, depending on how events played out in the coming days. Under certain circumstances, should they transpire, he would have no choice but to discuss the matter with both women.

However, the situation was the complete opposite when it came to the governor. Dantzler had no alternative but to discuss the details with him. He had to find out for sure if the story was factual, which he believed it was. Yes, Preston truly despised Mark Baker, but he wouldn't make up a tale that would cause irreparable damage to Hannah's name and reputation. Not even Preston was that cruel.

If the story turned out to be true, and if Mark Baker acknowledged it, then Dantzler had probably found the motivation behind the blackmail scheme. Information about a sitting governor getting a woman pregnant and then paying for an abortion would definitely be worth a lot of cash in the hands of the wrong person. It was a sad tragedy tailor-made for blackmail.

Such news, should it be made public, would bring about a quick and inglorious end to the governor's political career. That was an undeniable fact. His constituents would abandon him in the blink of an eye. In particular, none of his evangelical followers would continue supporting him, financially or otherwise. They would fall away faster than Civil War soldiers on the front lines at Gettysburg.

But as Dantzler pondered all this, one question kept nagging at him: Had he been wrong to conclude that Tim Nelson was blackmailing the governor because Ernie Kruger was an ex-Nazi? Maybe this had always been about the governor's sexual indiscretion. Maybe it had nothing to do with Ernie. But how could a mutt like Tim find out Hannah was pregnant? Or that Mark Baker paid for her to have an abortion? Hannah and the governor were two people way out of Tim's league. It didn't seem feasible their paths could have crossed at any point in the past. So, if that was why Tim blackmailed the governor, how did he learn about the pregnancy and abortion?

There was, Dantzler acknowledged, one obvious answer: Another individual knew about the situation and informed Tim. It couldn't have been Hannah—she didn't know the guy from Adam. Dantzler knew this because she said as much prior to doing the research on Tim. And if she had known him, she never would have confided such personal information to a stranger. Who, then? The individual who left the latest note? Dantzler had to admit this made the most sense.

But this left him with the overriding question: Exactly how many people knew about the governor's indiscretion? Preston indicated the circle of those in the know was very small, and he had not shared this information with anyone other than Dantzler. But this was no longer believable. Preston didn't snatch the information out of thin air. Someone had to tell him. Who was that person? And how many others know?

Clearly, Preston was wrong about the circle being small.

Dantzler had been so engaged with his thoughts he failed to hear Bloom enter the office. He had quietly come in and closed the door. When Dantzler finally looked up, Bloom was staring down at him, shaking his head.

"You have a serious look on that mug of yours, Jack," Bloom noted, sitting across from him. "What's got you so perplexed?"

"What makes you think I'm perplexed?" Dantzler asked. "Maybe I'm just a profound thinker?"

"Well, you are profound, that much I'll grant you. But that was perplexed I saw on your face just now. Remember, I've known you since you were fourteen. I'm very familiar with those looks of yours. You might say I'm an expert at reading your various facial expressions. Now, back to my question . . . what's got you so perplexed? Has to be something Preston said, right?"

Dantzler nodded.

"Care to share it with me, Jack? Or was it meant for your ears only?"

"Can't leave this room. Do I have your word on that?"

"I'm offended you'd ask that question."

"According to Preston, Mark Baker got a woman pregnant, then paid for her to have an abortion."

"Holy shit!"

"That was my initial reaction."

"Well, that clears up one question—why the governor is being blackmailed," Bloom pointed out. "He'd be a dead man politically if that news ever gets out. His career would be over before you could say *oy vey*."

"No doubt."

"Do you see Preston as being behind the blackmail scheme? I mean, given his feelings for Baker, he's the obvious candidate."

"No, it's not Preston."

"What makes you so sure?" asked Bloom.

"Like he said, it's not his style," Dantzler replied. "Also, he has no desire to embarrass the woman involved. I believe him."

"Did he reveal the woman's name?"

"Hannah Andrews."

"Hannah Andrews? That's . . . she's Erin's best friend, isn't she?"

"Yep, she is."

"Just proves once again that truth can be stranger than fiction.

And this particular truth puts your ass in a bind, my friend. Are you going to tell Erin?"

"Not unless I have to. Same goes for Hannah. But I will ask the governor about it. I have no other choice. He has to be confronted."

Bloom stood. "I wouldn't want to be in your shoes when you do have that talk. I doubt he'll be pleased. But . . . there would be no need for what promises to be an embarrassing chat if he'd kept his dick home where it belongs. If his house comes crumbling down, he has no one to blame but himself."

Dantzler didn't respond as Bloom left him alone with his thoughts.

TWENTY-ONE

BARRY FLEMING WAS PREDISPOSED TO DESPISE MUHAMMED before he ever laid eyes on the man. How could it be otherwise? Muhammed was a Muslim, and as every right-thinking American understood, Muslims were bound by three ideals—they hate this country, they slaughter innocent people, and their ultimate goal is to take over our nation and force us to follow Sharia law. And they have no intention of ending that dream until the overthrow is successful.

There was no damn way in hell the fine citizens of the United States would ever allow that to happen, Barry thought, just moments after meeting Muhammed. We'll drive them back into the desert where they belong. There, they can live in tents and ride camels just like their ancestors did centuries ago.

David Danforth had arrived at a little past nine in the morning, introduced his visitor to Barry, grabbed a bottle of water, and left. His final advice to Barry was to make certain Muhammed got everything he requested.

Barry's loathing for Muhammed intensified seconds after Danforth departed. Muhammed's first words to Barry were a direct order; he told Barry to pull three tables together, end to end, to make one long table. He followed that with a second demand—he directed Barry to move the chairs and line them against the wall.

Barry had a Colt .45 tucked under his shirt, and it took every ounce of restraint to keep from pulling out the weapon and putting a bullet between Muhammed's eyes. Send the fucker to Paradise, where he could hang out with all those virgins waiting for him up there. Let them follow his orders.

But Barry let the moment pass, knowing that killing Muhammed would put a crimp in Danforth's big plan, whatever that plan might be. It would also result in Danforth putting a bullet in Barry's brain, an idea that did not appeal to Barry in the least. He enjoyed living too much to ever challenge Danforth.

So, Barry held his tongue, silently arranged the tables into a single line, and then moved the chairs out of the way. Giving in to Muhammed's commands wasn't pleasant, but if Barry was being totally honest with himself, he had to admit he was intrigued by the prospect of seeing how a big bomb was constructed. He'd keep his mouth shut and stay out of Muhammed's way, while at the same time casually keeping an eye on the man as he went about his business.

Muhammed had arrived with a large duffel bag and two small boxes, which Danforth helped carry into the Quonset hut. Muhammed opened the duffel bag and spread the contents onto the first table. Next, he opened the two boxes and laid their contents on the second table. To Barry's great surprised, he recognized virtually all of the bomb's ingredients—a large metal canister, nails, shards of glass, fertilizer, battery, wires, a clock, timer, and three blocks of C4.

Damn, if I watch this dude, I can build a bomb, Barry concluded.

He plopped down in one of the chairs, leaned back against the wall, and stared straight ahead, his intensity level rising as Muhammed began putting each familiar piece into its proper place. Barry had to admit one thing—Muhammed was a true master at his craft, working as smoothly and efficiently as a brain surgeon.

Barry was left to wonder how many bombs Muhammed had built over the years. One thing Barry knew for certain: This was definitely not his first.

AS DANFORTH DROVE AWAY from the hut, he had a smile on his face. And for good reason. Everything was proceeding according to plan. No, he quickly revised his assessment. Things were going *better* than planned.

Danforth never bought into the insane plan to build three explosive devices for the purpose of taking out a synagogue, an Islamic mosque, a Protestant church, or a school building. That was pure bullshit, fake information once it circulated. He knew the guys in the group would eventually get wind that something big was in the works, and given their ignorance and blind hatred of people of color, they would naturally assume the plan involved killing those people. Furthermore, they would see themselves as instruments of destruction. What they didn't know was Danforth couldn't care less about Muslims, Jews, Christians, or Catholics. None of those folks factored into his thinking or into his plan.

Danforth had finally settled on a single target, one that would shock and disappoint everyone in the group. But that didn't matter to him; what those guys thought was irrelevant. The device Muhammed was building had a singular purpose, and Danforth wouldn't be happy until that purpose was fulfilled. Until the right people were dead.

Muhammed made a fuss when informed he would only be

building a single bomb, his chief concern being money. Danforth assured Muhammed that payment had not changed, that he would be paid for three bombs as promised. This was also bullshit. In fact, Muhammed would receive no payment at all. He would be dead, and the dead have no need for money.

Danforth's thoughts drifted back to the group, and more specifically, what to do with those men once his plan had been implemented? In truth, he never really considered it much of a group, certainly not like many others he was familiar with around the country. Men in those groups would kill you without giving it a second thought. They had blood on their hands. Think Charlottesville, where real hate and violence were on display. But this group was little more than a collection of punks and losers, none of whom held to any particular ideology. Sure, a few may have thought they did, but they were only fooling themselves. The majority of these men wanted to carry a gun and sound tough even though not a single man had ever marched in a real demonstration or confronted a person of color face to face. This group was made up of wannabes.

The smart play would be to simply disband the group and send those idiots on their way. And with only two or three exceptions, they were idiots. Of course, disbanding meant Danforth either had to abandon the sale of weapons, or bring together a new group of individuals for the purpose of continuing what was a profitable enterprise. But new faces would invariably bring on many questions, and questions, especially ones posed by idiots were never a good thing. Maybe the wisest route to take would be to keep six or seven of the top guys and pay them a heftier wage, provided they purchase a higher volume of weapons. Let their income be contingent on their output. More results, more money. Pure capitalism, right?

But in recent days, and in light of certain events, he had begun to question the wisdom of continuing the sale of weapons. It was a risky business, to be sure, and the income of those sales was nothing to sneer at. But what good was money if you were behind bars?

The expression on his face changed when a new thought crossed his mind:

Jack Dantzler.

If Dantzler asked to join the group—and he would—this meant he had to be closely monitored. Dantzler would never join such a group for any purpose other than to spy on it. His joining had to be in a law-enforcement capacity. What other reason would he have for joining? None that Danforth could think of. Dantzler was a genuine danger, a man to take seriously. Suddenly, Danforth's thoughts took a darker turn:

If Muhammed can be eliminated, who's to say Jack Dantzler can't also be taken out? After all, it's a known fact that anyone can be killed.

Even an ex-cop.

———

BARRY'S ATTENTION was so focused on Muhammed that it took several seconds before he realized his phone was buzzing. His eyes still on Muhammed, Barry picked up the phone without looking to see who the call was from.

"Yeah," he snapped, not peeling his eyes away from Muhammed.

"Barry?" the caller asked.

"Yeah, this is Barry Fleming. Who's this?"

"Mickey Wilson."

"Oh, hello, Mick. What's up?"

"I need to talk to you about Jack Dantzler. Got a minute?"

"What about him?" Barry inquired.

"He's changed his mind about joining the group," Wilson said. "He wants in."

"Why the sudden change of heart?"

"What can I say, Barry? He thought about it, reconsidered, and now he wants in. What do you think? You still interested?"

"Yeah, Mickey, if you're absolutely certain he's eager to join and is also willing to commit one-hundred percent to our cause, then I'll say yes. But if he shows any lack of interest, or if he refuses to follow orders, he's gone. You okay with that?"

"Sure, Dantzler won't be a problem. You have my word on it."

"You can't bring him here before five-thirty. Any time after that is fine."

"I'll bring him by tomorrow and introduce him to the guys," Wilson stated.

"See you then, Mick." Barry ended the call and immediately punched in Danforth's number. When Danforth answered, Barry said, "You were right, David. Dantzler changed his mind, now wants in. I said okay."

"I'm always right, Barry," Danforth said.

"You were right about something else as well."

"Let me guess . . . Mickey Wilson made the call."

"You're a true prophet, David," marveled Barry. "If you could do that at the racetrack or with the Lottery, you'd be a very wealthy man."

"I'm already a very wealthy man, Barry."

"Yeah, well, I meant *wealthier*."

"Dantzler could be a real problem for us, Barry. Don't lose sight of that. He must be kept in the dark about everything, especially the plan and the weapon sales. He cannot know about either of those things. He *cannot* know. Am I making myself perfectly clear on this?"

"Yeah, David, clear as crystal."

"How are things going with Muhammed?" inquired Danforth.

"Okay, I guess. Hell, the man hasn't uttered a word in an hour."

"He's not there to make conversation, Barry. He's there to build a fuckin' bomb."

"Well, that's what he's doing."

"Did he send you out for food?"

"No, he brought his own," Barry said.

"Tell him I'll pick him up at four-thirty. Until then, keep him happy."

"That's what I live for, David, to keep a damn Muslim happy."

"Sarcasm isn't your strong suit, Barry. I would advise you to put a lid on it."

With that, Danforth ended the call.

MIKE WATKINS PUNCHED in Dantzler's number, waited, then said, "Jack, you'll be pleased to learn you have officially been accepted into the group. Barry Fleming gave you the green light."

"Can't begin to express how honored I am, Mike," Dantzler said. "Being in that group will surely look good on my resume. A true jewel in my crown."

"Yeah, I can tell you're crazy with excitement. Can't blame you, pal. Now, down to business. We need to meet with Sam and decide what avenue to pursue. I suggest we get together sometime tomorrow. Will that work for you?"

"Only if it's in the afternoon," Dantzler replied. "I'm scheduled to meet with Governor Baker at ten in the morning. I have no idea how long that meeting will last."

"What about your place at two? I'll bring something from Subway. What's your choice?"

"Meatball sub with cheese and onions."

"You got it. See you at two, Jack."

TWENTY-TWO

When Mark Baker agreed to meet with Dantzler he asked if the two men could get together in the governor's office. Dantzler said he would prefer to meet in a more private setting, and then suggested the Vietnam Memorial as a possible compromise. Baker said yes, and the meeting was set for ten a.m.

Dantzler, as always, was early, and was looking at his father's name on the Memorial when Governor Baker showed up. Baker exited his car, and then walked briskly toward Dantzler. The governor moved like a man with a purpose, unaware he was on his way to having a nightmare revived.

"Kathy told me about your father, how he was in the Vietnam War but died in Laos," Baker noted as he moved next to Dantzler. "What the hell was he doing in Laos?"

"Tracking down a CIA agent who had gone rogue," replied Dantzler. "He was ambushed and killed. Shot in the back, actually."

"How old were you when this happened?"

"Six."

"Do you remember him?"

"Vividly. He was an impressive man. And a terrific father."

"Had to be tough on your mom. Did she ever remarry?"

"No. She was murdered eight years later."

"Damn, Jack, I'm really sorry. Kathy failed to mention that."

"We didn't discuss it." Dantzler pointed to his right. "Let's talk over there, out of this sun."

Dantzler led the governor to the same bench where he and Kathy had previously chatted. No other visitors were nearby, which protected this talk from prying eyes and eager ears. Private or not, Dantzler knew this was not going to be a pleasant conversation.

"Governor, the reason I . . ."

"You learned the name of the individual who is blackmailing me, right," interrupted Baker. "Is it someone I know? Preston Combs, maybe?"

"No, unfortunately I don't have a name for you, Governor," Dantzler said, slightly peeved at being interrupted. "But what I learned is likely the reason why you are being blackmailed."

"Well, good, that's a step in the right direction, isn't it? What is the reason?"

Dantzler took a deep breath, let it out slowly, then said, "Hannah Andrews."

Baker flinched, quick, almost imperceptible, but not enough that Dantzler failed to pick up on it. In that brief moment he knew the governor was guilty of having had a sexual relationship with Hannah. Now, the question was, would Baker own up to his indiscretion?

"What about Hannah?" Baker asked, giving his best impersonation of an innocent man.

"How well did you know her?"

"Not well, really. Oh, I know what I've heard about her, that she's a talented, dedicated, intelligent woman and a wonderful employee. That's why I suggested she help with research. I hope this doesn't sound sexist, but she is also quite beautiful. Why are you asking me about Hannah? You're not suggesting she's behind the blackmail scheme, are you?"

"Are you sure that's the answer you want to go with, Governor?"

"What are you getting at, Jack?"

"You know the answer to that, Governor."

"No, I don't. So why don't you tell me?"

"You had a sexual relationship with Hannah, she got pregnant, and you paid for the abortion."

Dantzler braced for an explosion, for a string of expletives, and possibly even a punch in the face. But none of those actions occurred. Instead, Baker's shoulders slumped and he stared straight ahead. It was almost two minutes before he responded.

"How did you find out?" Baker finally managed to ask. "Hannah didn't tell you, so it had to be one of my political enemies. Which one was it?"

"How I found out really isn't relevant," Dantzler said.

"Wait a second. It was Preston Combs, wasn't it? Yeah, it had to be that bastard. Tell the truth, Jack. Was it Preston who told you?"

"It doesn't matter who told me, because the person who did is not the person who is blackmailing you."

"You're sure about that?"

"Yes."

"Then who is blackmailing me?"

"Once again, Governor, ask yourself, who benefits the most if you leave office before your term is up?"

Baker shook his head, said, "I know where you're heading with this, Jack. You're convinced it's Bradley Cooper, but you're dead wrong. Bradley would never stoop to a criminal act like blackmail. That's beyond preposterous."

"True or false, Governor: You've been in talks with Marilyn

Lawrence about the possibility of her becoming your running mate should you run for re-election?"

"Yes, we've discussed the matter. But those talks are only in the preliminary stage, a feeling-out process. Nothing is for certain. And I don't see how Bradley knows about it."

"*I* know about it, Governor. And if an outsider like me knows, do you really believe Bradley Cooper doesn't? In my experience, when it comes to politics, everybody knows everything. There is no such thing as a well-kept secret."

"Bradley? I just have a hard time believing it's him."

"I'm gonna find out who it is, Governor, and Bradley Cooper will be my starting point. Are you on-board with that?"

"I hired you to do a job," Baker acknowledged. "I'm not about to interfere or tell you how to do it. So yes, you have my permission to go wherever your investigation takes you."

Dantzler stood and glanced at the Memorial. "Sorry to bring this up about Hannah," he said, shifting his eyes back to the governor. "But I had no other choice. I had to have the truth."

"Now that you do, can I persuade you to keep it to yourself?"

"I don't intend to tell anyone, Governor. However, I can't promise it won't come out at a later time. That'll depend on how certain future events unfold."

"Thanks for your candor, Jack. I appreciate it." Baker paused, then said, "And just so you'll know, Hannah and I didn't have a real relationship. We were only together one time. And the funny thing is, Jack, I'd do it all over again in a heartbeat."

Dantzler nodded but didn't respond. He wasn't certain if he was troubled by sadness for Hannah or anger toward the governor. Probably an equal measure of both, he concluded. Silently, he walked back to his car, got in, and drove back to Lexington.

THE MEATBALL SUB WAS DELICIOUS. Dantzler couldn't recall the last time he'd had one, and he dispatched this baby in a matter of minutes. Starved, he put away his sandwich, a small bag of chips, and a Diet Pepsi long before Sam Rosen and Mike Watkins had finished theirs.

When all three men were done eating and the table had been cleared, they went out onto the deck to formulate a plan for how to function within the group. Dantzler, however, was skeptical that his presence in the group would be much help.

"Those guys are not going to be very chatty with an ex-cop hanging around," Dantzler predicted. "They'll go all Simon and Garfunkel on us, which means about all we can expect to hear will be the sounds of silence."

"I'm not convinced those guys know very much, Jack," Watkins said. "If we learn anything of importance, it'll have to come from Barry. And I think there is a limit to how much he actually knows."

"He has to know who's calling the shots," Rosen interjected, "even if he doesn't know all the details."

"He's definitely the guy we work the hardest," Watkins agreed.

Dantzler said, "Who owns the property where the Quonset hut is located?"

"Don't know," Watkins admitted. "But we can ask Barry that question. That's something he probably does know."

"No, don't bring it up," Dantzler said, shaking his head. "I have better ways to get that answer."

"Then I'll pick you up at six tonight," Watkins said.

"Make it seven," Dantzler replied. "We don't want to get there too early."

Watkins grinned, said, "Fashionably late, huh? I like it. Makes us look classy, like Cary Grant or Fred Astaire."

"Stop dreaming, Mike," Rosen said. "No matter what, you'll

always look more like Charles Bronson or Ernest Borgnine than Grant or Astaire. Right, Jack?"

"Hey, leave me out of it," Dantzler protested.

DANTZLER NAILED it on the nose: He didn't recognize a single group member, but every one of them was familiar with him, which they demonstrated by their actions. Most of the men went out of their way to avoid being introduced, while the poor unfortunate few unable to escape being trapped in what for them was a disagreeable situation offered neither a hand nor said hello.

Dantzler wondered if Barry Fleming had alerted the men to his imminent arrival, or if they possessed an inner-cop radar detector that silently warned them to steer clear of anyone who had worn a badge. He had long ago come to believe certain criminal types could actually smell a law enforcement official, not unlike a zebra could smell an approaching lion.

Either way, the men dodged Dantzler like he carried the plague. For his part, Fleming made a second attempt to make the introductions, but the results were the same. The men simply didn't want anything to do with Dantzler.

None of this came as a surprise to Dantzler, who never expected to be a popular guy with the group members. He was destined to be a pariah. That's why he simply shrugged when Fleming apologized for the cold treatment dished out by the men.

"Never seen the guys so hostile," commented Fleming. "It's not like them to behave this way. Normally, they're pretty friendly."

"They don't like ex-cops," Dantzler said.

"Give them a little time. They'll eventually warm to you."

When Fleming walked away, Dantzler turned to Mickey Wilson, and said, "I seriously doubt it."

"I think it's safe to say you'll never be voted prom king," Wilson said. "They're gonna make sure you are always on the outside looking in."

Dantzler surveyed the Quonset hut interior. "This is a fairly elaborate set-up for such a motley crew," he stated. "Wonder who paid for it?"

"Isn't that what your phone call was about?"

As they were pulling up to the Quonset hut, Dantzler, having gathered information concerning the location, phoned Hannah Andrews, passed along the details, and asked her to find out who owned the property. Hannah agreed, saying she would get back to him sometime tomorrow.

"Yes, it was," Dantzler answered, "but we'll ask Barry, see what he can tell us. If he knows who paid for all this stuff, Hannah won't have to dig into who owns the property. It has to be the same guy."

They found Barry standing by the bar, having just opened a bottle of beer. He was speaking with the man known as Roadkill. The conversation appeared to be serious in nature, yet Roadkill quickly moved away when he saw Dantzler and Wilson approaching.

"This is a cool meeting place, Barry," Dantzler pointed out. "Pool table, card tables, ping-pong table, dart board, bar . . . not to mention the structure itself. Had to cost a small fortune. Did the guys in the group pay for all this?"

"No, the guys didn't pay for it," Barry said, after taking a drink of beer. "Hell, none of the men has a pot to piss in, much less the kind of bucks it took to build this place. To be honest with you, I don't know who did pay for it. But you're right. Whoever it was spent big dollars."

Wilson said, "We're gonna check out, Barry. Is there anything you need us to do?"

"Just keep bringing Dantzler around, give the guys time to

accept him," Fleming said, adding, "I'll let you know when you're needed."

Outside, as they were driving away, Dantzler said, "Barry has to be the worst liar I've ever encountered and I've dealt with hundreds over the years. Does he really expect us to believe he doesn't know who paid to have the hut built and then furnished with all those amenities? How dumb does he think we are?"

"Well, Jack, it's a group of thugs, not a convention of Mensa members," Wilson said, laughing. "A high IQ is not a prerequisite for membership into the group."

"That explains why you were allowed in," Dantzler said.

"Yeah, yeah, go ahead and finish your thought. I know you're dying to say it."

"And why I'm so out-of-place among that bunch of yahoos."

TWENTY-THREE

Two days and still no word from Hannah.

She had phoned Dantzler to inform him she was on her way to an important meeting in San Francisco, and she wasn't sure how long she would be gone. She told Dantzler that if she had some free time she would research the property's history, gather information on Bradley Cooper, and let him know what she found out. Dantzler had no choice but to wait until she got back to him.

But Dantzler hadn't been sitting around idle for those two days. During the afternoons and early evenings he kept a close watch on Bradley Cooper, which turned out to be a complete waste of time. Cooper followed a set routine—he left work at five, drove home, and never left the house. At no time did he, his wife, or anyone else enter or leave the place. Dantzler thought this was uncharacteristic behavior for the commonwealth's lieutenant governor. Most politicians are besieged by friends, hangers-on, or those seeking funds for their various pork barrel projects. Clearly, Bradley Cooper was not like most politicians.

It also forced Dantzler to question his belief that Cooper was the blackmailer. Maybe the guy was innocent. Maybe he had no desire to hold down the top job. Maybe he didn't care if he was replaced on the ticket by Marilyn Lawrence. Maybe he could live with it either way.

Maybe I just got it wrong.

But Dantzler didn't think so. No alternate scenario made any sense. Who other than the man hidden in the shadows would seek to move into the sunlight? To leapfrog into the big chair?

The person playing second fiddle, that's who.

There was one factor Dantzler had to consider: which of two possible scenarios was the correct one? Dantzler had always believed the governor was being blackmailed because his father-in-law was a former Nazi. But what if that wasn't the case? What if Cooper was blackmailing Baker because of the governor's sexual relationship with Hannah Andrews? If the second scenario was the right one, that dramatically altered the situation. Not only would the governor and his family be humiliated, but Hannah might be as well. Dantzler desperately wanted to avoid that outcome.

Shortly after sunset, Dantzler drove to the Quonset hut, spent an hour or so milling around, interacting with no one but Mickey Wilson or Barry Fleming. After two nights, not a single group member had "warmed" to Dantzler, as Barry had predicted. Nor was that likely to change.

On the third night Dantzler finally got a break. He was standing at the bar talking to Barry when Barry's phone began to ring. He answered, listened, stepped away from Dantzler, and then said in a voice louder than he realized, "How much longer is that damn Muslim going to be here? Oh, he'll finish tomorrow? Thank God for small favors."

Dantzler strolled away, making sure Barry didn't realize his side of the conversation was being overheard. Barry ended the call, tucked his phone into his hip pocket, came back to the bar, grabbed a beer, opened it, and took a swig.

"You okay, Barry?" Dantzler asked.

"Couldn't be better," Barry replied. "Why do you ask?"

"No reason. Look, if it's okay with you I'm going to book out. Truth is, Barry, I'm wasting my time coming here. It's obvious the guys don't want me around. That's not going to change."

"You just gotta give them more time. They'll eventually accept you."

"I doubt it, Barry, but I'll give it a couple more nights. See what happens."

Dantzler spotted Wilson, got his attention, and went over to him. "We need to scram, Mickey," Dantzler whispered. "I'm leaving now. You stick around for ten or fifteen minutes, then you leave. Phone Sam and tell him to meet us at my house. We need to talk."

"Got it," Wilson said, not questioning Dantzler's order. "See you in about an hour."

———

"A MUSLIM?" Rosen asked. "You know anything about that, Mike?"

"First I've heard of it," Watkins answered.

"Can't imagine a group like that tolerating a Muslim," Rosen said. "I'd think they would be more likely to shoot him at first sight."

"It's like I've been telling you, those guys don't have a clue what's really going on," Watkins stated. "But I can guarantee you one thing for sure . . . we now know why the hut has been closed during the day. Something is going on and it involves the Muslim."

"Mike is right," Dantzler chimed in. "If I had to hazard a guess, I'd say he is building some type of explosive device."

"Or devices," Rosen noted. "We need to get inside that hut, take a look around."

"Not possible without a search warrant," countered Dantzler. "And we don't have probable cause to get one. Plus, none of us are law enforcement officials."

"To hell with the warrant. We sneak in at night after everyone has gone."

"Too risky, Sam," Dantzler pointed out. "Besides, if we did it that way, anything we might find would be inadmissible in court. No, we have to play this by the book."

Dantzler rose from his chair, opened the refrigerator, and grabbed three bottles of Smithwick's. He handed the two men a beer, then sat back down.

"All right, Jack, we'll do it your way," Rosen conceded. "You contact your old buddies in the Lexington Police Department, bring them up to speed, and let them handle it in an official capacity."

"I have a better idea," Dantzler suggested. "Why not bring in the big guns? The FBI? I'll contact Glenn Rigby, fill him in on what we know, and see how he responds. I'm betting he'll be all over it."

"That works for me," Rosen said.

"Same here," Watkins agreed.

Dantzler checked his watch, said, "It's almost twelve; probably too late to give him a call tonight. I'll do it first thing in the morning."

"On the off-chance Rigby declines, we need to have a back-up plan in place," Rosen said.

"Rigby's not going to decline," Dantzler said. "Think about it. If he stops whatever it is the Muslim is doing, he'll also be putting an end to the weapons sales. He has as much skin in this game as we do. Maybe more than we do."

"Thanks for the beer, Jack," Watkins said. "We'll wait until we hear from you."

Dantzler walked the two men to the front door, shook hands

with each one, and then watched as they drove off into the darkness.

DANTZLER WAS in bed and had just turned off the lights when his cell phone buzzed. He checked—the call was from Hannah Andrews.

"Did I wake you, Jack?" Hannah said. "Sorry if I did, but I knew you'd want to hear what I found out."

"You didn't wake me," Dantzler said, turning on the light. "Are you in Frankfort?"

"Nope, still in Frisco. I'm probably stuck here for a couple more days. It's been an interesting and enlightening meeting to say the least. Lots of bad things happening around the world, now that all those populist, nationalist, far-right factions are taking hold throughout Europe. Scary stuff."

"Yeah, and it's not just happening in Europe. We have danger closer to home."

"World problems are not why I called," Hannah related. "I had some free time this afternoon, which I utilized by looking into the two areas you requested. I'll begin with what I learned about Bradley Cooper. He was born and raised in Fort Thomas, Kentucky, graduated from UK and UK's law school, and went to work for a small law firm in his hometown. Got married at twenty-four, had two kids, both girls, decided to run for state senator and won. He has since been re-elected two more times. Three years ago, he was selected to join Mark Baker on the Republican ticket. We all know how that election turned out. More important for your purposes, Cooper has no criminal record at all. No one in his family does. Pretty boring, I'll admit, but that's about the size of it."

"What about his finances?" Dantzler asked. "How well off is he?"

"He's not—his family was traditional middle class—but his wife did come from money. Not super rich, but more than enough to live a comfortable lifestyle."

"That's not surprising. Cooper strikes me as a classic run-of-the-mill kind of guy."

"Now, moving on to your second request, the one dealing with that piece of property in Jessamine County and who owns it," Hannah said. "The land, which comprises approximately three-hundred acres, was purchased in nineteen hundred by the Danforth family. It was jointly owned by two brothers, Daniel and Darrell. Tobacco and hemp were the two main crops they raised. All original structures are long gone, but there is a small building constructed three years ago that sits within a few hundred feet from a pond. The property is currently owned by . . ."

"David Danforth."

"Wow, was that a lucky guess, Jack, or do you know him?"

"He's a member of the Tennis Center."

"Well, he was an only child, so the property was handed down to him upon the death of his parents. He also inherited a shit-load of money. The guy is incredibly wealthy, one of those lucky trust-fund babies we all envy. I doubt the guy has worked a day in his life. Hell, I wouldn't if I had his money."

"Sure you would, Hannah. You were born to save the world from disaster."

"If that's true, I'm afraid we're all in big trouble," Hannah said, laughing. "What about David Danforth? How does he figure into your investigation?"

"Don't know. Maybe he doesn't. That's what I need to find out."

"Happy hunting, Jack. And if you need more assistance from me, just ask. I'm super busy, but I'll always make time for you."

"Thanks, Hannah. You're the best."

"Goodnight, Jack."

Dantzler ended the call, turned off the lights, and lay back down. Outside, a soft rain had begun to fall. He should have been sleepy, but he wasn't. A single thought was keeping him awake.

David Danforth? Who the hell would've figured he played a role in any of this?

And what about the mysterious Muslim? What was his involvement in all this?

We have danger closer to home.

Little did he know how dangerously accurate that statement would prove to be.

TWENTY-FOUR

MUHAMMED AND HIS FEMALE COMPANION WERE SITTING side by side in chairs placed at the center of the Quonset hut floor. More accurately, they were bound to the chairs by duct tape. Their ankles were taped together, their hands were tightly taped behind them, and several feet of tape virtually welded each of them to the chair where they were seated. A single piece of duct tape had been placed across the woman's mouth. The chairs sat on a twelve-by-twelve green tarp that currently lay where several tables had previously been located.

David Danforth stood directly in front of Muhammed, while Barry Fleming, a .45 pistol in his hand, was to Danforth's right. What was presently happening hadn't been spur of the moment. It had been planned out several hours earlier.

When Danforth showed up at the McDonald's parking lot a little after eight in the morning, he wasn't surprised to see Muhammed's lady friend in the car with him. Danforth had been informed the bomb was ready, and Muhammed expected payment. Danforth had other plans, none of which included money. He told Muhammed the money was at the Quonset hut, and Muhammed would have to follow him there if he wanted to be paid today. If he chose otherwise, the money could be mailed to him. Muhammed reluctantly agreed to follow Danforth to the hut. Twenty-five minutes later, Muhammed and the woman walked into the hut, where they were met by Barry, who pointed his weapon at them, then ordered Muhammed and the woman to sit in the two empty chairs, where they were immediately bound with duct tape.

Muhammed, his dark eyes shooting darts of fury at Danforth, asked, "Why are you doing this? The job has been completed. I did all that was required of me. Pay me the remainder of my money and we'll be on our way. There is no need for violence."

"You Muslims are experts when it comes to violence, aren't you?" Danforth said.

"And Americans aren't? Surely you know better than to believe such nonsense. But that's a debate for a later time. Now all I want is the money I was promised."

"You get nothing, Muhammed, until you answer one question for me," Danforth said in a calm and friendly voice. "Give me what I want, then we can discuss your payment."

"What question?"

"You told me when we began this project that once you were finished there would be one piece of the puzzle remaining, and that only you would know how that piece fit into place. You said I wouldn't be given the missing piece until you were long gone. Do you remember saying that to me?"

"Yes, of course."

"Well, I'd prefer to have that information now. Waiting just isn't my cup of tea."

"If I tell you, I'm a dead man," Muhammed said.

"Maybe, maybe not. Look at it this way . . . you have a fifty-fifty chance of leaving here alive. Not great odds, I'll admit. But it's better than no odds at all."

"Again, I must ask . . . why are you doing this?"

"That's a question, Muhammed, not an answer. Stop stalling. What's the final piece of the puzzle? What needs to be done for the bomb to be fully armed?"

Muhammed shook his head.

"Look, asshole, we both know you're eventually going to cough up the answer," Danforth barked. "Why not make it easy on yourself and simply give it to me? That'll save us both a lot of unnecessary hardship."

"Untie both of us, give me my money, promise us safe passage, and I'll give you the answer you're seeking."

"Sorry, pal, but I'm afraid that ship sailed long ago." Danforth nodded at Barry, who then placed the barrel of his pistol against the woman's temple. "I've never been officially introduced to the little lady, so I don't know if she's your friend, your wife, your sister, your mother, or just a fuck-buddy. But regardless of what your relationship is with her, she'll be dead unless you answer my question."

The woman began crying louder now, tears and snot ran across the tape covering her mouth and dripped into her lap. Her entire body shook like she was having an epileptic seizure. She tried to speak, but her words were muffled by the tape covering her mouth.

"Okay, I will tell you what you want to know, but please don't harm her," Muhammed pleaded. "She plays no role in this. She is innocent. Do I have your word no harm will come to her?"

"Yes, you have my word," Danforth replied.

"The truth is, I was making up that stuff about a final piece of the puzzle. It does not exist. There is no missing piece. Saying that was my way of guaranteeing my safety once the job was finished."

"I don't believe you, Muhammed. I think you were telling the truth then, and now you're lying, hoping to save your ass. That's not going to work. So . . . one more time—what is the final piece of the puzzle?"

"There is no final piece."

Danforth looked at Barry and nodded. Barry shot the woman in the head. She slumped forward, blood pouring from the fatal wound.

"You lying American infidel," Muhammed screamed. "You gave me your word. And now you do this? Your soul should burn in hell forever."

"Still waiting for that answer, Muhammed," Danforth calmly said.

"You stupid man . . . there is no final piece. It's not that type of bomb. There is a timer. You set the time when you want the bomb to go off, place it where you want it, and then walk away. The bomb will detonate at the chosen time."

"Not sure I believe that." Danforth again looked at Barry, said, "Knee."

Barry shot Muhammed in his left knee. Muhammed screamed in agony, tears flowing down his face. He dry-heaved several times, but nothing came up.

"You're telling me the truth now?" asked Danforth.

"I am."

"All I have to do is set the timer and the bomb is activated?"

"Yes."

"Know what, Muhammed? I believe you." Then to Barry: "Send this fucker to Paradise."

Barry fired two shots point blank into Muhammed's heart.

"Cut the tape and move the chairs out of the way," Danforth ordered. "We'll deal with them later. Wrap the bodies in the tarp and secure it with plenty of duct tape. Then we'll drag the bodies out to the pond. What about the concrete block and the rope?"

"Already in the boat," Barry answered.

"Good. We'll row the boat out to the middle of the pond and dump the bodies and the weapon overboard. No one will ever find them."

"How deep is the water in that pond?"

"I don't know for sure. Thirty, thirty-five feet at the center. Maybe even deeper than that."

"Why not burn the bodies? Wouldn't that be simpler?"

"Burning never gets rid of everything, Barry. Traces are always left behind. I want these bodies to disappear forever."

"Whatever you say, David."

Danforth said, "When we're done dumping the bodies, get in Muhammed's car and drive to Brannon Crossing. Wear gloves, a baseball cap, and sunglasses. Park in front of Kroger's, get out of the car, lock the doors, and go inside. Keep your head down on your way into the store. Right before you go inside, take off the gloves, cap, and sunglasses. Purchase a couple of items and come outside. I'll pick you up and bring you back here. Toss the car keys into the pond, come back inside, and drown the two chairs with bleach. Make sure all traces of blood are gone. Got all that?"

"Got it."

"Good. Now let's turn these bodies into fish food."

TWENTY-FIVE

DANTZLER TOLD ROSEN AND WATKINS THAT ONCE GLENN Rigby learned about the Muslim being involved he would be more than willing to offer his assistance. But what Dantzler hadn't taken into account at the time was the status of Rigby's health. The FBI agent might be cancer free, but what about the lingering effects of the surgery and the subsequent treatments he had undergone? To what degree had they impacted his ability to do his usual good work? This was a legitimate question that required an answer. Dantzler wanted Rigby's help—having the FBI in your corner was seldom a negative—but he had no desire to push Rigby beyond limits that could prove detrimental to his recovery. He'd said as much when he spoke with Rigby.

But Rigby casually brushed aside any concerns about his health or his stamina and quickly agreed to join forces with Dantzler, Rosen, and Watkins. He joked that he might "look like a corpse," and at times "felt like one," but every day was better than the one that preceded it. The only thing he wanted to know was when and where they would meet.

"You're positive you can do this, Glenn?" Dantzler inquired.

"If you're not up for it, that's okay. We can push on without you. Health has to be your top priority."

"Damn right I'm up for it, Jack. The Muslim is a game-changer. We have to find out why he's here."

"If you're good to go, I'll contact Sam and Mike. We can meet at my house this afternoon. Will two work for you?"

"Yeah, two is fine. But listen, Jack. I'm going to alert some folks higher up the food chain here, make them aware of what we're doing. I want them ready in case we need their help sometime down the road. And I would also suggest you inform Lexington PD. In the end, we might need everyone's help."

"I'll call them right away," Dantzler promised. "See you at two."

After ending the call, Dantzler phoned Eric Gamble, head of Lexington's Homicide Unit, and filled him in on what was happening. Eric listened but asked no questions. Only after Dantzler laid out all the details did Eric respond.

"I'll make sure we're ready to assist if it comes to that," Eric said. "But one of us should contact Nicholasville PD and the Jessamine County Sheriff's Department. After all, much of what's going on is taking place in their backyard. If bad shit does come down, we'll all have egg on our faces if we left them out in the cold."

"That's a great point, Eric. You should probably make the call. Better they hear it from someone official."

"Yeah, that makes sense. Let me know if you need us, Jack. We'll be ready."

"I will. And thanks, Eric."

Sitting alone in his Tennis Center office, Dantzler pondered the fact that he had not mentioned David Danforth's name when he spoke with Glenn Rigby. Nor had he informed Rosen and Watkins. Withholding Danforth's name had not been an accident or an oversight. It was a card Dantzler would pull out and play when the proper time presented itself. It was his ace in the hole.

For now, though, hunger was his primary area of concern. He had not eaten anything today, and his empty stomach was letting him know it was being neglected. Deciding it was time for lunch, he left the Tennis Center, got in his car, and drove to Ramsey's on Nicholasville Road. Once inside, he quickly placed his order— soup and a salad. That should be plenty enough to silence his rumbling stomach.

As for those other rumblings, he wasn't sure what it would take to silence them.

DANTZLER MADE THE INTRODUCTIONS, then asked if any of his guests wanted something to drink. Rosen and Watkins went with a Diet Pepsi, while Rigby, looking much better than he had a couple of days ago, asked for a bottle of water. After fetching the required drinks, including a Pepsi for himself, Dantzler joined them at the kitchen table.

"How did you find out about the Muslim, Jack?" Rigby wanted to know.

"Purely by accident," Dantzler answered. "I overheard Barry Fleming talking on the phone. No idea who he was talking to, but Barry wanted to know how much longer the Muslim would be around. Whoever Barry was speaking with said the Muslim's job was finished. Barry was extremely pleased to get that news."

"My money says the Muslim has already been eliminated," Watkins stated. "There is no chance they would ever let him leave there alive. He was a dead man the moment he agreed to work with that bunch."

Rigby said, "There is also very little chance the Muslim was involved in the sale of weapons. He was brought in for other reasons, probably to build some sort of explosive device. That's why we have to move on this with a great sense of urgency."

"Barry Fleming is the door we need to open and walk through if we want answers," Dantzler said. "He's the only one in the group who possesses any knowledge of what is going to happen and when it will take place. We should go at him with hurricane force, see how well—and how long—he can stand up to it. I'm betting he'll be quick to cave in."

"I think you're wrong about that, Jack," countered Watkins. "Barry's tougher than you give him credit for. After all, the guy did fight in Afghanistan. I also believe you're mistaken about another point . . . Barry only possesses partial knowledge of what's about to happen. For the most part, he's being kept in the dark by the individual behind the operation."

"Here's my suggestion," Rigby said. "I'll wait until three or three-thirty in the morning, after Barry is asleep, bang on his door, wake him up, and then begin to question him. He'll be groggy and pissed off, which is exactly how I want him to be. Once I've got him inside and seated, then it's like you said, Jack, I'll go at him hard."

"*We'll* go after him, Glenn," Dantzler responded. "No way I miss that interview."

"You might want to give that a second thought, Jack. If you're with me, that will effectively end your association with the group, along with any future information you might come across. Are you sure that's the smart way to go?"

"I don't give a crap about that damn group, Glenn. Being inside is a waste of my time. I'm never going to learn anything important from those guys. They shy away from me like I'm a leper. Besides, Mike won't be with us when we talk to Barry. He can continue to be our man on the inside."

"Won't work that way, Jack," Watkins corrected. "If your cover is blown, mine will be as well. I'm the guy who brought you in, remember? They won't overlook that."

"That just puts more pressure on us to make sure Barry Fleming tells us all he knows," Dantzler said.

"Do you have Barry's address?" asked Rigby.

"He lives alone in a small house he rents on Wilson-Downing. His closest neighbor is several hundred yards away. It's the ideal location for our purposes."

"Perfect." Rigby stood and stretched. "I will pick you up at two. We should get to his house by two-thirty."

"Good luck, guys," Rosen said, adding, "Mike and I will wait to hear from you early tomorrow morning. We'll go from there, depending on what you learn."

After the three men were gone, Dantzler picked up his phone and punched in Erin's number. He had no pressing reason to call, other than he wanted to hear her voice. He sought sanity in what he knew was an insane world. His call went to voicemail. Not his first choice but better than nothing. He patiently listened as she directed the caller to leave a message. He did—consisting of just two words.

"Love you."

TWENTY-SIX

DANTZLER BANGED ON THE DOOR FOR A FULL TEN MINUTES before Barry Fleming finally opened it. Fleming was wearing a T-shirt, boxer shorts, and white tube socks. He had obviously been drinking, and his blood-shot eyes resembled alien space craft hovering above two dark circles. His warm breath smelled of beer and garlic.

Through squinted eyes Fleming focused on Glenn Rigby, who had stepped in front of Dantzler. The door was only open a few inches, providing Fleming with a narrow field of vision. Fleming looked away, hacked out a deep cough, and then turned his attention back to Rigby.

"It's three o'clock in the morning," Fleming stated, his voice hoarse and raspy. "Who the hell are you and what do . . ."

Fleming's eyes widened when he recognized Dantzler standing behind Rigby. It took but a second before the realization kicked in.

"Dantzler? Fuckin' Jack Dantzler?" Fleming snapped. "We were right about you? We knew you were still a cop. We never . . ."

"*We?*" interrupted Dantzler. "Who exactly is *we?*"

"*I* knew you were still a cop," Fleming quickly corrected. "I argued that you never should have been allowed in the group. I said that was a big mistake."

"Barry, we want to talk to you about that group you just mentioned," Rigby calmly said. "Mind if we come inside?"

"Damn straight, I mind. Who the hell are you, anyway? You look like a man who died a week ago and no one sent you the message."

Rigby held up his credentials. "Glenn Rigby, FBI. And you already know Jack Dantzler."

"Yeah, he's a crummy copper."

"He called me a copper, Glenn," Dantzler said. "Haven't heard that one in years. Kind of makes me feel like I'm in an old Cagney movie."

"Yeah, definitely old school," replied Rigby. Then to Fleming: "You going to invite us in, or not?"

"Not."

"Enough of arguing with this little turd, Glenn." Dantzler moved in front of Rigby, used his shoulder to nudge the door open, and shoved Fleming forward. "Lead the way, asshole. We aren't leaving here until you answer a few questions for us."

"Screw you, Dantzler. And the same goes for your dead-man-walking Federal agent."

Dantzler roughly secured Fleming by the arm, said, "One more comment about Glenn and I'll wipe the floor with your sorry ass. Got it?"

Hoping to quell a potential physical confrontation, Rigby worked his way between Dantzler and Fleming. "Let it go, Jack. He's not hurting my feelings," Rigby said. "Look, Barry, we're gonna have a little chat and it doesn't have to be adversarial. We can converse like friends. But either way it does have to get done. It will get done."

"I ain't got nothing to say to either one of you," Fleming announced.

"Fine. Then how about I talk, tell you what I know, and you listen? Does that meet with your approval?"

"Okay, so talk." Fleming sat on the sofa, Rigby and Dantzler remained standing. "What do you two jerks think you know?"

"We know pretty much everything, Barry," Rigby said. "Let's begin with the sale of weapons. Tell us about that operation. Who purchases the weapons? Where do they go?"

"Don't know anything about no weapons sales."

"Aren't you curious to know how I learned about it?"

"Why should I be curious if I don't have a clue what you're talking about? Answer that for me, if you can."

"We had someone planted in the group," Rigby explained. "He informed us. That's how I know."

"Yeah, and who would that little songbird be?"

"The man you murdered. Tim Nelson."

"No way, man. I didn't kill Tim Nelson."

"Sure you did, Barry," Rigby said. "Who else could it have been?"

"Hell, I didn't know he was a rat, so what reason would I have to kill him?"

"But his being a rat is not why you killed him," Dantzler said. "Tim had to be taken out because he was using information about a certain individual to blackmail Governor Mark Baker. An individual your group reveres. Tim had to be silenced before that information leaked out."

"If you think you're scaring me, you're not," Fleming boasted. "I don't know anything about anyone being blackmailed, so you're just wasting your time."

"Then let's shift gears and move on to the Muslim," Rigby said. "Is he still alive, or has he also been eliminated?"

"What Muslim?" Fleming asked, clearly startled by the question.

"The one brought in to build an explosive device. Or perhaps several devices."

"You're just making this shit up, aren't you, old man?"

"Here's something I'm not making up, Barry. You're currently at the center of some future events that have death and destruction written all over them. Unless you step up and cooperate with us, get out in front of what's about to happen before they occur, you'll end up spending the rest of your sorry life behind prison bars. Is that what you really want?"

"No, what I want is to jump back in bed and get some shuteye. Any chance that might happen before I die of old age?"

"Barry, no one thinks for an instant that you are clever enough or wealthy enough to run an operation consisting of so many moving parts. That's way above your pay grade, your capabilities. You need to tell us the name of the person who is running the show. Who is putting up the money? Who's pulling the strings?"

Fleming smiled, winked, and shrugged his shoulders.

Dantzler had endured enough. Stepping in front of Rigby, he stared hard at Fleming. It was time to pull out his ace in the hole.

"David Danforth."

Fleming and Rigby simultaneously cut their eyes toward Dantzler, obviously baffled by the name Dantzler had just pulled out of the blue. Confusion registered on both their faces. Only the Lord himself could have discerned which of the two men was the most surprised.

"Tell me about David Danforth," Dantzler ordered. "And don't give me any bullshit about how you don't know him, because I know for a fact you do."

"You don't know jack-shit, *Jack*," Fleming said, smiling at his own turn of phrase.

"I know he owns the property the Quonset hut sits on. And I know he paid to have it built and furnished."

"Don't know anything about that."

Dantzler reached over, took Fleming's cell phone from an end table, and began scrolling through the list of recent calls. It didn't take long to find what he was looking for.

"Your last six calls went to DD," Dantzler pointed out. "Who might that be, I wonder?"

"Doris Day."

"Good answer, Barry. But in case you missed it, she died not too long ago. Care to try again? Maybe you should go with David Duke this time. He'd be more up your alley, wouldn't he?"

"Okay, let's go with David Duke."

Dantzler began miming punching in numbers.

"Wait. Who are you calling?" Fleming wanted to know.

"DD. I've never spoken to David Duke before. Think he'll talk to me?"

"Stop, you're right. DD is David Danforth."

"Cut the lying, Barry. It's not working."

"I ain't lying."

"Did Danforth bring in the Muslim to build a bomb?" Dantzler asked.

"Screw you, Dantzler."

Rigby pulled out his handcuffs. "Stand up and turn around, Barry," he said. "Put your hands behind your back. I'm taking you in."

"Yes, yes, he built the bomb, okay?" Barry acknowledged.

"How many bombs?"

"Originally, there were going to be three. But he only built one."

"Why the change?"

"Couldn't tell you."

"What was the Muslim's name?"

192

"Muhammed. Don't know if that was his first or last name. No one ever told me."

"Is the Muslim still alive?"

"Don't know."

"Come on, Barry, you're on the right track when you tell the truth. Now isn't the time to wander away from the right path. So, I'll ask again. Is Muhammed dead or alive?"

"I don't know. I swear."

"Yeah, you do, Barry, because you probably killed him. On orders from David Danforth, I would assume."

"How many more questions are you going to ask me?" Fleming mumbled. "I really want to get back in bed."

"Just one. Where is Danforth planning to place the bomb?"

"He never told me where."

"Know what, Barry? I believe you on that one," Dantzler said.

"Shouldn't I have a lawyer?" Fleming asked. "Yeah, I want a lawyer."

"You're a little late with that request, Barry," Rigby noted. "You should've asked for one at the very beginning of our little chat. But you don't need a lawyer. Not yet, anyway. Instead, you are going to work for me."

"No way, Jose. I ain't no fuckin' snitch."

"Here's the deal, Barry, and it's a one-time-only offer. You either agree to help us or I will arrest you, haul you off, and slam your ass in jail tonight, where you will reside for the rest of your natural life. It's your call to make, Barry."

"Arrest me? On what charge?"

"The murder of Muhammed."

"You can't prove I killed that Muslim."

"I'll get the proof, Barry. It won't be difficult to do."

"And just how do you plan to do that?"

"I'll bring in the FBI's finest forensics team and watch while they scour every inch of the Quonset hit. If there's a single drop of blood in there, they'll find it. And they'll match it to Muhammed, take my word on it."

"They won't find nothin', because there ain't nothin' there."

"For your sake, Barry, you'd better pray they don't."

"If I do agree to help, will I have to wear a wire?" Fleming inquired.

"Not immediately, but maybe at some future time you will. For now, though, I want you to go about your business in a normal manner. Do what you usually do. Try to engage David Danforth in as much conversation as possible. Ask questions, but don't sound too inquisitive. Don't give him the feeling he's being grilled. Your top priority is to find out where and when the bomb is supposed to go off. And one final thing—when Dantzler shows up at the Quonset hut, treat him like nothing has changed. Are you good with all this?"

"Do I have a choice?"

Rigby nodded, said, "Yeah, you can go to prison for the rest of your days."

"Some choice."

"Do I take that as a yes?"

"Yeah."

"Smart boy."

"Why bother with me? Why not just arrest Danforth? You know about the bomb. Isn't that enough?"

"We do that we'll never know where the bomb will be located, or if it's already in place," Dantzler said, taking over the conversation. "And in a your-word-against-his-word scenario, who do you think wins that debate? With his money, his resources, Danforth wins easily. No, Barry, we need to know where that damn bomb is. And you're going to help us find out where."

"Well, hate to tell you this, but David Danforth ain't gonna tell me."

"Make the effort to find out, Barry. It will work in your favor when the bad guys are being put away," Rigby said. "And that day will surely come. You do right by us we'll do right by you. That's a promise."

"Yeah, right, like your promises means squat to me," Fleming scoffed.

"Never forget one thing, Barry. This deal works both ways. Screw us and you'll get screwed ten times over."

"Are we done here?"

"Yeah, Barry, we're done for now," Rigby said. "Go to bed and get that sleep you so desperately need. Be fresh and rested, because beginning tomorrow you work for us."

"Do I get paid for this so-called work?"

"Yeah, your freedom."

"In case you haven't heard, you can't spend freedom," Fleming said, marching toward the bedroom.

Dantzler and Rigby quickly left the house. As they were walking toward their car, Rigby turned to Dantzler, and said, "Where did you come up with the David Danforth name? Sure would've been nice to have been given a heads-up. It took me completely by surprise."

"Sorry about that, Glenn," Dantzler said, getting into the car. "It was something I learned in the past couple of days, and I didn't have time to share it with you or the other guys. Won't happen again."

"Don't worry about it, Jack. That name changed everything. Without it, I don't think we would have gotten much information out of Fleming."

Dantzler looked at his watch, said, "It's almost six. I'll call Sam around nine and tell him what we worked out with Fleming. We should get together at some point tomorrow afternoon. We need to make sure we're all on the same page."

"Make it later in the afternoon, if possible," Rigby said. "I'm bushed. I need serious sleep."

"What about five? That sound okay to you?"

"Oh, you don't have to wait that late, Jack. I can be up and ready by three."

"How about we agree on four o'clock?"

"You should've been a negotiator, Jack. Yeah, four works for me."

"Now that we've settled on a time, get my ass home, Glenn. You're not the only one who needs some sleep."

"You're sounding like Barry now."

"Thanks, Glenn, that's just what I wanted to hear."

TWENTY-SEVEN

DAVID DANFORTH SAT IN HIS GAME ROOM AND EYEBALLED the bomb that rested on his pool table. It was inside a standard backpack, not unlike the ones used by multitudes of students, computer geeks, regular working folks, and, well, just about anyone who had items of a certain type that needed to be transported. It was perfect for moving the bomb without drawing undue attention. The backpack could be placed anywhere and no one would give it a second thought. He marveled at how something so small could cause such massive death and destruction. But it could.

And it most definitely would.

He had studied the bomb since taking it to his house, and had quickly determined Muhammed had not lied when he promised that the device was simple and easy to arm. Like Muhammed said, it was simply a matter of setting the timer, placing the bomb in the desired location, and then walking away. The blast would occur at the designated time.

Danforth filled his glass with more Macallan, took a sip, and let his thoughts drift off. And there was much for him to think about, to ponder.

Beginning with . . .

Barry Fleming and those stupid jerks in the group. This matter divided into two separate issues, both of which required different resolutions. How best to approach each one was the challenge Danforth faced.

To begin with, the group had to be immediately disbanded. This was a no-brainer. After all, what good was the group, anyway? None, best he could tell. The reason for this was simple: The men had no values. At their core they were fraudsters, goofballs who loudly professed to hate, Jews, blacks, Muslims, people of color, foreigners, gays, and atheist, when, in truth, not a single one of the men had ever spent ten minutes in the presence of any of those they purported to hate.

They were, to borrow John Wilkes Booth's infamous last words, "useless, useless."

Yes, the men had been helpful in procuring weapons to be sold. Danforth had to admit that much. But the enterprise had become too risky, too dangerous to continue. The money he made wasn't worth the chances he was taking. He had to put an end to it. He'd decided a few weeks ago that next month's shipment would be his last one. The various entities he sold to would be disappointed, but it was a decision they would have to live with. Besides, if they wanted weapons, there were plenty of individuals willing to sell.

Next on his list of issues to be dealt with was Barry. What to do about him? This was a tough one, no question about it. Barry had been a loyal and valuable soldier in every way. He kept the men in line, he had been a key player in collecting the purchased weapons, and perhaps most-important of all, he never flinched when given an order, even ones that included committing three homicides. A man like that deserved to be rewarded, maybe given a huge wad of cash, enough to last a lifetime.

However . . .

With the exception of the man who ordered the bomb, Barry was the only person on the planet who could connect Danforth to the gun sales, the murders, or the bomb. None of the men in the group were privy to any of this information. Only Barry possessed it.

The question then becomes, could Barry be trusted to keep this information secret for the rest of his life? Was he capable of hanging with his buddies, say, in five or ten years, and then after getting shit-faced one night, could he keep from bragging about all he had seen and done? Could he refrain from boasting about the three people he had murdered on orders from Danforth? Maybe Barry could keep this knowledge locked away forever. Maybe he could be trusted to keep his trap shut.

But . . .

Was it a risk Danforth was willing to take?

He wasn't sure, but he was leaning toward no. Allowing his fate to rest in Barry's hands did not sound like a winning proposition. Of course, there was an obvious alternative—eliminate the risk. Taking Barry out would certainly remove all worries. How and where presented no problem. Make it late at night, grab a case of beer, then he and Barry get in the boat and row out to the middle of the pond. Just two close friends talking, drinking, gazing at the stars. Then at some point pull out the pistol and shoot Barry. Wrap the body with heavy chains, then dump it—and the pistol—overboard, where they could both spend eternity with Muhammed and his lady friend. Go ashore, get in Barry's truck, drive it to a secluded location, park, get out, phone Uber, and head back home. Problem solved.

This was a possibility Danforth would have to seriously consider.

Another sip of Macallan, a different thought to chase. This one concerned ...

Jack Dantzler.

Of all the decisions Danforth had made in his life, allowing Dantzler anywhere near the group had been the dumbest. Hands down, it ranked as the king of his stupid choices. And what was so perplexing—and what made him so angry—was that he knew from the beginning Dantzler was joining the group for nefarious reasons. Dantzler may have played it cool and distant, feigning indifference about being accepted or rejected, but that was just an act, part of his ploy, his attempt to come across as being above the final decision.

Pure bullshit. Dantzler wanted in because he was seeking information. About what? Danforth wasn't certain. Most likely, it had to do with Tim Nelson's murder. This made the most sense. After all, Dantzler had been a homicide detective. He was plowing in a familiar field.

On a second front, perhaps Dantzler's involvement had to do with the sale of weapons, or with the presence of Muhammed on the scene. But the odds were slim that either of those scenarios were the reason why Dantzler wanted in the group. How could he have learned about either one? From Barry? Danforth didn't think so. No, Danforth decided, Dantzler was looking into the Nelson murder. This was the only scenario that rang true.

Danforth would have to think about what to do with Dantzler. Same goes for his sponsor, Mickey Wilson. Despite the glowing praise heaped on him by Barry Fleming, Wilson wasn't kosher. There was definitely something off about the guy. Whether or not he was actually working with Dantzler wasn't possible to know with certainty. But the two men were connected in a bad and potentially dangerous way. That fact was beyond doubt.

The scotch hit home and Danforth dozed off for a few

minutes, his thoughts morphing into a dream that included water, bones, darkness . . . a massive explosion.

Suddenly, his eyes snapped open. Wide awake now, a voice inside his head was screaming, telling him what to do, where to place the bomb, how to solve a pair of potential problems in a fraction of a second.

It hit him like a revelation—the perfect way to eliminate two men with a single blast.

Why hadn't he thought of this before? Why had it not come to him until this very minute? How could he have been so blind to what was clearly an obvious solution?

More Macallan, a bigger drink this time, another grin.

No, make that a ten-thousand watt smile.

Out of a dream he had solved a double-edged problem. Wasn't that worth a big smile?

TWENTY-EIGHT

It was all Dantzler could do to keep his eyes open. He was bone-tired, hadn't had a decent night's sleep in ages, and sitting inert in his car for the past ninety minutes wasn't making his staying awake any easier. Nor was the gentle rain that had recently begun to fall. A wiser man would've left, gone home and climbed into bed. But Dantzler knew that wasn't going to happen. There was too much at stake to give in to weariness.

He was parked about thirty yards from Bradley Cooper's house, on the opposite side of the street. This had been his standard routine for four nights, during which nothing out of the ordinary had happened. Once Cooper returned home from his office and went inside the house, no one came or went. The man and his family were like hermits.

Dantzler hadn't expected anything different on this late afternoon. But he was wrong.

About twenty minutes after Cooper got home, the front door opened and two women, Cooper's wife and one of his daughters came out of the house, each one carrying an overnight bag. They loaded the luggage into the rear of a white Honda CRV, got into the vehicle—the daughter behind the wheel—and quickly drove away.

Judging by the two large overnight bags, Dantzler figured the women planned to be gone for a short stay. Or perhaps only one was leaving, maybe to catch a flight, and was being driven to the airport by the one not traveling. Since the daughter was driving, Dantzler guessed if one was on her way to catch a flight it, was probably Mrs. Cooper, in which case the daughter would be returning home shortly.

Dantzler's speculation held true until a white vehicle pulled into the driveway next to Cooper's house. But this vehicle wasn't the one that had previously departed. Yes, it was the same color, but this one was a Lexus, not a Honda. There was yet another, more-important distinction—Dantzler recognized this vehicle.

He had seen it many times at the Tennis Center.

The Lexus belonged to Preston Combs, Governor Mark Baker's most-hated enemy. This was confirmed when Combs emerged from the driver's side, stretched, and began walking toward the front steps, where Cooper, having just come outside, stood waiting.

Interesting.

Dantzler's interest level spiked considerably when the passenger door opened and a well-dressed woman got out of the vehicle. She wore a blue pants suit, white blouse, and flat shoes. Her brown hair was pulled back and tied in a ponytail. After smoothing the wrinkles in her pants, she began walking toward the two men waiting on the porch.

The woman, when getting out of the Lexus, only half-turned in Dantzler's direction, yet even with the rain still coming down, he had a pretty good idea who she was. He couldn't swear to it under oath, but he was ninety-eight percent positive the woman was Marilyn Lawrence.

Only one way to know for sure, so he took out his phone, went to Google, and typed in **Marilyn Lawrence, Louisville, Ky. Attorney**. There were plenty of hits, including one for the firm where she was a partner. Dantzler opened that site and went to the section that said Partners. Her bio, accompanied by a color head shot, was second on the list. He studied the photo, and then mentally placed it against the woman he saw getting out of the Lexus. His conclusion: same woman.

Marilyn Lawrence.

Talk about a strange confluence of personalities. Three political heavyweights meeting in secret. Was this, Dantzler wondered, an unholy trinity, or simply an odd occurrence? After thinking about it for a few seconds, he concluded unholy trinity was the correct answer.

Unholy, yes, but these three in particular were also quite intriguing.

Dantzler could understand why Preston was here. He detested Mark Baker and would go to any lengths to deny the governor's re-election. Okay, but why was he visiting Cooper, a man who was second in command to Preston's arch-enemy? The very man Baker claimed lacked the ambition and the energy to challenge for the top position. But what if Preston knew better, that the governor was wrong? What if they were putting a plan in place to run Cooper against Baker?

Either way, Preston was now inside the lieutenant governor's house, which, to Dantzler's mind, threw a dark cloud over Baker's earlier proclamation regarding Cooper's seemingly low level of ambition.

But far more intriguing—and baffling—was the presence of Marilyn Lawrence. What purpose would she have for attending this meeting? What role did she play within this unholy trinity? After all, this was the woman being courted by Baker to replace Cooper on the Republican ticket. Yet, here she was at Cooper's house. What gives?

Preston hated Baker and wanted him ousted. Now, Preston was conferring with Marilyn Lawrence, Baker's probable choice for a running mate. And all this was taking place in Cooper's house? What the hell was going on here? Dantzler asked himself.

To Dantzler, none of this made sense.

Or, upon reflection, maybe it made perfect sense.

Preston, with his dominant, larger-than-life personality, was obviously calling the shots, whatever those shots were. The plan being devised behind those closed doors was being drawn up and laid out by Preston. It couldn't be any other way. He never took orders from anyone, and certainly not from a run-of-the-mill man like Bradley Cooper. That would never happen, not in a million years. He would treat Cooper as a subservient underling, a whipping boy, a chess piece to be moved around at will.

But back to the real question: Why Marilyn Lawrence was here? She was the mystery guest, the outlier.

Dantzler figured it had to be for one of three reasons: She was working undercover for Baker and was spying on his enemies; she was going to be put on the ticket with Cooper, run as his lieutenant governor, and challenge Baker; or she was being asked to run for the top spot, which would, of course, mean kicking poor Bradley Cooper to the curb. Probably not what Cooper had in mind, but chess pieces have no say in where they are placed. If that's what Preston desired, there was little Cooper could do to contest the order.

Dantzler quickly eliminated the second of those three possibilities. No way was Cooper going to run for governor, with or without Marilyn as a sidekick. And certainly not without Preston's support, which he would never get. There was another factor as well—Cooper was not leadership material, and therefore he could never get elected. His best plan for political survival was to keep his mouth shut and do exactly what Preston ordered him to do.

The first possibility was also weak, Dantzler judged. He

simply could not see Marilyn Lawrence as being a covert under-cover operative. She had the look of a woman with balls, one who would look you in the eye and tell you what's on her mind. Based on what he'd read about Marilyn on the firm's website, and now seeing her in person, he was convinced she was a formidable lady. But even if Dantzler was wrong and Marilyn was working under-cover, her efforts would be to no avail. Preston would sniff that out in less than an hour.

So, what was left? Only the final possibility was even remotely plausible. Preston planned to run Marilyn for governor against Mark Baker, the very man who wanted her to join him on the ticket. As for Cooper, most likely he was being ordered to keep his trap shut, make no waves, and with Preston's assistance, perform small favors during the campaign that would help undermine Baker's chances of being re-elected.

What this also meant, Dantzler realized, was that Marilyn was a snake in the grass who could not be trusted. So, how does that make her any different from most politicians? It didn't, not in his mind, anyway. To him, all politicians were spawned in the Garden of Eden.

Another possibility, one that shouldn't be overlooked or dismissed, was that the three insurgents were discussing a new scheme to blackmail Baker. But somehow he didn't see blackmail as the reason for this meeting. Not with Marilyn present. There was no way she knew anything about the previous blackmail plot against the governor. And even less chance she would be brought into a potentially new plot.

No, this meeting was purely about politics.

About getting rid of Mark Baker.

Suddenly, Dantzler was hit with another realization—Hannah Andrews.

Preston knew about the governor's fling with Hannah, the pregnancy, and the subsequent abortion. What were the odds that during a too-close-to-call election, he wouldn't use that sordid tale as the deciding factor? If it meant the difference between winning and losing, between seeing Baker remain in office or being voted out, Preston would almost certainly leak the story to the media. He was a win-at-all-cost guy, and if his winning hinged on hanging Hannah out to dry, he would do so without hesitation. She would be collateral damage in Preston's personal war against the governor.

Preston would win, but Hannah's life, reputation, and career would be shattered.

Dantzler wasn't about to allow that to happen, even if it meant going toe-to-toe with a bully like Preston Combs, or a snake like Marilyn Lawrence.

He would do everything within his power to assure that Hannah stays out of the firing line.

DANTZLER REALIZED he was no longer sleepy; witnessing the arrival of Preston and Marilyn; thinking about what was being discussed inside the house had taken care of that. His mind was now alive with possible scenarios being plotted out by this unholy trinity. What he wouldn't give to be a fly on the wall in that house.

But after twenty minutes of waiting, and with the visitors still camped inside the house, Dantzler's eyelids were starting to droop. He decided it was time to leave. He thought about driving to the Quonset hut to check out things there, but quickly shot down that idea. Nothing was to be gained by his being there. Barry Fleming's new mission as FBI informant hadn't been in play long enough for him to learn anything of importance from David Danforth. And if by chance Barry had come across some information, he could share it with Mike Watkins, who, along with Sam Rosen, had been brought up to speed on what was discussed during that late-night chat with Barry.

Realizing he was hungry, Dantzler opted to call Erin and ask if she would like to go out for a late supper. She answered immediately, said, "Hey, what's up?" and listened to his pitch.

"I have a superior plan," Erin said. "Why don't you come over here and I'll whip up something?"

"What do you have in mind?"

"How about scrambled eggs, hash brown potatoes, biscuits, and orange juice? Does that appeal to you at all, or would you prefer something more manly? A steak, maybe, with a baked potato and a salad?"

"Although we both agree I'm a manly man, I like your first option better. Besides, who says you can't have breakfast for supper? I'm all in for that."

"Great. One thing, though. I have an early meeting tomorrow morning, so you have to promise to be on your best behavior. That means nothing naughty will happen tonight. Are you good with that?"

"My dear, I'm way too tired to be naughty."

"Good. Then I'll start cracking the eggs."

TWENTY-NINE

"WHAT'S GOING ON WITH YOU, BARRY?" DAVID DANFORTH inquired after handing a small piece of paper to Fleming. "You don't look so good. Anything wrong, anything I need to worry about?"

They were sitting in Danforth's den drinking Macallan scotch whisky. This was the first time Barry had been in Danforth's house. It was also his first time drinking Macallan.

"No, everything is hunky-dory," Barry barked. "Why do you keep hounding me about that? I'm fine, okay? So let it rest."

"My, my, you're in a rather disagreeable mood tonight, Barry. Fact is, you are acting like a total asshole, and I don't care for it one bit. Don't forget who you're talking to."

"Sorry, David. Maybe I'm acting this way because I'm having trouble sleeping at night." Barry held up his glass. "Or maybe this swill I'm drinking is having a negative effect on me. And by the way, didn't you tell me you never drink?"

Danforth grinned, said, "Swill? Do you have any idea how much that bottle of Macallan cost, Barry?"

"No clue."

"Plenty enough that you should drink it with respect."

"Okay, it's not swill, you had to dig deep into your pocket to pay for it, and I think it tastes like liquid gold. Does that sound better?"

"No, it sounds like you're still being an asshole. One more time and we'll have a problem. You understand what I'm saying?"

"Yeah, Yeah, I know I'm acting shitty. Sorry. Won't happen again, David. Promise."

"If you can't sleep, Barry, I have pills that will take care of the problem. If you want a couple, just ask."

"Maybe I'll get one or two before I leave." Barry looked at the piece of paper Danforth had given him, then looked back up at Danforth. "Okay, so who is George Clayton, and why have you given me his name?"

"George Clayton is like one of those Jeopardy jerks who win a ton of money. He knows things no person should know."

"Such as?"

Danforth refilled his glass with the scotch whisky, took a sip, then said, "George is the man who hired Muhammed and ordered him to build three bombs. Of course, I had no intention of allowing Muhammed to follow those instructions. That's why I lied to him —and to George—about only needing a single bomb because we were in a time crunch. When I informed George about the change of plans, he had no choice but to agree that we only had time to build one bomb. For what George had planned, apparently there was a real time issue. However, when I told George the deal was off and I was keeping the bomb, he went ballistic. And in my experience, angry men tend to make unwise decisions. I can't afford to let that happen."

"What can he do?" asked Barry. "It's not like he can go to the cops and tell them about it. They would arrest him before they had you in cuffs."

Danforth nodded, said, "True. But what if he made an anonymous call to the FBI? He could rat me out that way and no one would be wise to who phoned in the tip."

"Yeah, but what good would that do him? You would just turn around and rat him out as your accomplice."

"George Clayton is a well-respected judge who comes from a prominent Southern family. If he and I start pointing fingers at each other he's likely to come out on top. You have to understand, Barry, there is nothing that connects the two of us, which also means there is nothing that connects George to the bomb."

"What about phone calls? They're easy to trace."

"Come on, Barry, you know better than that. We used burners and we tossed them after each conversation. Like I said, there is absolutely nothing to connect him to me or to the bomb."

"So . . . what are you saying, David? That you want me to go to Georgia and take him out?"

"That's exactly what I'm saying. Think about it, Barry. It's the only way to ensure our freedom."

"But I can't just drive to Georgia without knowing anything about the guy," Barry protested. "Is he married, does he have kids, does he live alone, where is his house located? I'd need answers to those questions before I would even think about making that trip."

"He's in his early eighties, he's a widower, and he lives alone. His kids are all grown and live in nearby Atlanta. Trust me, Barry. This will be the simplest job you'll ever have."

"Easy for you to say, David. You won't be the one pulling the trigger."

"No, but if you refuse to do the job, I just might be the guy standing next to you when the cops arrest us and haul us off to jail. I don't want that outcome and I'm fairly sure you feel the same way."

"Okay, David, I'll do it. But first, tell me why George Clayton wanted the three bombs."

"George is a true son of the South, one of those old school

Johnny Rebs who don't consider the Civil War, or what the South-erners call The War of Northern Aggression, to be either over or lost. As such, they continue to hold tremendous animosity toward Northerners—especially the ones they label as elitists—for the role those snobs played in the destruction of the South. First, they freed the slaves, which Southerners have always claimed killed the South's economy. Then, according to people like George, things went from bad to worse when the Northern establishment will-ingly allowed our country to be taken over and ruled by Jews, Muslims, Orientals, Mexicans, liberals, women, and atheists."

Danforth took another drink before continuing, "Now, I don't know for sure, nor do I care where George planned to set off his bombs. But I am sure it would have been in locations that resulted in the deaths of many of those people he finds so repulsive."

"Then I regret his dreams went unfulfilled," Barry said.

"Why do you say that, Barry?"

"Because it's exactly how I feel about the direction this country is heading. It's what all the guys in our group think. It's what you think, isn't it, David?"

"Let me share a little secret that will probably come as a surprise to you, Barry. No, I don't think that way. Why should I? How would it benefit me? To worry about others you have to think about them. And I don't, not for a second. I couldn't care less about any of those groups, or the individuals within those groups. Not coons, Yids, Spics, gooks, wetbacks . . . none of them. I'm so far above all of those folks. To me, they are little more than ants running around on the ground. Nothing and no one else matters when you have the kind of money I have. As for the men in our sorry group, the sad truth is, they don't know jack shit about anything. They've somehow fooled themselves into believing they do. They call themselves white supremacists. Really? Who are any of those guys superior to? No one and that's the truth. It's all part of some stupid fantasy they wrap themselves in. But then, when you're as dumb as they are, how can they be expected to have a real clue about what's going on in the world?"

"You're a fuckin' phony, David, a damn hypocrite. You know that?"

"Remember who you're talking to, Barry. You'd be well-served to keep your hostility and your disappointment to yourself." Danforth poured more scotch into Barry's glass, then more into his own. "You are the only smart guy in the group, the only one I can trust. That's why I've always counted on you to handle difficult situations, to be the group's leader. So, put aside those hurt feelings, agree to go down to Georgia and eliminate George Clayton. Then when you come back here, I'll have one final task for you to complete. After that's done, I'll write you a check that will make you a very rich man."

"What final task?" Barry inquired.

"Torch the Quonset hut."

"You're not serious?"

Danforth nodded. "One-hundred percent serious."

"Why?"

"No hut, no group. Scattering the guys is the best way to end it all. The group has outlived its usefulness, Barry. It also has the potential to become something of a liability for us."

"When do you plan to do this?"

"Immediately after you return from Georgia."

"When am I going down there?"

"Day after tomorrow. You should leave early in the morning which will put you there late in the afternoon. That's a Saturday, so the judge won't be in court. Wait outside his house until after dark. Once you're sure he's inside, walk up and knock on the door. When he opens it, put one bullet in his heart and one in his brain. He'll likely be alone, but if you do see anyone else in the house, you'll have to put them down as well. Your gun will have a silencer, so no one should hear the shots. Once the deed is done, you get in your car and drive back to Lexington. Sleep in on Sunday. Give me a call when you get up and we'll work out the details regarding the Quonset hut. I'm thinking we'll set the fire at two or three in the morning. The way that place was constructed, and considering the materials we used, it will be reduced to a pile of smoldering ashes within twenty minutes."

"After I take care of this Clayton dude and get back here, how can I be sure you won't put a bullet in my brain?" Barry asked. "You kill me and then dump my dead ass in the pond. That would be the sure way to silence me. Is that your plan, David?"

"You get money, Barry, not a bullet. Trust me, you have nothing to worry about. I reward loyalty, I don't eliminate it."

Barry drained the scotch from his glass, looked down, a deep scowl on his face. A few tears began to collect in his eyes. After a few seconds, he lifted his head, glanced quickly at Danforth, and then let his gaze wander around the room.

"You look like the classic tortured soul, Barry," Danforth said, breaking the silence. "Something on your mind? Something you need to share with me?"

"The Feds know about us, David," Barry whispered. "They know everything . . . the weapon sales, the bomb, Muhammed. They know it all."

"And how did you come by this information?"

"They paid me a surprise visit in the middle of the night and questioned me. That's when they told me."

"Who questioned you?"

"A cadaverous-looking FBI agent. And Dantzler."

"Dantzler, huh? So, I was right about him all along—he's still a cop." Danforth set his glass on the table. "How did they get on to us in the first place? They must've had someone on the inside. That's the only possible explanation. Who was it? That Mickey Wilson fellow you like so much?"

"Tim Nelson."

"You gotta be kidding me. That little piece of shit was a Fed informant?"

"Yeah, according to the FBI guy, he was."

"There's not much Tim Nelson could have told them? He was dead before Muhammed showed up. Nelson was aware of the weapon sales, but he couldn't have known anything about Muhammed or the bomb. So, tell me . . . how did the Feds know about that?"

"I don't know, David. But they do."

"And you swear they didn't learn it from you, right? Be honest, Barry. I need to know everything."

"No, I didn't tell them anything. They told me." Barry paused before continuing. "One more thing, David. They know about you."

"Are you sure about that?"

"Positive. While I was dodging the FBI guy's questions, Dantzler jumped in and said your name. Pulled it out of the blue. He wanted to know if I knew you. I said I didn't."

"And? Don't stop there, Barry."

"He knew you own the property where the Quonset hut is located."

"But how did Dantzler make that connection in the first place? And why would he?"

"Can't say, David. All I know is what he said."

"They didn't just question you and leave. That's not how those guys work. They had to want something from you. So what did the Feds ask you to do?"

"Get as much information from you as possible. Mainly, they wanted me to find out all I could about the bomb. Has it been planted? Where it's to be planted? When it's set to go off? Shit like that."

"You don't know the answers to those questions, Barry, so you couldn't have told them anything. What else did they ask?"

"That's about it," Barry answered. "Oh, they wanted to know if Muhammed was dead or alive. I said I didn't know. And they ask me if I killed Tim Nelson. I said, hell no, I had nothing to do with his death. Don't know if they believed me or not."

"Doesn't make any difference. Tim Nelson is the least of our worries at the moment."

"What do we do now, David?"

Danforth was quiet for a moment, then said, "For starters, we stay cool. *You* stay cool. Continue to behave no differently from the way you normally do. Go to the hut, interact with the guys same as always. I need a day or two to figure out some things. When I do, I'll let you know what the plan is."

"Am I still going to Georgia?"

"No reason to make that trip now. George Clayton is no longer a matter of concern for us."

"What about torching the hut?" Barry asked. "Is that also out?"

"No. At some point that will have to be done. I'll let you know when." Danforth stood. "Go home, Barry. Sit tight and wait to hear from me."

Barry stood and began following Danforth up the stairs. When they arrived at the front door, Barry turned, and said, "Can we survive this, David?"

"Only if we play it smart, keep our wits and make no mistakes," Danforth said, opening the door. "That means you have to follow all your set routines. Don't vary anything. If Dantzler shows up at the hut, don't give him any hints you've spoken with me. Maybe later we'll feed him false information, send him on a wild-goose chase. That might buy us some time. And it's essential you share with me anything he or the Fed guy tells you. I need to know what they know. Got it?"

"Yeah, I hear you."

"Go home, Barry, and get some sleep. You could use it."

Danforth stood at the door a full minute before closing it. He required more Macallan and more time to get a better grasp of what he'd just learned. Slowly, he headed back down the stairs and into the den, intent on drinking and thinking.

One factor required no further thought: His plan had to be implemented sooner rather than later.

And it had to be successful.

THIRTY

THE INCESSANT BUZZING OF HIS CELL PHONE ROUSED Dantzler from a deep sleep. For a brief moment after waking up, his thoughts were cloudy and disoriented. Then he realized he was in Erin's bed. He was alone, Erin having left an hour ago to attend her early morning meeting.

Dantzler groaned, rolled over and fumble for his phone. After securing it, he checked to see who the caller was. Mark Baker. Dantzler wasn't surprised to get a call from the governor—he had been expecting it. He also had a pretty good idea what Baker wanted to talk about.

"Morning, Governor," Dantzler said, blinking hard to clear away the clouds. "I was going to call you later today."

"I know it's early, and I can tell from your voice that I woke you up," Baker said. "Sorry about that. But since I haven't heard from you for a few days, I wanted to check on the status of your investigation. Are you getting any closer to finding out who is blackmailing me?"

"No, Governor, sorry to say I haven't. But that doesn't mean I've given up hope. There are still a couple of promising leads I plan on pursuing. I'm hoping one of them will pan out."

"I don't mean to pile on additional pressure, Jack, but time is growing short. The clock is ticking. That thirty-day deadline is less than two weeks away."

"I'm aware of that, Governor. Believe me, I'm doing everything possible. No stone will be left unturned until I get a name for you. That's a promise."

"I have every confidence you will do whatever is necessary. Just stay in touch, okay?"

"I will, Governor."

Dantzler ended the call, knowing he had just told an untruth to the governor. Or, perhaps half-truth was the more-accurate assessment. Yes, he was making progress—that part was true. And even though deep down in his gut he felt like he knew the identity of the blackmailer, he couldn't be certain his suspicion was anything more than an educated guess.

And yet . . .

When he lined up all the pieces, factored in all probable possibilities, only one individual was left standing.

Preston Combs.

Despite Preston's vociferous denials, despite his bold talk about confronting the governor face-to-face if he had something to say, despite all that, Dantzler was left with a single question:

Who else could it have been?

No one was his conclusion. Preston was the individual behind the scheme to blackmail Mark Baker. Couldn't be anyone else.

But if his calculation was true, then the recent meeting at Bradley Cooper's house was a pivotal moment, one that triggered a new and different set of scenarios. In short, that meeting changed everything, beginning with the blackmailer's thirty-day deadline. When it does run out, Dantzler now believed nothing would happen. No incriminating or embarrassing information about

Baker or his family would be leaked to the press. That plan had been shelved in favor of a new and more realistic plan.

The plan to run Marilyn Lawrence for governor.

That plan made more sense politically and it was less dangerous from a legal standpoint. No one goes to prison for backing a political candidate in an election. Conversely, prisons are filled with failed blackmailers.

The big question for Dantzler now was whether or not Cooper knew about the blackmail scheme. Dantzler doubted that he did, but it was possible. Maybe Preston trusted Cooper enough to tell him, although Dantzler couldn't see any reason why he would.

And what about Marilyn? Did she know? Dantzler would wager heavily she didn't. There was no reason for Preston to share that dark secret with her. After all, he would have no way of knowing how she might respond. Being a representative of the judicial branch, she might conclude Preston had gone too far by breaking the law, and she wanted no part of it. She might feel bound to reveal Preston's plan to law enforcement.

No, Dantzler concluded, Preston was the only one who knew.

Putting thoughts of Preston aside, Dantzler dragged himself out of bed, went into the bathroom, and took a quick shower. After drying off and getting dressed, he headed for the kitchen and filled a glass with orange juice. He had an important call to make, but at eight-ten it was a little too early, so he decided to hold off until after nine.

Instead, he picked up his phone and punched in Mike Watkins's number. Dantzler wanted to know if Mike paid a visit to the Quonset hut last night, and if so, did he learn anything. The phone rang several times before Mike picked up.

"Yeah, I spent about two hours there last night, didn't hear anything of importance," Watkins said, his voice sounding exactly like Dantzler's had when he answered the governor's call. "I will pass along one detail, though, and while it wasn't informative, it was at the least somewhat intriguing. Barry Fleming was acting very squirrelly last night, especially around me. Twice, when I attempted to engage him in a conversation, he couldn't get away from me fast enough. He concocted some lame excuses to break it off, like needing to take care of things at the bar, or wanting to ask Roadkill about restocking the fridge with beer. Total bullshit. He just didn't want to have anything to do with me."

"You nailed it when you said he would be suspicious of you for sponsoring my admittance into the group," Dantzler responded. "He'll never trust you again."

Watkins coughed, said, "Look, Jack, I think we both know Barry is never going to give us any important information. That's because he's never going to be made privy to anything that will help us. I vote to bring in your FBI pal and turn him loose on David Danforth. See what he can pry out of the guy. We're taking a huge risk by putting off going after Danforth."

"Wish it was that simple, Mike, but I'm afraid it's not. The fact is we don't have enough right now to bring Danforth in. All we have is what Barry told us, and it's only hearsay evidence that wouldn't be admitted in a court of law. On top of that, if we did haul Danforth in for questioning, within fifteen minutes he'd be surrounded by a team of expensive high-powered attorneys. He wouldn't utter a word. And we wouldn't be one step closer to finding out the status of the bomb. No, our only recourse at this point is to keep digging and to pray Barry can get some information that will allow us to move forward on Danforth."

"All I know, Jack, is if that bomb does go off, and if hundreds of men, women, and children are killed or wounded, I would spend the rest of my life second-guessing the choices we made, or didn't make."

"I'm in the same boat with you, Mike. I don't want that, either. So, how about we do this? We give Barry the weekend to come up with something useful. If he doesn't, I'll talk to Glenn, see what he suggests is our best course of action. Can you live with that?"

"Hey, I'm a team player. I'll follow your lead."

"Give Sam a call and bring him up to speed on what we discussed this morning. I'll be out of town this afternoon, but if you guys want to chat, I will be available after five."

"An important meeting?"

"Well, to borrow your word . . . it should be intriguing.

DANTZLER WAS IN LOUISVILLE, sitting in an outer area at the law firm of Thacker, Lawrence, Harper, and Samuelson located on West Jefferson Street. He was there to meet with Marilyn Lawrence. He had phoned earlier that morning, and the meeting was scheduled for one o'clock. That deadline had passed twenty minutes ago.

The firm took up the top three floors in an eight-story building. Dantzler guessed that if you counted all the attorneys, paralegals, assistants, investigators, secretaries, and receptionists he had encountered on his way up, there had to be about one-hundred employees. Each floor was like a small city, with dozens of busy workers racing around, all at seemingly top speed.

Marilyn's large office was, as Dantzler expected it to be based on her position in the firm, located on the eighth floor, in a corner, with a glass window that provided a terrific view of downtown. Surprisingly, despite the relatively close proximity between Lexington and Louisville, Dantzler had spent very little time in the city that gave the world the great Muhammed Ali. Other than to participate in a few tennis tournaments, or for the occasional dining-out visit, he was practically a stranger to Louisville.

At precisely one-thirty, Marilyn's receptionist was given the green light to send Dantzler in. He stood, thanked the receptionist,

222

who led him down a narrow hallway to the office, opened the door, and ushered him inside.

Marilyn Lawrence was standing behind her desk when he came in. She was all smiles, but Dantzler detected a puzzled look in her eyes, a clear indication to him that she was baffled by his request for this meeting. She leaned forward, offered her hand for him to shake, which he did.

Up close, Marilyn was an impressive lady. She was tall, easily five-nine, with brown hair, hazel eyes, a thin-bridged nose, and full lips any female movie star would kill to have. Or pay big bucks to have. She was dressed in much the same way she had been that night at Bradley Cooper's house—dark blue pants suit, white blouse, expensive shoes. An earring dangled from each ear, and a gold cross stood out against the white blouse. Dantzler noted the absence of a wedding ring.

"Why don't we sit at this table, Mr. Dantzler, where . . ."

"Jack."

"Where we will be more comfortable," she said, moving from behind her desk to the large oak table. "Please, have a seat, make yourself at home."

Dantzler, ever the gentleman, remained standing until Marilyn was seated. She did not take offense, or seemed trouble by his old-fashioned gesture. In fact, Dantzler suspected she was pleased by it."

"Being inquisitive by nature, Mr. Dantzler, I . . ."

"Jack."

"I was vaguely familiar with your name, so I looked you up on the Internet. You've had a very impressive career. Ph. D. in Philosophy, many years as a highly decorated homicide detective, and now a successful private investigator. And the cherry on the topping . . . you are also something of a tennis whiz. Hard to find many men with those credentials."

"Considering what those dastardly Russians are up to these days, how can you trust anything you read on the Internet?"

"What are you saying? That it's all propaganda?"

"The Ph. D. part is. Never got around to writing the dissertation."

"So, Mr. Dan . . . Jack, why did you ask for this meeting?"

"To have a leisurely talk, ask a few questions, get some answers."

Marilyn laughed, said, "If you knew my hourly billing rate you would probably want a speedy conversation rather than a leisurely one. But this meeting is off the clock, so go ahead, fire away with your questions."

"How well do you know Bradley Cooper?" Dantzler asked.

"Not well. I mean, we're both Republicans, so I occasionally bump into him at political events or certain charity functions. Why are you asking about Bradley?"

"Is he planning to challenge Mark Baker for governor?"

"I couldn't say, but I seriously doubt it."

"Ah, come on, Marilyn, you more than doubt it. You know for sure he's not looking to take over the governor's office."

"Why would I know that for sure? Like I said, Jack, I hardly know the man."

"You know, because *you* are going to run for governor."

"That's preposterous. I have no such intention."

"Preston Combs? Do you know him?"

"Everybody knows Preston," Marilyn replied. "His finger-prints and his money are all over the place. He's the top Republican donor, and he hates Mark Baker. Truth be told, he hates all liberals, which is how he views the governor. Personally, I think Preston is dead wrong. Mark Baker is anything but a liberal."

"And yet you are joining forces with Preston to oust Mark from office."

"Where are you coming up with this nonsense, Jack? Who is

feeding you such bullshit? And why on God's green earth do you believe it?"

"No one is feeding me anything, Marilyn. I saw it with my own eyes."

"Saw what?"

"You and Preston at Cooper's house two nights ago. Then the three of you go inside, where, I'm sure, the groundwork for Preston's plan was laid out, discussed and put into action. I can't imagine Cooper being particularly thrilled with the plan, but there was nothing he could do about it. I'm sure Preston told him to sit down, shut up, and behave like a good little lad. Cooper is weak; he'd have no choice but to follow Preston's orders."

Dantzler smiled, said, "How am I doing so far, Marilyn?"

"Not bad, Jack. Not bad at all. But why were you at Bradley's house in the first place? Were you following Preston or me?"

"I wasn't following either of you. I was watching Cooper's house for a totally different reason, one that had nothing to do with you or Preston. And then, lo and behold, out of nowhere, who shows up? Preston Combs and Marilyn Lawrence. Have to admit, I didn't see that coming."

Marilyn nodded, picked up a pitcher of water from a silver tray on the table, and filled two glasses. After giving one to Dantzler, she took a drink, then said, "Yes, Preston wants me to run for governor. His dislike for Mark is such that he's willing to back me, a novice, for office. What he doesn't realize is that his plan might end up being a miscalculation on his part."

"Because he thinks that once you are in office, he'll be the puppet master pulling all the strings, right?"

"That's correct. And I'll never allow that to happen, I don't care how much money he spent getting me elected. I'm my own person and that will never change." After another sip of water, she continued," At my core I'm a true old-fashioned conservative. Just like my father and his father before him. I am not one of the new breed of Tea Party neo-cons. However, there is one area where I disagree completely with Preston—when it comes to Roe v Wade. That ruling must never be overturned under any circumstances. Every woman should have the right to choose when it involves situations regarding her own body."

"Somehow, I don't see you as being all that conservative, Marilyn," Dantzler stated. "Sure, being a conservative plays well in Kentucky. In today's climate, if you want to have any chance of winning one of the higher offices, you have to be a hardline conservative. So you happily go along to get along. But I can't see you settling for the governor's office. If that's all you wanted, you could run for lieutenant governor on Baker's ticket. Then when his term is up in four years, you'd be a shoo-in to get elected to the top spot. But that's not in the cards, is it? You're more ambitious than that."

"What do you see? Tell me, I'm curious."

"The senate would be your best bet. McConnell can't be around forever, and the other guy is a lightweight. You win a senate seat, then who knows? With your looks, talent, and charisma, there's no limit to where you might end up."

"Sounds like I should hire you as my campaign manager."

"Of course, there is a downside to being backed by a controversial individual like Preston Combs. Should you win, that's not going to endear you to that group of Republicans who have a low opinion of Preston. They will acknowledge that you rode in on Preston's coattails. They'll likely brand you as Judas, a traitor, and turn against you."

"And that's why I told Preston I needed time to think about it."

"Let me give you a piece of friendly advice while you're mulling it over. For your own good, don't fly too close to Preston Combs. That would be like flying too close to the sun. You do, you'll get burned."

"Sounds ominous. Why the warning?"

"Are you aware that Preston is behind a scheme to blackmail Mark Baker?"

"No, I most certainly am not," Marilyn said, forcefully.

"He didn't share that information with you during the meeting at Bradley Cooper's house?"

"He did not. And if he had, I would have immediately walked out the door." She took another sip of water. "How, exactly, is he blackmailing the governor? And how do you know about it?"

"About two weeks ago, the governor found a note on his car windshield ordering him to resign his office within thirty days or embarrassing information about him and his family would be released to the media. Now, unless I'm badly mistaken, Preston won't follow through with his plan, not now, not if he can succeed in enticing you to run for governor. Doing so is not worth the risk he'd be taking. From a legal perspective, winning an election is a lot safer than blackmailing someone. Putting an individual in public office is better than ending up behind prison bars."

"What you are telling me is all very hard to believe," Marilyn said, shaking her head. "What embarrassing information does Preston have against the governor and his family?"

"Can't share that with you, Marilyn. Sorry."

"Then why should I believe you?"

"That's your call. But it would be unwise to not believe me."

"You have given me a lot of data to process." Marilyn stood, a clear indication the conversation was finished. "I will think about what you've told me and then decide how I want to proceed."

"Proceed down whichever path you choose, Marilyn," Dantzler said, standing. "But I do have a request. Don't share this conversation with Preston. I'm asking as a favor, not for me, but for a certain woman whose fate is in Preston's hands. Also, there is the blackmail issue. I can't bring that to a successful resolution if Preston knows I'm on to him."

"While I sympathize with the woman, if I do decide to spurn

Preston's offer, he's going to ask me why. I'll have no option but to tell him it's because I have no desire to part of a criminal enterprise like blackmail."

"Come on, Marilyn, you'd have plenty of options. Tell Preston you changed your mind because, after thinking it over, you have no interest in being governor. Tell him you have your own political aspirations and they would die a quick death if your Republican friends found out he was backing you. Or tell him it's a matter of money, that what you are pulling in now is twenty times what the governor's salary is. Any of those would work."

"I'll think it over." She opened the office door. "Thanks for coming by, Jack. It's been an enlightening conversation."

Having said that, Marilyn summoned her receptionist and promptly closed the door, leaving her young assistant with the task of leading Dantzler out of the huge office.

THIRTY-ONE

On Saturday morning, at precisely ten o'clock, two phone calls were made simultaneously. Though neither call was in any way connected, both would end up playing crucial roles in two very different outcomes.

Dantzler phoned Preston Combs to request a meeting in Dantzler's Tennis Center office. Preston grumbled a pair of excuses—he was too busy to meet, and on top of that, he had nothing new to say—but when his protests were met by Dantzler's stony silence, he relented and agreed to the meeting.

With an hour to kill, Dantzler went to the lounge area, purchased a bottle of water, sat at one of the tables and pondered what he was going to say when Preston showed up. His decision came quickly . . . he would go straight at Preston. Face to face, to borrow Preston's approach. Give the man a taste of his own medicine, whether he liked it or not, which he probably wouldn't.

"You look like a man carrying a heavy burden," Amy Countzler remarked, sliding a chair back and sitting across from Dantzler. She was dressed in her typical summer work attire—cutoff jeans, sandals, and a T-shirt, this one with Bruce Springsteen's picture on the front. "What's weighing you down? You can confide in me, because, hey, I'm working on a master's in clinical psychology. I'm an ocean of knowledge and wisdom."

"How old are you, Amy?"

"Twenty-four. Why do you ask?"

"Just curious. You've been working here for, what, three years now?"

"Almost five. Ever since my first semester in college."

"Why not work someplace that will help you career-wise? You know, maybe an internship in a psych facility, or shadowing a famous psychiatrist? I'm sure Bloom could set you up in a hundred different places."

"Two reasons. First, I love it here, and second, at this job I interact on a daily basis with all sorts of weirdos and oddballs. Being here is like working in an institution that affords me the opportunity to study the psychology of many different personalities. This is the best classroom I've ever been in. Anything I need to observe is always right here in front of me."

Dantzler laughed and nodded his agreement.

"Hey, guess who I have a date with tonight?" Amy asked.

"Jake Thomas."

"How the heck did you know that?"

"Haven't you heard the rumor, Amy?" Dantzler said, standing. "I'm a world-class detective."

Dantzler returned to his office and checked his watch. Ten forty-five, still fifteen minutes before Preston was scheduled to arrive. That was being optimistic, Dantzler silently acknowledged. He had no doubt Preston would show up a few minutes late, his way of demonstrating who was really in control. Dantzler thought about making a quick call to Erin, but decided not to. Instead, he would sit and wait for Preston to make his grand and tardy entrance.

As predicted, Preston showed up at eleven-ten. He came in

without knocking, charged toward the desk, and plopped down in the chair across from Dantzler. Everything about the man—demeanor, body language, the look in his eyes—telegraphed clear signals this meeting was to be brief.

"All right, Jack, I'm here at your request," Preston said, his voice sounding like it came through a bullhorn. "What do you want to discuss? Whatever it is, make it quick. I am a very busy man. I have several important items on my plate that have to be taken care of this afternoon. So, let's get on with it."

Hearing that directive only served to anger Dantzler. It also prompted him to make the decision to seize control of the conversation. He wasn't about to allow Preston to bully him. This conversation, Dantzler decided, would last until he determined it was finished.

Or until Preston got up and stormed out, which was a very real possibility.

"First, I want to thank you for stopping by," Dantzler said, pushing his anger aside. "I understand you are busy, and I . . ."

"Yeah, yeah . . . we both know I'm pressed for time. Stop being so damn patronizing and tell me why I'm here. Do it quickly, or I'm gone."

Now Dantzler was boiling mad. His natural instinct was to reach across the desk and slap Preston's face. But that couldn't happen and he knew it. He had to stay calm. Losing his temper would result in shifting the battlefield to one more favorable to a hot-head like Preston. Dantzler didn't intend to play on Preston's home turf.

"You're here, Preston, because I know you are behind a scheme to blackmail Mark Baker," Dantzler said. "And I want the plan shut down today."

"Really?"

"Yeah, really. Your blackmail scheme ends now."

"That's a load of crap, Jack. And we both know it."

"No, it's not. You are blackmailing Mark Baker."

"You can't prove that," Preston replied.

"Don't have to now, Preston. You just proved it for me."

"How do you figure that?"

"You didn't deny it. If you were truly innocent, given your temper you would have bounded out of that chair, screaming at the top of your lungs, while contemplating taking a swing at me. You're guilty, Preston. Someone left a threatening message on the governor's windshield, and that someone was you."

"Not that I have any reason to, but I will gladly deny doing any such thing."

"Your denial is hot air and nothing more. You see, Preston, what you didn't factor in when you were leaving that note on Baker's car were the cameras. There were several of them, and they cover every inch of that parking lot."

This was, Dantzler knew, a lie, one that could easily backfire if Preston wasn't guilty, or if he hired someone else to put the note on Baker's windshield. It was a huge risk, but one Dantzler was willing to take. Either it worked, or it bombed badly. Preston's response would let Dantzler know if he had pressed the right button or if he had been caught in a lie.

Preston's answer told Dantzler his risk had paid off.

"Mark Baker must be removed from office," Preston said in a matter-of-fact tone. "He's ruining everything positive about our state. Four more years of his diabolical administration and Kentucky will be so far down the rabbit hole we'll never recover. I can't allow that to happen."

"That's for the citizens to decide, isn't it?" Dantzler asked.

"The citizens . . . what do they know? Hell, it was the citizens who put the bastard in office in the first place." Preston shook his head dismissively, then smiled at Dantzler. "As for that blackmail scheme, you can stop worrying. It's dead. I have since formulated a new plan to get rid of Baker."

"Hate to tell you his, Preston, but I also know about that plan."

"What plan are you referring to?"

"The one where you back Marilyn Lawrence for governor."

"That's insane. She's a nobody within the Republican Party. And she's a rookie. What makes you think I'd ever back her?"

"Preston, you hate Mark Baker so much you would back the Devil himself if you thought he could win."

"Where do you come up with this nonsense, Jack?"

"A few nights ago, I was watching Bradley Cooper's house when you and Marilyn showed up, went inside, and unless I'm badly mistaken, you had a little strategy session. You also informed poor Bradley that he's out, and that his new role is to be a behind-the-scenes cheerleader for Marilyn. During this meeting, you made it clear that all your mighty power and influence, along with your big bucks are squarely behind Marilyn. Rookie or not, you see her as your acolyte in the governor's office taking orders from you."

"What difference does it make to you who I back for governor?"

"It doesn't. I don't give a damn who you back, Preston. You want Hannibal Lecter, I say go for it. But here's what I do care deeply about. So, listen to what I'm going to say, and do exactly what I tell you to do."

"I don't like your tone, Jack. Not at all."

Dantzler shrugged, said, "I'm totally indifferent to what you think of my tone, Preston. Virtually every criminal I've interrogated over the years didn't much care for my tone. Didn't bother me at all."

"Are you saying I'm a criminal?"

"Hear this, Preston: Under no circumstances will you ever make public what you know about Hannah Andrews and her involvement with Mark Baker. You got that? I know you, and I know how you operate. If Marilyn does run, and if it's a tight race down the stretch, your killer instinct will be to make that story public, which, were that to occur, would all but ensure Mark Baker's defeat. You'd win, but at Hannah's expense. That's not going to happen. Hannah's name had better not become part of your winning strategy. You understand what I'm telling you, Preston?"

"Or?"

"Your blackmail scheme, the parking lot tapes, your name . . . it all goes public. And just in case you need a refresher course on our laws, blackmail is a crime punishable by prison time. Toss in tampering with an election, and several other crimes I'm leaving out, and your days as a free man will be numbered."

"That sounds like a threat, Jack."

"Nope, not a threat at all. Think of it as a piece of sound advice. The ball is in your court, Preston. Choose wisely, because if you don't, if Hannah's name is smeared during the campaign, your downfall will be swift and permanent."

"Now, that is a threat, Jack," Preston said, coming out of his chair. "And it's the last one you'll ever make that's directed at me. You got *that*?"

"Fair enough, Preston. Just keep in mind what I've said."

"You're the wrong man to be giving me orders, Jack."

As Preston was opening the door, Dantzler said, "By the way, I don't think you should count on Marilyn being on the ticket. I have a strong suspicion she's going to spurn your offer. She's too intelligent to attach herself to a ship that has an excellent chance of sinking."

Preston Combs left without responding.

———

AT THE MOMENT Dantzler was making his call, David Danforth was punching in Barry Fleming's number. Based on Barry's late-night hours at the hut, and the long series of rings,

Danforth felt sure Barry was still asleep. This was confirmed when Barry finally answered. His voice had that scratchy sound familiar to anyone who has ever answered a ringing phone after having been roused from a deep sleep.

"Damn, David, what time is it?" Barry groused.

"Ten o'clock," Danforth replied.

"Shit, man, I didn't get to bed until six. I was sleeping like a dead man."

"Sorry to wake you, but I have a couple of tasks you need to take care. Once those are out of the way, you can go back to bed. But what I want done needs to happen ASAP."

Barry yawned, said, "What tasks are you talking about?"

"Go to the hut, make a sign in all caps that says, 'NO ADMIT-TANCE UNTIL FURTHER NOTICE', and tape it to the front door."

"The guys won't be pleased when they see that sign."

"Barry, what did I say about those guys?"

"That you don't care about them."

"Not in the least. Besides, after tomorrow, there will be no hut for them to get upset about."

"Are we lighting the torch tonight?" asked Barry.

"Tomorrow. But we're going to soak the place tonight, say, around eleven. That brings us to your second task. You need to purchase six five-gallon cans and fill them with gasoline. I have three cans at the hut already. That should be more than enough to bring the place down in a matter of minutes. It'll be ashes before the fire department can get there."

"It's a great hangout. Hate to see it go up in flames."

"Take off, Barry, go and put that sign on the door," Danforth directed. "Purchase the cans, get the petro, then head home and get some sleep. Just make sure you are at the hut around eleven. Got it?"

"Yeah, David, you can count on me."

"Good. See you tonight, Barry."

ALTHOUGH HE WAS fifteen minutes early, Barry wasn't surprised to see Danforth's BMW convertible sitting in the parking area, top down, maybe twenty feet from the front door. Barry pulled his big truck next to the sleek BMW, cut the engine, and climbed out. He could hear movement coming from his right, but in the darkness he didn't see anyone. Had to be Danforth, he figured, already pouring gasoline on the hut.

"Get those cans out of your truck and let's get down to business," Danforth said, emerging from the darkness holding an empty can. "We'll use the six you brought on the outside. There are still two inside, and those we can use to flood the interior. I'll continue to the right, you go left. We'll meet on the backside. Pour most of the gasoline at the base of the structure, but also splash some on the sides. Be generous. I want this place soaked to the hilt."

Barry grabbed two of the cans from the truck and set them on the ground. Danforth took those two and headed to his right. After removing the final four cans from the truck, Barry picked up one with each hand and took off walking to his left. Each man would come back and take one of the final two cans to finish the job.

Thirty minutes later, they were standing side by side near the front entrance. The smell of gasoline permeated the area.

"Not bad, Barry, not bad at all," Danforth commented, nodding his head in approval of the job they'd done. "All that remains is to finish up inside. Then I come back in the morning, turn this joint into a giant fireball, and get the hell out of here. This time tomorrow the Quonset hut will be nothing more than ashes and a memory."

Surprisingly, dousing the inside took almost an hour to get

done. Danforth was precise as to where he wanted the gasoline poured, often directing Barry to "put more over there" or to "let that area go, it's not important." On several occasions, pouring gasoline in the proper place meant having to move tables or other larger pieces of furniture out of the way. It was those laborious chores, all performed by Barry alone, that lengthened the time it took to finish the job.

Once the job was completed and Danforth was satisfied with the work, the two men stood at the center of the hut looking the place over for the final time.

"I know this is necessary, David," Barry said, wistfully, "but I hate to see it go. This has been a great place."

"Well, take a look around, Barry, because it's the last time you'll ever see it."

As Barry turned to admire the place, Danforth pulled out his .357 and shot Barry in the back of his head. The powerful weapon sent the bullet through Barry's head, out the front, shattering his face in the process, and then continuing on until it embedded in a large piece of oak furniture. Barry tumbled forward, blood streaming from his ruined head.

"Like I said, Barry, this was your final look," Danforth said, placing the weapon in his back waistband. "You stupid fool. Did you really think I was going to let you walk away, knowing the things you know? Not a chance in hell. You had to go, you poor bastard."

Danforth had brought along some items he planned to place on Barry's body as a way of prolonging law enforcement's attempts to identify the dead man. If successful, they might assume he was the dead man. But that wouldn't work, not now, not with a bullet in the back of Barry's head, which, effectively, ruled out suicide. Maybe, Danforth thought, he should have stuck with his original plan to poison Barry. But the gun was quicker and more efficient. Therefore, Danforth's passport, driver's license and the ring he planned to plant on Barry were of no use now, even if they did somehow miraculously survived the inferno. But the plan to mislead the authorities never would have worked. Within a day or two, the coroner would use dental records to identify Barry's charred body.

With his false identification scheme no longer feasible, Danforth gave some thought to torching the place tonight rather than tomorrow as planned. But he quickly vetoed that notion. Tonight was the wrong time. No, it was much better to wait until tomorrow morning. Do it on a quiet, peaceful Sunday, when all things were right in heaven and on earth. When humans and angels rested from their troubles and dreamed their dreams.

Let peace reign until all hell broke loose.

THIRTY-TWO

EARLY SUNDAY MORNING WAS A TALE OF TWO DIFFERENT weather fronts. From approximately five until just past six-thirty, a soft rain fell from a ceiling of dark clouds. But as soon as the rain stopped, those dark clouds were replaced by fluffy white ones. At the same time, the sun was making its first appearance. The air was crisp and clean, the temperature rose from cool to warm. Unless another weather system showed up out of nowhere, Sunday was going to be damn near perfect.

Dantzler's early morning sleep seemed to follow the shifting weather pattern. He slept through the rain and woke up just as the rising sun overpowered those dark clouds, happily rendering them a quickly forgotten thing of the past. By the time he was wide awake, the day had completed its transformation from gloomy to beautiful.

Dantzler showered, dressed, went into the kitchen, poured a glass of orange juice, took a single bite of a rock-hard bagel, then tossed it into the garbage, thankful he hadn't chipped a tooth in the process. After finishing his orange juice, he set the glass in the sink, grabbed his car keys, and left for the Tennis Center.

It was still early, barely seven-thirty, the perfect time to show up at the Tennis Center. Few players would be present at this hour, which allowed him plenty of uninterrupted time to take care of past-due paperwork and other minor tasks before the statute-of-limitations ran out on those long-neglected issues. Sean Montgomery or David Bloom could have competently performed this grunt work, but over the years, more out of habit than anything else, these chores had fallen on Dantzler's shoulders to complete.

Dantzler pulled into the parking area and wasn't surprised to see Amy Countzler's blood-red Nissan Rogue sitting there. Amy often came in early to clean up any mess that might have been left in the lounge area at closing time last night. However, Dantzler was surprised to see two familiar late-model SUVs parked next to Amy's Rogue. This told Dantzler a heated doubles match was being waged inside by four seventy-something men who had once again opted for tennis over church. Dantzler couldn't fault the foursome for the choice they made. Their absence from hearing the Word of God would surely be forgiven by the Big Guy upstairs, who, Dantzler had long ago concluded, was a serious tennis fan.

Inside, Amy was bent over, a broom in one hand, a dust pan in the other. She was sweeping up a pile of white powder that Dantzler prayed wasn't cocaine.

"Talcum powder," Amy announced, much to Dantzler's relief. "Someone must've spilled it while leaving late last night. As you can clearly see, no one bothered to clean it up."

"I'm just happy to know it's not your nose candy," Dantzler said.

"Ha, ha . . . very funny. You know I don't do drugs."

Amy dumped the white powder into a wastebasket, then disappeared when she went into a small closet, where she left the broom and dust pan.

"How did your date go last night?" Dantzler asked, as Amy

emerged from the closet and moved behind the counter. "You and Jake hit it off okay?"

"Great. I mean, the guy is like a saint, you know? Kind, classy, respectful . . . just terrific."

"Did he ask you for a second date?"

"He did," Amy said, nodding. "And if he hadn't, I was going to ask him."

"Good for you, Amy. There's nothing wrong with a woman asking a guy to go out with her."

"That's exactly how I feel." Amy opened a bottle of water, took a sip, then said, "Those four codgers playing tennis. How old are they?"

Dantzler shrugged, said, "I don't know. Mid- to late-seventies would be my guess. Why do you ask?"

"Because if one of those old geezers has a heart attack, I'll do the chest compression, but I will not do mouth to mouth."

"That makes two of us, Amy," Dantzler said, heading for his office.

"Oh, almost forgot," Amy said. "There was a guy in here earlier. Showed up a few minutes after I opened the place."

"Yeah, who was the early bird?"

"David Danforth."

Hearing this stopped Dantzler in his tracks. He turned and walked back to the counter.

"David Danforth was here?" he inquired.

"Yep, sure was."

"Did he say what he wanted?"

"Yeah, to challenge you on the tennis court."

"David Danforth wanted to play tennis against me?" Dantzler said. "You're sure about that?"

"Yes, I am. What's the big deal? He's pretty good, isn't he?"

"Not that good."

"Well, he came prepared for battle," Amy noted. "He left his equipment bag with me, said he'd come back when he was sure you were here."

"Where did you put his equipment bag?"

"Here, on the floor," Amy said, pointing.

Dantzler went behind the counter, saw the equipment bag, picked it up, and set it on the counter. He then began to slowly drag the zipper from left to right until the bag was open.

"Holy shit!" Amy screamed. "That's . . . that's a fucking bomb, isn't it?"

"Amy, run downstairs and get those four men out of this place." As Amy started to leave, Dantzler told her to wait, then dug into his pants pocket, took out a key ring, removed one of the keys, and handed it to her. "Leave through the outdoor courts. That key opens the back gate. Get them as far away from this place as possible. Now, go."

"What are you going to do with that bomb?" Amy asked.

"Put it in the steel safe in my office," Dantzler responded. "That way, some of the damage might be minimized if it does detonate. Get out of here, Amy."

As Amy ran down the steps, Dantzler carefully picked up the equipment bag, carried it into his office, and placed it on a table. After opening the safe and removing papers, a checkbook and several folders, he picked the bag up and put it inside the safe. He then closed the door but didn't lock it. He wanted the bomb squad guys to have easy access, if it came to that.

Once the bomb was in the safe, Dantzler ran for the front entrance, cell phone to his ear, making the call to the police department, knowing they would alert the bomb squad, or as it is officially titled, the Hazardous Devices Unit. By the time he'd ended his call, he was outside standing behind his vehicle. Within five minutes, two Lexington patrol cars had arrived, and five minutes later, sirens could be heard in the distance.

While waiting, Dantzler also put in a call to Eric Gamble,

head of the Homicide Unit, to inform Eric that it was David Danforth who had placed the bomb inside the Tennis Center.

"He lives in Griffin Gate," Dantzler told Eric. "You need to locate him and bring him in for questioning."

"I'll dispatch a couple of cruisers out there immediately," Eric replied. "I will order them to sit on the place until Jake and Vee show up. If Danforth is home, they can bring him in."

"And if he's not at home, which I doubt he will be, what's your next option?"

"I'll give Jake and Vee the green light to get inside the house, look around and see what they can find."

"Thanks, Eric."

"Meanwhile, I'm on my way to the Tennis Center. See you when I get there."

The bomb squad arrived just as Dantzler ended the call to Eric. Several men jumped out of the vehicle, most of them new and unknown to Dantzler, but there was one old face he did recognize—Lenny Stuart, head of the unit, and a veteran of the Lexington Police Department.

"Heard you saw the bomb," Lenny asked, after shaking hands with Dantzler. "What are we looking at?"

"Hell, Lenny, I glanced at the damn thing, I didn't exactly study it," replied Dantzler. "What I can tell you is I saw a bunch of wires, and I heard a ticking sound."

"Where is the bomb now?"

"In a steel safe in my office."

"Is it on the floor?"

"No, it's about six feet off the floor."

"Okay, so that pretty much rules out using the robot." Lenny turned to a couple of men standing there waiting for orders. "Suit up, guys. You're going in."

Five minutes later, Dantzler felt like he was watching a scene from the movie *The Hurt Locker*. But this wasn't a movie; this was real life. And there was no guarantee those two brave men who entered the Tennis Center would come out alive.

What surprised Dantzler was that it only took fifteen minutes (though it seemed like hours to him) before the two men emerged from Tennis Center, one of them carrying the equipment bag in his hand.

The man holding the bag, who apparently knew Dantzler by reputation, said, "What time is it, Detective Dantzler?"

Startled by the question, Dantzler looked at the time on his cell phone, said, "Nine thirty-five."

"You are one lucky dude," the second man said. "Thing was set to detonate at nine forty-five."

"What have you got?" Lenny inquired.

"Sophisticated, professionally done, very powerful, but easily diffused," the man, whose name was Sid Kelly, answered. "Simply a matter of cutting a couple of wires."

Dantzler said, "How much damage would it have done had it exploded?"

"Well, the Tennis Center would be a thing of the past, and virtually anyone inside would have been killed or wounded. This device was meant to do serious damage."

"Jack, I always suspected you had more luck than ten Irishmen," Lenny said, laughing, "and now I know for sure that's true."

Before Dantzler could respond, one of the uniformed officers said, "Damn, this is one crazy Sunday morning."

"Why? What's up?" Lenny asked.

"There's a big fire in Jessamine County, just across the county line," the patrolman replied.

Dantzler knew immediately what this meant—the Quonset hut was on fire. After thanking Lenny and the two men who diffused the bomb, he raced to his car, jumped inside, and quickly headed for Jessamine County.

Meeting with Eric would have to wait.

THIRTY-THREE

AFTER CREATING AN INFERNO AT THE QUONSET HUT, DAVID Danforth drove away in Barry Fleming's big Ford truck. He was listening to the radio when a local station interrupted regular programming with breaking news that a bomb had been found— and diffused—at the Lexington Tennis Center. Hearing this, realizing his plan had failed, Danforth cursed himself for giving the equipment bag to Amy Countzler rather than simply placing it in a corner where it likely would have gone unnoticed. Not doing so was a huge and quite possibly a fatal error on his part.

Cursing himself wasn't going to change things. In fact, he silently admitted, it was counterproductive. What he had to do now was to think, to plan, to come up with a realistic way out of the shit storm he had created for himself. This was his one and only priority.

With the bomb having been discovered, probably by that goddamn Dantzler, Danforth realized certain facts: Dantzler would know from having spoken with Amy who planted the bomb, and he would have alerted the cops, who by now were swarming Danforth's house in Griffin Gate. Danforth also knew he had to lose Barry's truck and get a different vehicle if he hoped to escape. At some point after Barry's body had been identified, the cops would figure out Danforth had left his BMW behind and driven away in Barry's truck.

Damn, how could things go so wrong? Danforth mumbled out loud.

Getting out of town meant leaving behind most but not all of his vast fortune. But doing so didn't mean he was destitute. Far from it. He had two accounts in a Cayman Islands bank, each one totaling five-hundred-thousand bucks. A million dollars was more than enough to live comfortably on, provided he had the opportunity to spend it.

But he had to commandeer another vehicle before he could even begin to think that far ahead. Crossing Nicholasville Road, he pulled into the Brannon Crossing shopping center, briefly circled the area before finally stopping in front of Kroger's. Cutting the engine, he began looking around for a convenient target. It didn't take long for him to spot one—an elderly white-haired woman emerged from Kroger's pushing a shopping cart with five bags of groceries loaded on it. She walked to a blue Toyota Avalon, used a fob to pop the trunk, put the bags in, and then closed the trunk lid. Next, she pushed the cart over to the area where other carts were left after shoppers were finished using them. It was when she had returned the cart and was walking back to her car that Danforth began to move in her direction. They both reached the Avalon at the exact same moment.

Danforth pulled his .357 and stuck it in the old woman's ribs. "Stay quiet, stay calm and nothing bad will happen to you," he whispered, as he gently began guiding her to the passenger's side. "Get in and act normal. I don't want to harm you, but I will if you don't do as I say."

He opened the door for her and helped get her inside. Then he closed the door, hurried to the driver's side, opened the door, got in, adjusted the seat, started the engine, and slowly drove away.

"Here, take this," the crying woman said, offering him her purse. "You can have my money, my credit cards, anything you want, just please don't hurt me."

"The only thing I want from you is your cell phone," Danforth said. He pulled out onto Nicholasville Road and headed back toward Lexington. "You do have one, don't you?"

"Yes, yes, please take it," she whispered, digging it out of her purse.

Danforth took the phone and put it in his shirt pocket.

"Please don't harm me," the woman pleaded. "Let me go. I won't turn you in."

"Shut up."

Danforth drove down Nicholasville Road until he came to Wilson-Downing. Making a right turn, he proceeded for another mile or so until he came to Southern Elementary School on the right. After turning onto school grounds, he continued until his car was hidden from view behind the big brick building. Leaving the motor running, he got out of the car and ordered the woman to do the same. Trembling, she began walking hesitantly toward him. He motioned with his pistol for her to walk closer to the rear of the building. When she turned away from him, he cracked the back of her head with the butt of the pistol. She instantly crumpled to the ground, unconscious, blood leaking from her wounded skull.

Danforth tucked the weapon into his waistband, quickly got back behind the steering wheel, and began driving away. His destination: A small house on Smoky Mountain Drive he had purchased several years ago. There, he would hole up until he could collect his thoughts, get them squared away, and formulate an escape plan.

And he had better come up with one quick, or he most likely would spend the rest of his life sitting inside a cold prison cell.

And that's the one place I never want to be.

THIRTY-FOUR

BLOCKED BY A FLEET OF OFFICIAL VEHICLES—FIRE TRUCKS, patrol cars, unmarked cars, an EMT bus, and the coroner's wagon —Dantzler was forced to park approximately twenty yards from where the Quonset hut once stood. The combined efforts of fire departments from Jessamine County and Lexington had done a terrific job putting out what had obviously been a serious blaze. Dark smoke continued to rise toward the sky, and smoldering embers popped up at various locations within the hut's ruins, all of which were quickly doused with water. As a preventative measure, two of the fire trucks had their hoses aimed at the surrounding woods, thereby making sure the fire didn't spread out of control.

Dantzler exited his car and began strolling toward a circle of men standing next to a BMW. One member of the group was an old buddy of Dantzler's, Frank Tankersly, better known as "Tank", a nickname that perfectly described the man. Tank was built like a block of granite; there was not an ounce of fat on the man. He had stone pillar legs, Popeye forearms, no neck, and a square head topped off by yellowish hair cut in a fifties-style flattop. The ex-

Marine and Vietnam veteran exuded strength and power and menace, yet despite all outward appearances, he was one of the kindest, most-gentle humans you were ever likely to cross paths with.

"Well, as I live and breathe, if it's not the legendary Jack Dantzler," Tank said, as he moved away from the group and shook Dantzler's hand. "What the hell brings you to this neck of the woods?"

"You know me, Tank. I'm drawn to excitement like a shark is drawn to a drop of blood," Dantzler replied.

"Word is you had more than enough excitement at your Tennis Center this morning. Is the situation there under control?"

"It is now, thank heaven, but we were damn lucky. The bomb was set to detonate about ten minutes after the guys diffused the thing. If it had gone off, I wouldn't be standing here right now. I'd be in pieces. Like I said, we got lucky."

"Any idea who planted the device?"

Dantzler nodded, pointed at the BMW, and said, "Yeah, the guy who owns that car—David Danforth. He also owns this property. The Quonset hut was his."

"Yeah, that jibes with the name Jessamine County detectives came up with when they ran the plates. Didn't know this property belonged to David Danforth, though. Or, at least, I didn't know."

A plainclothes Jessamine County detective Dantzler had seen before but didn't know personally caught the tail end of the talk between Dantzler and Tank. He made his way over to where the two men were standing.

"They found a body inside," the man stated, introducing himself as Gary Hensley. "Based on the car being registered to Danforth, we're assuming the body is his. He must've set the fire and then failed to make it out before being engulfed in flames. Poor slob. Being burned alive would be a horrible way to go, you ask me."

"Gonna have to disagree with you, Gary," Dantzler commented. "There is no way that's David Danforth's body in there."

"Then whose body is it?"

"Barry Fleming."

"Hell, I know Barry," Hensley remarked. "I mean, he's a few years younger than me, but I was in the same class at school with his sister, Isabel. Izzy, we all called her. What makes you think it's Barry?"

"He did a lot of work for Danforth," Dantzler replied. "He was also involved in most of Danforth's criminal activities. Danforth probably viewed Barry as a liability, so he silenced him forever. As a famous Mob boss often said, 'When in doubt have no doubt.' One more thing, Gary. I'll wager that when the coroner examines the body, he'll find that Barry was dead before Danforth started the fire."

"Well, hell, I'd damn sure rather be dead than burned alive," Hensley acknowledged.

"How much do you know about this place?" Dantzler asked Hensley.

"Not much, really. I didn't even know the Quonset hut was here until Eric Gamble advised us to keep an eye on the place, which we made an effort to do. Unfortunately, every time I sent a patrol car here the place was closed." Hensley paused for a second, then said," What criminal activities are you talking about?"

"The sale of weapons to foreign entities was the main one. However, I'm certain there were others I'm not aware of."

"I don't mean to sound like an asshole or anything, Dantzler, but how is it you know all this? Didn't I read somewhere that you retired?"

Not anxious to go into great detail, Dantzler simply said. "A guy doing some undercover work informed me."

"Huh. Undercover? Really?"

Dantzler's cell phone buzzed. The call was from Eric Gamble.

"What's up, Eric?"

"Vee called, said Danforth isn't at his house. No surprise there, right? Anyway, I gave Jake and Vee the okay to go inside the house, see if they can find anything of interest, or something that might help us locate the guy. I'm on my way to see Judge O'Malley to secure a search warrant."

"Listen, Eric, could you meet me at the Tennis Center when you get the warrant? I'd like to tag along when you go to Danforth's house."

"Not a problem. Be different, though, you being my sidekick."

"I'll see you there," Dantzler said, ending the call. Then to Tank: "Take it easy, Tank. And stay safe."

"You know me, Jack," Tank said. "Safe is my middle name."

Dantzler started to walk away, stopped, turned back, and said, "Gary, you might want to drain that pond behind the hut. Unless I'm badly mistaken, you'll find at least one body at the bottom. And don't be shocked if you find more than one."

"Gotta hand it to you, Dantzler," Hensley said. "You sure know a lot for a retired dude."

"Believe me, Gary, my life would be much simpler if I *didn't* know so much."

DAVID DANFORTH CUT across Tates Creek Road onto Armstrong Mill, drove to Man o' War Boulevard, turned left, and went another mile or so before making a right onto Buckhorn. Unsure if there was booze at the house, he paid a quick visit to a liquor store and purchased a bottle of Maker's Mark. Leaving the small shopping center, he got back on Buckhorn, made a left, wound around the street, turned right at Smoky Mountain Drive, and then proceeded until he reached his house on the left.

Rather than pull the Avalon into the driveway, he opted to back in, reasoning that to do so would ensure his license plates could not be seen from the street, and that it would provide a faster getaway, should it come to that. Parking his car in the garage was not an option; it was filled with stacks of boxes containing the most-recent supply of purchased weapons.

Danforth climbed out of the car and went inside the house, a one-level structure with a spacious living room, three bedrooms, and two baths. There was a deck out back and a small backyard that ended at a wooded area bisected by a large creek.

The house was rarely used—Danforth had only been inside the place perhaps a dozen times, mostly for the purpose of engaging in sex with women he deemed unworthy of being taken to his opulent mansion in Griffin Gate. Only ladies he judged to be "prime subjects" were granted the experience of visiting his main hacienda. This house was for second-tier women.

Danforth bought the place on Smoky Mountain Drive for a simple reason—to serve as his own personal safe house in case things ever went sour. And now they had. That's why he kept one-hundred grand in cash here, along with a leather pouch containing two-dozen diamonds valued at more than four-hundred-thousand dollars. This was money earmarked to pay for a flight to the Cayman Islands, where his million bucks were safe from law enforcement and from nosy IRS officials.

The challenge now was getting to the island. For that to happen he would need a plane. This meant placing a call to Juan Diego-Lopez, an Atlanta-based attorney, and first cousin to Manny Garcia, head of a wealthy and violent Mexican drug cartel. It was Diego-Lopez who served as go-between for Danforth's gun sales to Garcia.

Danforth went into the kitchen, found a plastic cup on the counter, rinsed it out in the sink, and then filled it with bourbon. Taking a sip, he moved down a hallway and slipped into one of the bedrooms. Picking up a box from the floor, he opened it and removed one of the pre-paid cell phones still in its original package. He headed back to the kitchen, sat at the table, took the phone from its package, and punched in Diego-Lopez's private number. The attorney answered, listened to Danforth's request—and how much he was willing to pay—then responded with a single word —"Traditional"—and ended the call.

That one word was the standard reply used for past communications between the two men. It said Diego-Lopez would instruct his pilot to land in an open field at midnight on a piece of property just off of Ironworks Pike. The land had previously belonged to Danforth's family but had been sold years ago. This was also the site where Danforth had often delivered weapons to the drug cartel.

There was nothing for Danforth to do now but sit tight and wait. Not an easy thing to do given the dire situation he found himself in. Midnight was still more than twelve hours away. A lot could happen in such a long period of time, most of it bad. Danforth tried to put negative thoughts out of his head. *Think positive*, he kept reminding himself. At that moment, the blaring sound of a siren caused his heart to sink. Racing to the window, he peeked out of the curtains in time to see a police cruiser flash by. His spirits lifted when he realized the cop car wasn't coming for him.

Think positive, he reminded himself once again. *Make it to midnight and I'm home free.*

He took another sip of bourbon.

The clock was ticking.

BY THE TIME Dantzler arrived back at the Tennis Center, a large crowd had already gathered in the parking lot, many of whom, based on how they were dressed, had come to play, and who only now were hearing about what had transpired there earlier that morning. They all had that are-you-kidding-me expression on their faces. None of them appeared to be upset with not being able to play. The Tennis Center was closed, and would remain so until a thorough search for other explosive devices had been completed. Those who had come to play all agreed that a follow-up search was a grand idea.

Eric Gamble, cell phone held away from his ear, was standing next to his car while speaking with a uniformed patrolman. The young patrolman was furiously scribbling down whatever instructions Eric was passing along. When Eric had finished talking, the patrolman nodded, then sprinted to his vehicle, got in, and drove away.

As Dantzler approached, Eric resumed talking on his phone. He listened, said, "great work, guys," listened some more, then said, "the warrant is on the way," before punching off.

"Was that Jake or Vee you were speaking with?" Dantzler inquired.

"Jake. He said Vee found two pieces of information that are relevant to us," Eric answered. "According to documents she found, David Danforth has two accounts worth one-million dollars in a Cayman Islands bank. She . . ."

"That means he has to secure a plane to fly him down there. It also means we need to locate the guy fast. We may never track him down if he gets airborne."

"You didn't let me finish, Jack. Vee also came across the deed for a house Danforth purchased eight years ago. It's located on Smoky Mountain Drive. I think we should pay a visit to the place, don't you?"

Dantzler asked, "Where is Smoky Mountain Drive?"

"Off Buckhorn."

"Then we need to head that way."

"Got your weapon, Jack?"

"What do you think?"

"My car," Eric said.

Five minutes after they drove away, Eric got a call on his cell phone. He answered, listened, thanked the caller, and ended the call.

"The Southern Elementary principal found an elderly woman unconscious behind the school building," Eric said. "He apparently forgot it was Sunday and showed up to do some work. He called nine-one-one. By the time an EMT bus arrived, she was conscious and talking. She said her car—a Toyota Avalon—was hijacked in Brannon Crossing by a man waving a very large gun. He ordered her to pull in at the school, then told her to get out of the car. When she did, he hit her over the head, knocking her out cold. Jessamine County officers found Barry Fleming's red truck parked in front of Kroger's. We have to assume Danforth ditched Barry's truck there, then attacked the old lady and took her Avalon."

"When did this happen?" asked Dantzler.

"A little more than an hour ago, which means he's still close by."

"Yeah, there's little chance he would risk securing a plane before nightfall."

"We can only hope," Eric said, mashing down on the gas pedal.

DAVID DANFORTH HAD JUST DOZED off on the sofa when he was abruptly awakened by the sound of slamming car doors outside his house. He shook himself awake, jumped up, rushed to the front window, opened the curtains a couple of inches, and peered outside. He didn't like what he saw. Two men he instantly recognized—Dantzler and the black detective named

Eric Gamble—had exited their vehicle and were approaching the house. Danforth realized his worst nightmare was coming true. The dreaded bad news had arrived at his doorstep.

Danforth picked up his .357 from a table, used the butt to crack the window glass, and fired two shots, both of which slammed into the rear of the Avalon.

Dantzler and Eric ducked behind the wounded Avalon, each man on opposite sides of the car. Both men had weapons drawn and safeties off.

"He's got a cannon, Eric," Dantzler whispered.

"You don't have to tell me that."

A third shot took out the Avalon's left rear tire, causing the car to become tilted. It was Dantzler's side that went down, forcing him to duck even lower for protection. Seconds later, Dantzler noticed the curtain closing, which indicated to him that Danforth was on the move.

"He's heading out the back way, Eric," Dantzler pointed out. "Go around the house on the right, I'll go left. Stay low, and take no chances."

Dantzler and Eric reached the back of the house just as Danforth leapt from the deck and begin a mad dash for the wooded area. As he was running, he fired twice—wildly—over his left shoulder, neither shot coming close to hitting either Dantzler or Eric.

What Danforth wasn't aware of was the wire fence hidden behind trees and other foliage that blocked his entrance into the woods. The thin wire was virtually invisible to the naked eye. In full panic mode, he began to frantically search for an opening but couldn't find one. This left him with two choices—to either lay down his weapon and surrender, or engage in a gun battle with the two cops rapidly closing in on him. He chose the second option.

It was the last decision David Danforth ever made.

As he turned to fire, two bullets slammed into his upper torso not more than an inch apart, tearing through flesh and shredding his heart to pieces. Dantzler and Eric had each fired once, and they had made it count. The two bulls-eye hits knocked Danforth backward to the ground, the .357 clutched tightly in his right hand, his open, glassy eyes staring up into nothingness.

Slaves to their years of training, Dantzler and Eric approached with caution, although they both realized Danforth was dead. Eric bent down and removed the weapon from Danforth's hand, careful to avoid the blood flowing from the two fatal wounds. He thought about closing the dead man's eyes but decided not to. *Screw him*, Eric said to himself. *Let the sun fry the damn things.*

"You okay, Eric?" Dantzler said, putting his Glock away.

"With this, yeah," Eric answered, pointing at Danforth's body. "With the mountain of paperwork that's coming, not so much."

"That's why they pay you the big bucks, Eric."

THIRTY-FIVE

TWO DAYS DANTZLER DREADED TURNED OUT TO BE surprisingly pleasant. His reasons for being at police headquarters —filling out a mountain of paperwork, giving an official statement, providing further details about David Danforth—were tedious and time-consuming, necessary though they were. However, spending time in the place where he toiled as a homicide detective all those years, and hanging out with former colleagues while meeting new faces made those two days enjoyable and special. As a bonus, while he was there, several retired cops, having heard he was in the house, stopped by to say hello and to chat about old times. Although Dantzler would never acknowledge it, he was highly respected by the older dudes and idolized by the younger crowd.

Finishing his tasks late Tuesday, he left the police station with the idea of stopping by the Tennis Center to make sure things were getting back to normal. But that notion quickly vanished. He had already heard from Sean and from Bloom that the only topic of conversation at the Tennis Center was what happened there Sunday morning. Dantzler knew that was all anyone would want to talk about. And he had no desire to rehash that scary experience. Instead, he decided to go home, dress down, fix a drink, and chill.

As hour later, as darkness descended, he sat on his deck, glass of Pernod and orange juice in hand, listening with eyes closed as the night critters surrounding the lake made their music. It was a sound he never tired of hearing. But their symphony was interrupted by a phone call from Sam Rosen.

"What's up, Sam," Dantzler asked.

"Heard you had a double-dose of excitement Sunday," Rosen replied. "Staring at a bomb, getting shot at . . . that's almost too much danger for one day."

"You think?"

"Happy to hear you made it out alive."

"Yeah, living is always preferable to dying."

"Listen, Jack, the reason I called is to beg for a favor."

"Sure, Sam, what do you want me to do?"

"Call Mark Baker and ask him if he and his wife will meet you at his father-in-law's house tomorrow at six. It's time we bring an ex-Nazi to justice."

"Who will be going with us?"

"Glenn Rigby. But, Jack, I think it would be best if you didn't mention that Glenn and I will be with you."

"I think it's only fair that I tell Mark the reason for our visit."

"No, that would be the worst possible mistake you could make," Rosen said. "If the governor tells the old man, which he would, you know what would happen then, don't you? Kruger would take his own life, like a lot of those old Nazis did. That way, he escapes without having paid for his crimes. It'd be the easy way out for him. And I can assure you he always has a cyanide capsule within reach. He would swallow it in a flash if he knew we were coming for him. For that reason, no one should know why we're meeting."

After concluding his talk with Rosen, Dantzler spent the next few minutes formulating a reason for the visit, should Mark Baker ask. He ran through several possibilities before finally settling on telling the governor he had more information to share concerning the blackmail scheme. Dantzler knew such a story would spark the governor's interest.

But to Dantzler's surprise the governor didn't ask any questions. He said he and Kathy had already planned on being at the Kruger house tomorrow night. According to Baker, Wednesday's were set aside for a weekly game of bridge. He concluded by telling Dantzler he was more than welcomed to drop by.

"Hopefully, Ernie will be in a more talkative mood," Baker said, "and you can finally hear some of his great stories. They really are terrific."

"We'll see," was all Dantzler could say before ending the call.

MARK BAKER'S friendly expression quickly transformed to quizzical when he saw the two men standing behind Dantzler. "I wasn't aware you were bringing company," he noted. "Who are your friends?"

"Can we go inside, Governor?" Dantzler asked. "I'll make the introductions then."

Baker's body language signaled his reluctance to grant Dantzler's request, but after a brief hesitation, he finally relented and opened the door. He went in first, followed by Dantzler, then Rosen and Glenn Rigby. In the small living room, Mary Kruger and Kathy Baker were sitting on the sofa. Ernie Kruger sat in a recliner to their immediate left. Mark Baker eased his way to the end of the sofa, waiting for Dantzler to introduce the two strangers.

"Governor, this is Sam Rosen," Dantzler said, putting a hand on Rosen's shoulder. "The gentleman to his right is Glenn Rigby."

"I'm guessing there is a reason why you brought them here tonight," Baker stated. "Care to share that reason with me?"

Dantzler looked at Rosen and nodded. Taking his cue, Rosen stepped forward until he was standing directly in front of Ernie Kruger.

"Do you want to tell them, or should I?" Rosen said to the old man, whose expression never changed. But his eyes grew cold and hard.

"Hold on a minute," Baker said. "Why are you questioning Ernie? And what is it you want him to tell us?"

After taking a deep breath, Sam Rosen said, "Governor, what I have to say will be shocking and not very pleasant to hear. But it will be the truth, you can be sure of that." Once again, Rosen looked at the old man. "Do you want to tell them? It's your last chance."

When the old man remained silent, Baker said, "Please, tell us what you have to say."

"This man is not Ernie Kruger," Rosen stated. "In fact, his real name is Franz Kindler. FBI Agent Rigby and I are here to arrest him."

"What?" Kathy yelled. "Arrest him on what charges? My father has done nothing criminal in his life. He's a good man."

"No, Mrs. Baker, you're dead wrong. Your father has a horrific criminal past that dates back more than seventy years."

"What are you talking about? What crimes?"

"Your father is a Nazi war criminal, Mrs. Baker. He worked with Josef Mengele at Auschwitz, conducting horrible experiments on hundreds of people, including many children. He also shot and killed seven Jewish prisoners, and he was responsible for sending thousands more to the gas chamber. Your father is truly a monster."

"My father has never set foot in Germany," Kathy argued.

"Franz Kindler was born in Munich in nineteen twenty-five."

Rosen took out the 8x10 photo of the four Nazis and handed it to Mark Baker. "He is the third man in that picture, standing between Mengele and Albert Speer. He was nineteen at the time. When Germany lost the war, Kindler, like many fellow Nazis, escaped to Argentina, where he lived safely for approximately eight years. While there he learned to speak English. He also took a new name—Ernie Kruger—secured a passport, a Social Security number, and other documents necessary for relocation to the United States. He settled in Milwaukee and married his first wife, Lisa, in nineteen fifty-four. She died five years later after falling down a flight of stairs. Her death was ruled accidental, but the Milwaukee detectives had their doubts. They were convinced she was murdered by her husband, but they never could come up with the evidence to prove it. Then, a few years later, he met and married your mother."

"What you are saying is pure fiction," Kathy said, her eyes filling with tears.

"If it is fiction, Mrs. Baker, your father will have his chance to prove it in a court of law," Rosen replied, turning his attention back to the old man sitting in his chair. "Franz Kindler, you are under arrest for murder and for crimes against humanity. Please stand up and put your hands behind your back. Agent Rigby will read you your rights, and then put the cuffs on."

"Is this really necessary?" Mark Baker asked before Rigby began reciting the Miranda warning. "The man is ninety-six. How much danger can he be?"

"I'm afraid it is necessary," answered Rosen. "Please stand up, Herr Kindler."

When Rigby finished reading the old man his rights, Mark Baker said, "Don't say a word, Ernie. Not until I get you an attorney."

"Where are you taking him?" Kathy inquired. She had an arm around her stricken mother.

"He will be taken to the city jail, where he will be booked and processed," Rosen explained. "I am making every attempt to have him extradited to Israel, to stand trial in that country. But given his age, I doubt that will happen. More than likely, he'll be tried in federal court here in this country."

"Do you need assistance getting up?" asked Rigby.

The old man waved off Rigby's helping hand, stood up, and moved so close to Sam Rosen that their faces were inches apart. His eyes were hard, and his mouth curled into a sneer. He resembled a wild animal ready to pounce on its prey.

"*Juden*," the old man said in a loud voice. "Vermin, swine, Christ killer." Then: "Heil Hitler."

"No, Father, don't say those awful things," Kathy pleaded.

Sam Rosen smiled, said, "Just as I expected, Herr Kindler. Your allegiance hasn't changed one bit over the years, has it? You're what you've always been—a murderous Nazi thug."

Mark Baker stood silent, stunned by the old man's venomous outburst, while Mary Kruger's face registered a look that somehow managed to incorporate confusion, disbelief, and betrayal. This wasn't surprising to anyone in the room. After all, her entire life had been shattered in a matter of minutes.

As Rigby was leading his prisoner out the front door, Mark Baker managed to shake himself out of his trance. To Dantzler, he said, "I feel like we were ambushed tonight, Jack. This could have been handled in a more appropriate manner. I hold you responsible for the awful way this situation was conducted."

Sam Rosen stepped forward, said, "Governor Baker, if anyone is to be blamed, it's me. Jack wanted to give you a heads-up but I advised against it. The way events transpired here tonight was strictly my call. While I have the utmost sympathy for you, your wife, and your mother-in-law, that sympathy was not going to prevent me from doing what I came here to do, which was to put away a truly bad man. Again, I am sorry for what your family had to go through tonight, but this was the only way things could have gone down."

Dantzler followed Rosen out the front door, his feelings decidedly mixed. He agreed with Rosen on the sympathy thing, but that was the weaker of his feelings. He had built his entire career around a single goal—to take bad guys off the street. And that's what had happened tonight. Yes, it was long past due, and yes, Franz Kindler had lived these many decades as a free man. But his freedom ended tonight. Inevitably, he would be held accountable for his past sins, if not in this world, then perhaps in the world to come.

And that was good enough for Dantzler.

THIRTY-SIX

*T*IME DOESN'T DIMINISH, IT ENHANCES.

So long ago now. So many summers and winters fallen away like fresh leaves blown by the wind. Blown into a past that was glorious, yet badly misunderstood by those with blind eyes and limited intelligence.

Oh, how they misunderstood.

But time doesn't diminish, it enhances.

Memories, closer now than ever, flood back, crashing against the failed arc of history, ever mindful of what might have been. What should have been.

If only the righteous had prevailed.

But memories have a way of outliving success or failure. Clear and precise memories of giants who should've ruled. Individuals with superior intellect, superior minds. Men with high ideals, higher goals, greater dreams. Men with a burning passion to revenge past wrongs.

Everything comes back, always present, like the air we breathe. It's a movie that never ends. A movie with its own visuals, its own soundtrack. Trains rumbling across steel tracks, dogs barking, loud

voices shouting orders, cold weather, smoke, chaos, people scream-
ing, crying, lost, confused, terrified, snow that wasn't snow falling
from the sky . . .

Magnificent times indeed. If only we had prevailed, what a
better world this would be.

Sadly, the authors of history have failed to recognize or grasp
this magnificence. Writers, mostly Jews with small minds have
distorted the past, assigning blame, turning heroes into villains,
positives into negatives. But who are these authors? And what could
they truly know, truly comprehend?

Nothing, because they weren't present when this history, this
story was actually being written. They are outsiders, far removed
from those heady times, those marvelous events. They write looking
over their shoulders, not from any genuine first-hand knowledge.

Liars, all. They can never know the truth.

For such fools, times doesn't enhance, it diminishes.

They should all be consumed in the fires of their false narrative.

They are ants unworthy of commenting on those giants of the
past.

30 April 2011

"HOW COULD any sane human being write something this vile, this sick?" Erin asked. She was in her den, along with Dantzler, Sean, Bloom, and Hannah Andrews. "He wrote it ten years ago, when he was eighty-six. How pathetic that a man lives his entire life filled with such hatred. That's beyond tragic."

"That's just one page, Erin," Dantzler pointed out. "In all, he filled three notebooks with this insanity. Glenn Rigby found them in a locked box in the old man's garage."

"Really, this shouldn't surprise any of us," Hannah said. "We all know anti-Semitism is on the rise all around the globe."

"Anti-Semitism is one thing, Hannah, but this was something else entirely," Bloom noted. "What Franz Kindler and his fellow Nazis had in mind—and attempted to do—was to eliminate an entire race of people from the Earth. And they came damn close to accomplishing their goal."

"Where is Kindler now?" Sean asked.

"In a Manhattan jail," Dantzler answered. "Sam Rosen is attempting to get him to Israel for trial, but given Kindler's age, that's not going to happen. He'll eventually stand trial in this country."

"If he doesn't die first," Sean pointed out.

"Which he would have had he known we were on to him. He had a cyanide capsule in his shirt pocket. Glenn found it when he patted the man down."

"Can you imagine how his family is handling this?" Erin said. "They have to be totally devastated. I mean, there is no way they saw this coming."

"You have to believe Mark Baker will resign as governor," Sean stated.

"He won't resign, Sean," countered Dantzler. "He might not win re-election, but he's not going to willingly step down."

"Even though he's being blackmailed?" Erin inquired.

"That is no longer an issue," Dantzler said, glancing at Hannah.

"Changing the subject, what about those weapons found in David Danforth's garage?" Sean asked. "Did you find out who purchased them, or where they were headed?"

Dantzler shook his head, said," That's just one of several questions that likely will never be answered, Sean. No records were found at Danforth's house that indicated who bought any of those weapons. We'll also never know if Danforth worked alone, or if he was taking orders from someone else. Did another individual put him in touch with Muhammed, the man who built the bomb?

We'll probably never know the answer to those questions. But you know, Sean, if I could ask Danforth one question, I'd want him to tell me where he originally planned to detonate the bomb. It couldn't have been the Tennis Center. He only placed it there because he knew I was on to him. So, where did he hope to set it off?"

"According to Eric, four bodies were found when they drained the pond behind the Quonset hut," Sean said. "You're positive those men in the group weren't aware of that?"

"Not a chance. They were clueless. Here's another bit of information Eric shared with me. Danforth was worth approximately thirty-million dollars."

"Jesus, why does a guy with that much dough get involved in criminal activities? He could have lived like a king anywhere in the world. It makes no sense."

"Boredom, the challenge, excitement, a need for thrills . . . who can ever really know?"

"You're the psychiatrist, Bloom," Erin said. "What's your take on all this?"

Bloom was silent for almost a minute before answering. "As a famous Jewish rabbi once commanded, 'Love they neighbor as thyself.' Sadly, that's a concept we humans have yet to grasp, or to follow. We continue to prove the notion that humans are risen apes, not fallen angels. Simply stated . . . little has changed in thousands of years. And unfortunately, I don't see change coming in the foreseeable future."

"That's a rather grim outlook," Erin said.

"If you foresee a brighter future, show me the evidence," Bloom responded. "I would love nothing more than to be wrong."

TWO HOURS LATER, after everyone had departed, Erin and Dantzler were alone. They were sitting at the kitchen table. Dantzler was drinking Jameson and Diet Coke, Erin had a glass of Merlot.

"Do you agree with Bloom's assessment?" Erin asked.

"Hey, I'm an ex-homicide detective who worked more than one-hundred murders," Dantzler replied. "Surely you don't expect a rosy response from me. Remember, I normally saw the dark side of human nature. So, yeah, I'm inclined to agree with him."

"Well, color me an optimist, but I continue to see the basic decency in most people."

"Nothing wrong with being optimistic."

Erin sipped her wine, said, "I caught your glance at Hannah when the subject of blackmail came up."

"So . . .?"

"You know about her unfortunate situation with Mark Baker, don't you?"

"Yes."

"How long have you known?"

"Couple of weeks."

"How did you find out?"

"That's not important, Erin. All that matters is the blackmail scheme is dead. It's not going to happen. I've taken care of that. Hannah's name and reputation are secure. Now, my question to you is, how long have you known?"

"Hannah informed me a few minutes after she found out she was pregnant with Mark Baker's child. I was also with her when she had the pregnancy terminated."

"What in the world was she doing with him, a married man?" Dantzler asked.

"Timing, poor judgment, a moment of weakness, failing to consider possible consequences . . . take your pick. And you can toss in bad luck. It was the only time they were together."

"And she never used it against him? Good for her."

"One thing I'm confused about," Erin said. "Was Tim Nelson working with Preston Combs? You know, blackmailing Mark Baker?"

"No, they had very different cards to play against the governor. Tim had the ex-Nazi angle, while Preston knew about Mark and Hannah. Those blackmail schemes happening at the same time were pure coincidence."

Erin reached out and took Dantzler's hand in hers. "David Bloom told me something in private that I find very interesting. He said there was something different about you. He said it was in your eyes. I tend to agree with him."

"What was Bloom's keen observation?"

"That you have the look of a man ready to search for a new adventure."

"Did he say what that might be?"

"That you were going to chase the sunset."

"You know, Erin, the old shrink just might be right for once in his life."

"Will that journey include me?"

"'No bird soars too high if he soars with his own wings.'"

"The Book of Psalms?"

Dantzler grinned, said, "No, the Book of Blake."

ACKNOWLEDGMENTS

The list of those I need to thank for their support and encouragement continues to grow. Thanks to Julie Watson, Sarah Small, Wanda Underwood, Jake Small, Chris Boggs, Scott Boggs, Christina Young, Carol Palmer, Michael Palmer, Suzanne Slinker, Denny Slinker, Bonnie Vincent, Jim Vincent, Grant Sparks, Jimmie Nell Jenkins, Joe Gillespie, John Gillespie, Kelsey Gillespie, Roger "Roddy" O'Byrne, Peter Kiely, Bobby O'Byrne, Oisin Kiely, Sean Sutton and Joe Bryant. As always, thanks to Frank Hall for bringing me into the Hydra family, and to Tony Acree, who successfully manages to handle multiple issues while keeping Hydra Publications and Enigma House Press rolling smoothly along.

ABOUT THE AUTHOR

Tom Wallace is the award-winning author of nine previous Jack Dantzler mysteries, including *The Journal, Heroes For Ghosts, Murder by Suicide, The Poker Game, The Fire of Heaven, The List, Gnosis, The Devil's Racket* and *What Matters Blood*. He also wrote the thriller, *Heirs of Cain*.

His novel, *Gnosis*, won the prestigious Claymore Award at the Killer Nashville Writers Conference, and *The Devil's Racket* captured the Mystery Writers top award. *Murder by Suicide* was an Amazon best-seller.

Tom, a former sportswriter, has written several successful sports-related books, including *The Kentucky Basketball Encyclopedia* (now out in its fourth edition), *So You Think You're a Kentucky Wildcats Basketball Fan?* and *Golden Glory: The History of Central City Basketball*.

Tom is a Vietnam vet who currently lives in Lexington. His web site is www.tomwallacenovels.com

www.ingramcontent.com/pod-product-compliance
Lightning Source LLC
Chambersburg PA
CBHW070845250626
47159CB00003B/931